ROCKIN' ROBIN

ROCKIN' ROBIN

STEPHANIE JOHNSON

WHERE DRAMA MEETS THE STREETS

ROCKIN' ROBIN
Stephanie Johnson

Urban Books
6 Vanderbilt Parkway
Dix Hills, NY 11746

ISBN: 0-7394-5429-3

Acknowledgements

I would like to thank my husband, our children and my entire family for their support and encouragement. I thank God for the many blessings that he's given me. The gift of writing, however, has allowed me to express myself freely and for that, I'm extremely thankful.

Very special thanks to Nick Moore and Mrs. Lyda Mooney for reading Rockin' Robin in manuscript and giving their much appreciated feedback.

To my Urban Family, thank you so much for your support.

To Tysha Lockame-Jackson and Tyshel Lockame, you are some talented sistah's. Thank you so much for your support on the West side. For more information on these fabulous designers, go to www.lockamedesigns.com.

To those who have stood by me and allowed me to do me without judgment, thank you so much. To name you would take forever. Just know that each of you will forever be in my heart.

Peace Tyson

S. Johnson

Chapter One

"I was sleeping. My daddy parent was looking at me. I could feel him. He came really close to my face and said, 'You look just like your mother. Run your mouth like she runs hers, and you'll get your ass beat like she gets hers beat,'" Robin told the therapist who had put her into a deep hypnotic state.

"I didn't know how to say, 'Come closer so I can spit that thick white stuff that my mommy parent gave me right in your ugly face. Bird dog! Bird dogs don't get wings, and that's why you can't fly'.

"So I cried, and my mommy parent came and picked me up. I heard my daddy parent tell her to hurry up because he wanted to eat and for her not to make him come and get her.

"Then I heard Chrissy say, 'Not to worry. We gonna handle him in our way and at the right time.' I knew who Chrissy was but could never see her where I am now. She was in the shadows of my soul. It seemed like forever since I heard from Chrissy. She must've found her wings and fell completely out of the hole to come and be with me.

"The bird voice that I used to hear wasn't bird-like anymore, either. My mommy parent was holding me too tight, and her voice was skipping. Some wet stuff was dripping on my face. She wiped my cheek and pushed away some hair that was on the top of my eyes. Our bodies were moving back and forth. I was getting dizzy.

"Then my daddy parent came and hit my mommy parent in the head. She held me close so that she wouldn't drop me. She hurried up and finished feeding me, changed my hot and funny smelling clothes, and kissed me good night.

"Mommy parent's eyes were big and had blue circles around them. She was still so pretty." Robin's voice was weary.

"Robin, when I count to three, you'll wake up. One. Two. Three." Robin opened her eyes to find herself in a fetal position on Dr. Christopher's leather couch. She looked at the doctor, a handsome black man, then looked around the office at her surroundings. His Ph.D from Georgetown University hung on the wall alongside the many awards he had won over the years. A photo of his wife was displayed prominently on his large, honey-colored oak desk.

"Can I have some water, please? My throat is really dry," Robin said to Dr. Christopher. "Tell me, how did I do? Did I talk about anything in particular?"

"Yes. In fact, you did. I thought I heard you indicate that there was someone else with you. You spoke in past tense, and it sounded like you were speaking of another child. You mentioned the name Chrissy. It was actually quite confusing, Robin."

"Really? Another child named Chrissy?"

"Yes. Let's talk more about that more at your next session. How are you feeling? Are you tired? Hungry? Upset?"

"No. I know that name Chrissy from somewhere."

"Ok. But as I said, we'll talk about that at your next session. I don't you want to overdo it today. What are your plans for the rest of the night?"

"Nothing really. I'm probably going to go home and relax. I have to work tomorrow, but then I'm on vacation from this Thursday until next Thursday. I'll probably call it an early night."

Robin had hoped that her therapy sessions would help her understand the shadow that she felt she always had, the voice that finished her sentences, and the times that she couldn't account for. Dr. Christopher said she was making progress, but Robin just didn't see where. She felt like she could talk forever about her childhood and her parents, but it was never going to answer the questions she had about what was going on within her.

Robin's relationship with her mother, Toscha, was what helped them to survive the abuse that they endured every day. They protected each other as much as they could when her father, Jiles, would beat them.

Jiles Sessoms suffered from little man's syndrome. He and his brother were brought up by their father to believe that women must be subservient. There were many nights when Jiles and his brother Jarvis would find their mother crying in the laundry room. They would walk by as if they didn't even see or hear her, because they didn't. In their eyes, she was neither seen nor heard unless they or their father needed her to be.

The sexual abuse that Robin endured was catastrophic. Every time Jiles violently raped her, Robin walked backwards into her soul. Her mother knew it was happening when she wasn't around, and it tore her up inside. But she knew that her husband's beatings would prove deadly if she ever confronted him with it. Instead, Toscha tried to be home all the time so that Robin would know that she would protect her if he tried anything while she was home.

Even as a child, though, Robin felt like her mother should have done something else to stop the abuse. Toscha was a classic example of a domestic abuse victim, and through her therapy sessions, Robin learned it wasn't that her mother didn't want to do something about the abuse; it was that she couldn't do anything else.

When Robin was seventeen she left home. The abuse had gotten worse, and she knew if she stayed, her father would eventually kill her. Now she lived in a small suite at the hotel where she worked. She and her mother still talked several times a week and had lunch every now and then, but Robin never went back to the house. Toscha would always have to meet her somewhere.

The day she left was the last day she'd looked at her father and said her last words, "Payback is a bitch." The horrible memories of him were never spoken of outside her therapy sessions with Dr. Christopher.

When Robin left, her father took to beating her mother once, sometimes twice a day. Robin would call the house for days at a time, but only the answering machine would pick up. The longest period of time that Robin went without speaking to her mother was a week. When she did finally see her mother, Toscha downplayed her bruises and told Robin that she'd been busy.

"I got your messages, but I was running around like crazy and forgot to call you back."

Robin knew better, but there was nothing she could say to convince her mother to leave her father.

Chapter Two

In Long Branch, New Jersey, the leaves fell to the silent music of the brisk wind. Fall was Robin's favorite season of the year. Whenever a guest opened the doors in the lobby of the hotel where she worked, Robin enjoyed the breeze that rushed in.

"Thank you. Your room number is 5535," she told the guest standing before her. "Take the elevator to the fifth floor, and it's the room at the end of the hall. Enjoy your stay."

Robin loved her job as manager of operations at The Gray Pearl, which was aptly located on the beachfront. It was Wednesday, the busiest night in the hotel's restaurant lounge, Breezes. Every week, Breezes had a buffet consisting of clams on the half shell, baked fish, ribs, cornbread, pasta, almond rice and an assorted variety of vegetables, cooked and uncooked.

Her staff was always on time, and that made for a very profitable happy hour. When the customers were happy, they spent more money.

Robin went to Kim's register in the lounge to get any large bills Kim may have had. In walked Mr. and Mrs. Todd Kendricks, the owners of the hotel. They resided in the building's finest suite. Chanel was always very polite when she spoke, but Todd never spoke at all. Ironically, he was currently furthering his education as a student at Monmouth University, where he was studying to get a degree in communications, of all things.

"Robin, how are you doing tonight? Looks like a full house for you and your wonderful staff," Chanel commented. "Can I get a white wine spritzer, please?"

"Sure, Chanel. I was about to count this drawer, but as soon as I'm done, I'll make that for you. Can I get something for your husband?"

"Please. Does it look like he's concerned about getting a drink right now? He's mingling with all of the single women here tonight. When he's ready, he'll order his own damn drink."

"Alrighty then. That's cool with me."

Todd and Chanel met at the hotel's grand opening, back when Chanel's parents owned the place. Todd was her first real love. He, however, was married before, and according to rumors around the city, his ex-wife left him because he was mentally and physically abusive. It had also been said that he had a bad drug addition. Funny how these types of things never got back to the second wife until it was too late.

"Robin, did you ever contact Dr. Christopher and have a session?" Chanel asked.

Whenever Robin went missing for a day or two, Chanel became worried. Robin would come in wearing a rumpled, stained uniform, clearly the same one she'd been wearing before she went missing. Robin would be distant and sometimes downright indignant toward Chanel, and the drastic change in behavior concerned her. Finally, when Robin came to work dressed in her street clothes, talking all crazy, Chanel suggested that she get some help. She referred her to Dr. Christopher.

"Yes. I see him once, sometimes twice a week," Robin said as she fixed Chanel her drink. "Tuesdays are my regular sessions, and every now and then I'll see him on a Thursday when I'm really feeling down."

"That's great," Chanel said. "How's it going? Do you think it's helping?"

"It's been a few months since I started seeing Dr. Christopher, and he thinks my sessions are going well, but I'm not as confident of my progress as he is. And thanks again for referring me to him, Chanel. How are things with you and Todd?" Robin asked, eager to change the subject.

"As good as they're ever going to get. I married him, and now I have to live with that. Where I come from, when you say 'I do', you do. For better or for worse, until death do you part." Chanel sipped her spritzer through the tiny cocktail straw, seeming lost in her own thoughts. After a pause, she admitted, "I'm lying. I can't stand his ass. He's a liar, and I think he's still fucking his ex-wife, Eryca, that druggie bitch."

Robin didn't know what to say. She began to feel very uncomfortable talking about her boss's marital problems, so she changed the subject again.

"Yo, I need me another gig. I'm thinking about taking another job as a garbage woman."

Chanel spit out a mouthful of alcohol when she heard Robin speaking in that ignorant tone Chanel had just recently come to know. "Really, Robin? You're joking, right? A garbage collector?"

"For real. I want a second job."

"Why? You make pretty good money here. Do you feel that you're not getting paid what you should be? We can talk about that." Chanel tried to keep her tone even with Robin. "I want to keep you happy and here."

"Nah, you hook me up enough. I need out of this piece sometimes."

Chanel tried not to get offended. Clearly, Robin's issues were more important than Chanel's hurt feelings right now.

"I got some thangs I need to take care of. You know what I'm sayin'?" Robin said in that same strange tone. "And the Department of Sanitation don't pay half bad. Besides, I think it's sexy."

"All right," Chanel answered, wondering what was sexy about picking up trash. "But when you find out how smelling like hot garbage and over-ripened vinegar is sexy, please let me know. Maybe I can spray myself with the combination and get myself a real man."

"Ay, how your boy Kyle?" Robin asked.

"Oh, Robin, he's so big. He just turned thirteen and is in the eighth grade. The girls are ringing my phone all times of the day and night. It's scary that my baby is growing up right before my eyes."

"I bet. Is he still playing basketball?"

"Yup. He made M.V.P. two years in a row. Hey, why don't you come with us to his game next week? I'm sure you'll have a good time."

"I'll think about it and get back. Thank you for the invite, baby girl."

Chanel looked at Robin one last time, took her drink and went to find Todd.

Chapter Three

Robin called her mother to see how she was doing. A week ago, her father had gone to the hospital complaining of shortness of breath. They admitted him, and after some tests, determined that he had pneumonia, which left her mother home alone.

"Mom? How are you?"

"Robin. I'm fine. I'm just having a bite to eat before I go to see how your father is doing. Do you get off soon? Maybe you can come with me."

"No. I have to work until 2 a.m. Sorry, can't make it this time."

"Robin, please," her mother pleaded.

Every time Toscha asked her to go with her to see her father, Robin's stomach would get sour. He repulsed her. She hated him for the abuse he subjected her to just because she wasn't a boy. He would dress her in jeans and baseball hats to make her look as boyish as he possibly could. He even cut her hair when she was sleeping one day. And she resented her mother for not taking a stand and objecting to his torment. All Toscha did was try to coordinate her clothes with all the different colored bruises he left all over her body. "Thanks, but I'll pass."

"He is still your father, Robin. Please come with me."

Before Robin could respond, she heard yelling in the front lobby. "Mom, I'll have to call you back," she said then hung up quickly, rushing to the front desk to see what all the commotion was about. Apparently, someone had double-booked suite number 5535, and a guest was very unhappy.

"I'm sorry. My name is Robin Sessoms. I'm the manager of operations. Can I help you with something?"

"Yes, you can. When I booked my hotel, I specifically asked for room 5535, and now I'm being told that it's not available. I've been coming here for years, sleeping in the same room. You have all my information on file, and I'm insulted that I'm not being taken care of. What kind of business are you running here? I'm a loyal customer. I got my confirmation paperwork right here. What's up? Huh?" He jostled the paperwork so close to Robin's face that when she breathed, the bottom of the paper swayed back and forth.

Robin tried to remain calm as she reached for the paperwork. She placed it on the counter that separated her from the irate guest. As she was examining his papers, she heard a voice.

Man, another bird dog. Tell him we don't have any more rooms. He kind of cute, though.

The need to respond was great, but she didn't see anyone to respond to, so Robin tried to ignore it.

"All right, Mr. Nelson Bray of 954 Trail Boulevard. Is this your correct address?"

Nelson picked up the papers and shook them in her face again as if to say, "Miss, what does it say right here?" His 6-foot 5-inch, 290-pound body made his deviant mannerisms even more intimidating.

"Let me see what I can do for you," Robin responded, trying to remain professional. She pushed some buttons and clicked the mouse a few times.

"There. I wasn't able to give you the original suite that you reserved, but I upgraded you to the Presidential suite. Is that sufficient?"

"I don't want that suite."

"You don't have a choice," Robin snapped as she handed him the keys. He glared at Robin as he reached for his paperwork and his bags. Robin stopped him.

"No. Please let me have someone help you with your bags. Go ahead up to your room and I'll have them brought up to you. You have been inconvenienced enough."

"Well, I'm glad we agree on something. I didn't pay four hundred and fifty dollars a night to stay in this place to get treated like a second class citizen. Thank you very much!"

As obnoxious as Mr. Bray was, and with all the verbal abuse that Robin had been subjected to in her life, she was quite drawn to his sophisticated unruliness in a scary kind of way. "Sandra, have Kevin take up Mr. Bray's bags to Presidential Suite three. Call the kitchen and have them make up a 1A on the house. Also advise them that I'll be taking the cart up to our guest personally."

Robin pushed the cart to Mr. Bray's room and knocked lightly on the door. No sooner than she did, he appeared, drink in hand, looking good as hell in his ankle-length black velour robe.

"Mr. Bray, I took the liberty of arranging a night cap for you. A selection of cheeses and fruit along with the house champagne has been prepared for you in an attempt to make the rest of your stay at The Gray Pearl as pleasant as possible."

"Leave it right there. Ay, where's the safe in this room? Aren't Presidential suites supposed to have safes?"

Robin heard the voice again. *What a derelict. Let me answer this one.*

"No." Robin looked around to see who was talking, but there was no one there. "I mean yes. Presidential suites are supposed to have a safe, but this one particular suite has just been completed, and the workers haven't had a chance to install it yet. I have a safe in the main office that can hold any valuables until I can have them install the safe in the morning, if that's okay with you."

"Whatever. I'm leaving in the morning, but give me a minute to get it together and you can take my case with you when you leave."

Robin stood outside the door and he closed it in her face. A few moments later, he opened the door and handed her a black plastic box, the kind you would get when if bought a new drill.

It was heavy, but Robin asked him if there was anything else she could take downstairs for him. Not that she could carry anything else.

"No, that'll be it. Take care of her, right?"

Robin nodded, turned around and walked to the elevator. She knew he was watching her, but didn't look back until she was about to get on the elevator. She shot him a disapproving look then boarded the elevator.

Curiosity was killing Robin as she set the box on her desk. Jewelry wasn't that heavy. She noticed that the only thing stopping her from looking inside the box was her opened office door, which she could close, and a clamp that could be easily lifted then closed again.

Robin got up and closed the door. She went back to the desk and sat in front of the black box that Mr. Nelson "Testosterone to the Bone" Bray had given her. She reached for the clamp that held the box shut. It was tight at first, but after Robin messed with it a little, it opened. In front of her sat a polished nine-millimeter with five full jackets. Robin's mouth hit the floor.

She turned around to make sure the door was closed then got up and locked it. As she stared at the gun, her hands reached out and picked it up. She turned it around in front of her face. Her hand looked like a child's hand holding a gas pump. That's how big it was. It looked brand new, and it looked good in her hands.

After admiring this impressive, shiny piece of metal, she returned it to its haven. She closed the box and placed it in the master safe.

In the early hours of the following morning, Robin made it her business to be at the front desk. She wanted to be around just in case there were some other customer problems, in particular with Mr. Nelson Bray. She called her co-worker, Paula, and told her she could start her shift later in the day.

Paula was more than happy to agree. She hated coming in at 2 o'clock in the morning anyway. Robin and Paula were hired at the same time, six years ago, but Paula was a partier. She would often call out of work to go to Breezes. She had a set of balls on her. And her mouth was as big as those balls too.

Before Nelson had checked out, Robin sent him a complimentary breakfast. And no, it wasn't a bagel, butter and a coffee. Ol' girl went to the kitchen herself and made some grits, eggs, sausage and pancakes. Cinnamon sticks garnished the homemade rice pudding she prepared.

This time, she had it sent up by the bellhop. A card was placed over a platinum covered dish, again expressing the hotel's apologies for the mishap with Mr. Bray's requested room. It included a complimentary day stay that would grant Mr. Bray a full body message, pedicure, manicure and facial.

Robin personally signed it and included her direct line phone number, in case he had any questions . . . or wanted to ask her out. She left at 6 o'clock in the morning and arranged for the breakfast to be delivered at 7 o'clock, but not before jotting down his address on a Post-it note and shoving it into her purse.

That's right. Go get your boo, the voice told Robin.

Chapter Four

Robin was rushing. She only had fifteen minutes to get to her job interview at The Department of Sanitation.

The truck yard was loud with the sound of garbage trucks being refueled or repaired. Gasoline puddles formed a walkway up to the office.

Ms. Paulette Grimes, the manager of The Department of Sanitation of Asbury Park, looked at Robin through her bifocals as she sat across from her. Her smoke and coffee breath danced around Robin's nostrils.

"Now, what's a cleaned-up gal like you doin' lookin' for a job as a garbage man?"

"Well, that would be garbage woman, Ms. . . . ." Robin looked at her nameplate. "Ms. Grimes."

"When can you start? There really isn't any need to check your previous job experience. Anybody can pick up a garbage can and dump in into a bigger garbage can."

"I can start as soon as possible because I need the money. How much does it pay, anyhow?"

"Fifteen dollars an hour, usually a two or three-hour run. It's a big neighborhood. Why do you want to be a garbage man?"

"That's none of your business. All you need to know is that I'll show up for work if you give me the gig."

Ms. Grimes eyed Robin, not sure if she liked this girl's attitude.

"Now, can I get a uniform or whatever garbage people wear?"

"You ain't no stalker, is ya?"

"What the hell kind of question is that? I can't imagine that you get people coming off the streets wanting a job dumping garbage everyday, so—"

"No. Any old sweats and boots will do."

Robin completed all of the necessary paperwork, gave a copy of her driver's license and left.

While Robin was out, she figured she'd go by her mother's house to visit. When she got there, Robin found her mother sitting quietly in the kitchen.

"Ma, what's wrong?"

"Robbie . . . " Her mother always called her that when she had something serious to talk about. "They think that your father may have bone cancer. They took a few tests and want us to get down there as soon as possible."

"Okay, so . . . " Robin responded carelessly.

"I would like for you to come with me."

"I gathered that when you said 'us.' " Robin stood with her arms across her chest.

"We should both be there, Robin. This may be it for him."

Robin let out a big sigh. She guessed the time had come when she needed to pretend she was upset that the old bastard's last day on this earth might be sooner than he and everybody else had expected.

"Let's fuckin' go," Robin said.

When they arrived at the hospital, they went right into his room.

"Mrs. Sessoms, he's resting comfortably. A low dose of Morphine was administered to him for his pain," a nurse explained before leaving the room.

Toscha sat next to her husband's bed while Robin stood at the foot of the bed, emotionless. The look on her face said, *Die, you sorry fuck.*

Mr. Sessoms wasn't awake and didn't know they were there, so Robin addressed her mother. "I never thought there would be a day where he wouldn't be able to run his fucking mouth. For once, we're in control and he's dependent on us. I say we leave his old ass right here alone."

"Robin!" her mother exclaimed.

"Robin what?"

"How could you say such a thing about your father? What is wrong with you?"

"You act upset. Personally, I could give a shit."

"You can't mean that. I never heard you speak of or to your father like that before. Why are you behaving this way?"

"Well, I do mean it. He's a rotten motherfucka and we hate his fucking guts," Robin said, raising her voice.

"We? This is my husband. I don't hate him. Now shush or you'll wake him. I will not allow you to continue to behave like this. It's like you're somebody else standing in front of me."

"It's all right, Toscha. Let the ugly child speak," Jiles croaked from his bed.

"Jiles?"

"Yeah. Jackass?"

"Robin, that's enough! I will not condone you disrespecting your father like that. Mind your manners."

"That's right." Her father let out a grizzly cough. "That's just like when she would eat, Toscha. She could never chew with her mouth closed. She sounded like a cow grazing in the meadows. Untamed warthog!"

Robin's mother looked down at the floor, then at Robin. Her eyes seemed to be pleading. *He may not be here tomorrow. Please stop this.*

Robin walked over to his bedside and placed her hands on his arm. Mr. Sessoms looked unsure of what she was going to do.

"Ma, why don't you go and get some ice for Daddy to suck on?" Robin suggested.

"No." With Robin's behavior, Toscha was reluctant to leave her alone with her father. She didn't know what Robin might say or do.

"Yes, I think you could use a cup of coffee or something. You look exhausted."

"Ain't you heard her?" Jiles interjected.

Robin looked down at her father, but kept a straight face so as not to reveal her true emotions while her mother was still there to witness it.

"Really, Ma. If anything happens, I'll be sure to have the nurse page you."

"Well, all right," Toscha finally agreed. "Are you sure you two will be okay while I'm gone?"

"Yes, Momma. We'll be fine," Robin assured her mother.

Robin and her father watched Toscha walk out of the room, one eager to see her go, the other wishing she had stayed to protect him in his vulnerable state. When she could no longer hear her mother's footsteps, Robin pulled a chair alongside her father's bed and spoke her true feelings to him.

"I just want to let you know that you have fucked us up for life. The shit you did to me when I was a little girl has turned me into someone that you should fear for the rest of your miserable and numbered days, motherfucka. Ma may be able to deny or deal, whichever she does with your sick mentality, but trust us when we tell you, payback is a bitch."

"You're the most miserable child I've ever known. If you were my son, you would be looking up to me, not disobeying me when you're told to do something. Can't believe I thought you were a good piece of anything." He coughed again, this time right in her face.

"I obeyed you, Mr. Jiles Sessoms. When you told me to be quiet, I was, even though it was hard not to scream when you were pounding that thing you call a dick," Robin lifted the sheet and laughed at his penis, "into my seven-year-old pussy. We took it, though. It ain't something I'd be too proud about if I were you." Jiles peered into Robin's poker face and listened with fear in his eyes.

"I even listened to you when you said that if I told, you would be forced to stick it in my butt. I didn't say anything. Did I? And by the way, your ass smelled like pure shit." She finally let go of the sheet and continued.

"Everything you asked me to do, I did because I thought that one day you would accept me and stop hating me for not being a boy. But instead, you continued to beat Ma and me and abuse us when you were drunk."

Jiles finally spoke. "I don't know what you're talking about. You need to stay off of those drugs."

"Ain't nobody on no drugs, Daddy."

"I always told your mother that you were a bad child. Something rotted inside of her right before you were born, but not enough to kill ya." Spit camped out in the corners of his mouth.

Robin heard footsteps coming back down the hall. She leaned over to his ear and got so close that he could feel her lips moving against it. "I tell you what, you old, black, poor excuse of a man. You bitch-ass nigga, you better hope Ma lives long enough to keep us away from you, because if she dies before you do, rest assured we'll have no reason not to get you back for every goddamned thing you ever did to us."

Just then, Robin thought she smelled something. She lifted up the sheets and saw that he had urinated on himself. "You pissy piece of shit! I'ma do everything that you did to us, back to you. You got that, Mr. Jiles Sessoms? And you will be wishing you had died starting right now."

As she got up, she pulled the hairs that were growing out of his ears and twisted them in her fingers. He let out a whimpering moan just as his wife came back into the room.

"Jiles, baby, are you all right? Why are there tears in your eyes?"

"She tried to kill me, Toscha."

Robin's mother looked at her. "What did you do to him, Robin?"

"What the hell could I have tried to kill him with, Ma? He's doing just fine. We just settled some shit that was bothering the both of us. Right, Daddy?"

Her mother looked at him and waited for his response.

"Get this wench out my face," he snarled, turning his head away from Robin. Mrs. Sessoms wiped away his tears that were too big to be held back.

"Ay, I need to be going anyhow. You need me to give you a ride home?" Robin asked her mother.

"No, but I want to speak to you in the hallway before you leave."

"For what?"

"Robin," her mother said sternly. Robin sighed and walked into the hallway.

"I'll just be a moment," Toscha said to Jiles as she walked out and closed the door behind her.

"I don't know what has gotten into you, but you better stop it right now," she told Robin.

"Or else what?" Robin's voice was getting loud again.

"Lower your tone. Robin, the past is the past. Your father may be dying in there, and all you can do is come here and act like an ass."

"I tell you what," Robin began, but her mother cut her off.

"No, you listen to me. I'm not going to do this here. We will address this when I get home. I'll call you."

"I don't want to hear the shit, so don't bother." With that, Robin turned and walked away. "Have a good night, Ma. Oh, and Daddy pissed on himself," she yelled.

Chapter Five

Robin put on her Timberlands, a pair of jeans with holes in them, and a T-shirt. She turned her hat to the back and waited at the corner for her ride. It was 5:20 a.m. on her first day as a garbage woman.

Can't believe you doing this shit. A garbage woman? What the fuck are you thinking about?

Robin looked to her right. "Chrissy?"

Who else would it be, Robin?

"How and why are you here?"

Because I have to be. I was born with you, or should I say you with me.

Robin grabbed her head.

It's not that bad, Robin. You and I, we need each other.

"I don't need you. I just need you to go away."

Ain't happening. Besides, where would I go? I'm in your head.

"Go away, please," Robin cried as she sat on the curb and lowered her head.

A garbage truck pulled up and stopped in front of Robin.

"Robin?" the female driver asked.

"Yeah."

"Get in," she said.

Sharon, Robin's truck buddy, stood about six feet and weighed about 180 pounds, a dark brown-skinned woman, attractive in her own way. She was a divorced mother of one, a boy named James. During the day, she worked as a garbage woman, and at night she worked at a collections agency to make ends meet.

Cory, her deadbeat ex-husband, was the mistake of all mistakes. He rarely paid child support, and she refused to let James feel the brunt of her mistake.

"Okay, pretty girl, let's get one thing straight. I want to do my run and get it done right the first time. The majority of the people know to set their shit out the night before, but there are a few who forget. A select few get a courtesy walk up to the door and pick-up of their trash, but the rest will wait until next week if they don't put their shit out on time," Sharon explained.

"Are you on for Mondays and Wednesdays, too, or are you just working on Fridays? And who were you talking to when I pulled up?" she asked Robin.

"I assumed all that shit," Robin responded, ignoring Sharon's questions.

"That's cool."

"How long have you been driving?"

"Driving? Only a few months, but I had the gig for about a year now. The hours coincide with James' school hours, and at the very least, I want to have dinner with him and put him to bed."

"I hear you. I don't have any kids and I don't think I want any."

"Children are a blessing, girl," Sharon said as she flipped her visor down to show Robin a picture of James.

"I guess so."

During their run, everybody on the first couple of blocks had the garbage neatly placed on the curb with the lids on. The houses were moderately kept, and most had fences around them.

The next block looked like it was misplaced. The houses were almost double the size, the lawns were greener than she had ever seen, and their cans were at the tops of their driveways, which held Mercedes Benzes, Lexus and Range Rovers.

"Man, did we get pulled into another world? Look at the difference between that block and the ones we just did," Robin commented.

"Trail Boulevard is the shit. Wait until we go further in," Sharon said.

"Trail Boulevard?" Robin recognized that as the street where Nelson Bray lived.

Yeah, girl. That's where yo' boy live, the voice encouraged her.

"Shut up!" Robin's shout startled Sharon.

"Girl, what the hell is wrong with you?" Sharon yelled. "Who the fuck you think you talking to?"

"No, who the fuck you talking to?"

"Look, chick, if you having second thoughts . . ." Sharon started, but Robin cut her off.

"I ain't having second thoughts. You don't know me like that to be cursing at me."

"You trippin', a'ight. Maybe you need to go on and get you another gig. This ain't working out already." Sharon sucked her teeth and shook her head.

"I'm good."

"You sure? I don't want no shit out of you," Sharon replied, all the while thinking this girl was a bitch.

Robin changed the subject to keep the peace for now. She needed this job.

"Ay, you know any of these people personally? I mean are they nice, or do they be acting all stanky-dank-dank?"

"Most of them are cool, and when it's Christmastime, they look out for real. Last year, I got a book bag full of school supplies from Mrs. Curry, and

Mr. and Mrs. Benton gave me dinner tickets for two. Still ain't used them."

"I guess they figure this job is grimy enough, and showing their appreciation will encourage you to empty the garbage in the truck, not on the grass." Sharon laughed at Robin's observation.

They pulled up to the block where all of the houses looked like they should be on *MTV Cribs*. The lawns were as plush as the most expensive carpet. The flowers and professional landscaping meticulously lined the custom-designed cobblestone driveways. The people who owned these houses obviously had mad money.

One house in particular was the shit. It sat about thirty yards from the street on a cul-de-sac. The chromed-out Excursion parked in the driveway was the icing on the cake. It was money green, and a gold shimmer pulled every color of the rainbow to it. This shit was tight.

"And what did the resident that lives at that address give you?" Robin asked as she pointed to the house.

"Oh, girl, let me just pull over and tell you right quick. Every time I come here, I'm always amazed at his spot. He—"

"Dayum!" Robin interrupted. "Would you look at this shit?"

They both stared in awe at the house, which looked more like a mansion. With the truck stopped, Robin was able to take in every detail. All of the accents on the exterior were silver, and the huge flowerpots in the front yard were planted with at least three rose bushes each. The place definitely looked like it had been decorated with a woman's touch. Robin figured the owner was married, or a woman lived there at the very least.

"Man. What does this guy do?" Robin asked.

"I don't know," Sharon answered.

"How the hell don't you know?" Robin pushed for an answer. "I thought you were cool with these people. They giving you shit at Christmas and whatnot."

"Just what I said. I don't know! We cool and everything. We talk a little every week, but I don't get all in his business like that."

"So, you've never wondered what it was that he did for a living? Have you ever looked through his garbage?"

"Hell no! What's wrong with you? I don't hardly like this job that much to spend no more time than I have to handling it. I certainly ain't trying to lose it behind being nosey."

"I see. Well, are we going to get his garbage or not? I don't see it on the curb."

"He's one of the people who gets special treatment. You not only have to get the garbage, but you have to go through the back and into the shed to get it. But first, we back the truck into the driveway just enough so no one can see what we're bringing out from his backyard."

"Get the hell outta here!"

"Nah, I'm so serious."

"Okay. Let's go," Robin said, intrigued with Sharon's information.

Sharon backed the truck into the driveway then got out and told Robin to follow her. They headed toward the shed in the back, but stopped when they saw two Akitas, one black and one white, guarding it and looking very hungry.

"What are we supposed to do about them?" Robin asked.

"Be cool and don't make no fast moves."

"You don't have to worry about that," Robin said, standing as still as she could.

"I have to ring a bell and someone will be right out." Sharon went to the patio. She put her hand under a laser built into a flower box, and chimes softly danced with the cool air.

Not one minute later, a man came to the door. Dressed in a sage and hunter green suit and a pair of light gray and hunter green Pumas, he slid the glass door open and walked out on the patio. Robin recognized him immediately but said nothing.

"Whatchu got for me today?" Sharon asked him.

"Just some shredded paper, baby girl. Who's your sidekick?"

"This is Robin. She's my new partner in this funky-ass job."

He looked walked over to Robin. "Thank you for the food. It was delicious."

Nelson knew who she was before they even got out of the truck. He had security cameras installed throughout his yard and had been watching the two women from the moment they stopped the truck to stare at his house.

"And the hospitality at the hotel was commendable as well. However, I would appreciate if you wouldn't go through my things. You should be careful who you give your prints to. They could put you anywhere," he said to Robin.

"Whatchu talking 'bout," Sharon asked as she looked from Nelson to Robin.

"She knows," Nelson responded. Sharon turned to Robin with a questioning grin.

Robin looked at Nelson. She ignored his obvious warning that he knew she had looked inside his box. Instead, she told him, "It was nothing. You were inconvenienced, and I wanted to make up for that."

"And you did. You were rockin' that uniform too. Do they make you pay for those?"

"No. They supply them, and thank you," Robin answered. "I'm impressed, Mr. Bray. Your home is very nice," she said.

"That makes two of us, Rockin' Robin, because like I said, you were rockin' that suit."

Robin looked at him like he was crazy. He didn't know her like that to be giving her a nickname. "My name is Robin."

"I know," Nelson responded.

"And I would appreciate if you called me by my name, asshole. Now, could you please get your mutts so I can get this garbage and be on my way?"

"Chill out. Robin it is," Nelson said with a laugh. "Black and White, come here," he yelled to the dogs. They came running, their tails wagging, and sat at his feet.

"Now you can get it. Leave the wood on the side of the shed."

Robin went into the shed and as soon as she opened the door, she found the bag filled with shredded paper. She grabbed it and headed for the truck.

"This is a small world. Where do you guys know each other from?" Sharon questioned Nelson. "Did y'all used to do it or something? Because I'm feeling a bit of perspiration out this piece. You better be glad there ain't no food in these here cans. We'd be stinking for real," she teased. "And speaking of food, what you have for me today? Last week you said that you'd have something for me." Ever since Sharon began picking up Nelson's garbage, they had talked a little each week. When she told him about her situation as a single mother, he started giving her things for her son.

Nelson motioned quickly, and a small white man brought out a box full of cereal, bread, canned goods, and pastas. He went back then returned with a few duffle bags full of name brand jeans and shirts, underwear, socks and personal hygiene items.

"Nelson, thanks again, baby. You don't know how much me and my boy appreciate this."

"Yes I do. Ay, Rockin' Robin, I'll be talking to you soon," he yelled as he walked Sharon to the gate. Robin was already in the truck.

"Bye," Sharon said as she hopped in the truck.

"Well, you wanted to know what he gave me for Christmas," she said to Robin as they pulled out of the driveway. "You're looking at part of it. In the beginning of the school year, he hooks me up with things for James, and at Christmastime, he gives me a gee. That's right, one thousand dollars."

"And how much ass are you giving him?" Robin asked as she leaned on the window and stared at Sharon.

"None. Absolutely none!"

"Yeah, okay. Now I got 'jackass' flashing on my forehead. You want me to believe that he just gives you this shit for free?"

"Yup."

She a lying bitch.

"I know, right. Just a lying bitch," Robin spoke aloud, answering the voice in her head.

"Home girl, you can believe what you want. I ain't that kind of girl, okay? And damn sure not your bitch. You better watch it."

"Where to next?" Robin snapped.

"Nelson was the last stop. We're finished. Where can I take you?"

"Take me home."

"And where is home?"

"The Gray Pearl."

Chapter Six

Robin went into the lobby of The Gray Pearl where she saw Paula signing for a package.

"Robin, this package just came for you. Do you want it now or should I have it sent upstairs?"

"I'll take it." She looked at the peculiar package, which was wrapped in black paper with a big white bow on top. "Huh. No name. Thanks. Are there any messages for me?"

"One. Here you go," Paula said as she handed her a slip of paper. It read: *Just a little something for you. Call me when you get this.* There was a phone number listed with the message.

Robin's imagination was running wild. She was anxious to open the package now. "Paula, hold all of my calls and have my cleaned suit sent up when you got a chance," she asked as she headed out of the lobby.

Her suite was on the fourth floor, and it certainly wasn't the best in the hotel. Only the high rollers get those, but it was definitely better than the raggedy apartment she lived in before she got manager's job.

When Chanel hired her, Robin was really down on her luck. She had just finished an 18-month course in hotel management, but no one would hire her. When she went for her interview with Chanel and Todd, they liked her immediately and offered her the position of reservation clerk. They were happy with her job performance, and six months later, they gave her a raise. On the same day, five other people quit, one being the manager of operations. They offered Robin the position, and Chanel made the deal even sweeter when she suggested that Robin reside at the hotel. This worked for Robin, and she'd been there since.

In her suite, Robin carefully opened the package so that she could keep the paper and bow, and examined the lightweight package about the size of a necklace box. She opened it slowly and found a pair of sunglasses and a simple note: *I think these would look nice on you.* There was no signature to indicate who the gift was from.

Robin heard a knock at the door. She opened it to see her mother standing in the hall.

"What are you doing here? I told you not to bother me."

"I came to talk to you about how you treated your father when we were at the hospital."

Robin's body temperature must've gone up twenty degrees, and sweat beads began to form on her nose. She stepped aside with her hand on her hip so that her mother could come in.

"Robin," her mother started, "whatever it is that you and your father are having trouble resolving needs to be dealt with. I feel that since his tests came back negative for bone cancer, it could be a new beginning for you two. He is your father, you know."

"Look, because of the foul things that 'my father' did to me, I'm in therapy, dealing with a lot of issues. The fact that you wish to ignore the abuse that he subjected both you and me to is your choice. I choose, now that I don't live under his roof, to forget about him completely. And you should too. Why is it that you feel the need to stay with this man who, at every chance he got, punched you in your face and beat you like a dog?" Robin shook her head and folded her arms across her chest.

"You just don't understand. Your father is the only man I've ever been with. We were boyfriend and girlfriend since I was fourteen, and we got married when I was eighteen, right before he went off to college. I chose to be a stay-at-home mom and make a home for my family. Is that so bad, Robin?"

"No, I guess it wouldn't be if you were married to a compassionate and appreciative man. But to me, the fact that you stayed home—and I believe it was *not* your decision but his way of having total control over you financially and emotionally—is a problem. Because if you interacted with other people, they would've seen that you were being abused, and he would have been called on it. He's a dog! I hate him."

"Robin," her mother protested.

"Ma, I'm going to tell you this one time only, and you can do with this information what you please. Do you remember the day when Daddy came home and said he needed you to pick up his dry cleaning for the next day? Well, as soon as you left, he came to my bedroom while I was doing my homework. I tried to ignore him but he . . . " Robin closed her eyes as she remembered that day like it was happening at that very moment. "He forced me to put his penis in my mouth. And although he had done this many times before, Mother, this time was different."

"I'm leaving, Robin. I don't have to listen to this nonsense from you. You hated your father because he wanted you to be a boy, and you have always been ungrateful, even when he did pay attention to you.

"Robin, your father worked hard to take care of us. You have no idea what it's like to have the pressures of taking care of a family. He did the best that he could for us."

"Oh, excuse me, but yes, you will listen!" Robin shouted as she grabbed her mother's arm and turned her around. "Don't interrupt us again." Robin's emotionless eyes were stuck on her mother, and her whole body was tight. Her ears felt hot. She saw herself falling back, no longer in control.

Let me handle this one.

"He proceeded to make me suck his dick and shit, and before I knew it, he came in my fucking mouth. Then he told me to mind my manners, to say thank you when somebody gives you something, and to eat with my mouth closed. How the fuck would you like that if it was done to you? Or was it done to you, Mommy?"

"You're delusional, Robin. It appears that you would say or do anything to make your father look like the bad guy here, when in fact you were the most defiant and unhappy child that I've ever seen. I tried to buy you everything you wanted and needed, but that wasn't good enough."

A look of disgust engulfed Robin's face. "I'm going to finish, and then you can leave. He told me to eat with my mouth closed, and so for once, I listened to him. I slowly started to close my mouth then I shut my jaws as fast and as hard as I could. He screamed, and I tugged and turned like a Pit Bull throwing down on a T-bone steak. I wanted to rip his uncircumcised, slug-looking dick right off."

Her mother smacked her teeth, smacked the shit out of Robin then walked out. Robin stood in the middle of the room, somewhat confused about what had just happened.

Oh, thank you so much for letting me handle this one. It was killing me to be quiet. First you let that Nelson guy talk to you like that, and then you were listening to your mother call you a liar. It's okay, though I believe you. I know you're not a liar. And shake that shit off. You've been hit harder.

An uneasy feeling came over Robin, like she left for a minute and came back. She was unsure why her mother smacked her, why her foul feelings about her father felt like they were subsiding, and why she wasn't as upset as she had been in the past when she spoke of her father.

Suddenly, she had an overwhelming feeling that someone else was in the room, and this made her search every inch. She went into the bedroom, the sitting area, the walk-in closet, and finally the bathroom.

She looked at herself in the mirror. Her eyes weren't the same eyes she looked into that morning. They weren't her eyes.

"I need some rest," she said out loud, turning out all of the lights and going to bed.

Good night, girlfriend.

Chapter Seven

Robin opened the windows of her suite. The sheer curtains that hung to the floor in Robin's bedroom flowed in the fall breeze. It was 7:30 on Saturday morning, and Robin was famished.

She took a hot bath while she ate pancakes and sausage from room service, delighted at the fact that she had no actual plans for the day. It was hers to do with what she pleased. Thirty minutes later, she got out of the tub and put on her favorite pink-and-blue sweatsuit.

The mall was just a few blocks away, so she decided to leave her car in the parking garage and walk there. People were out, shopping and having coffee at the little café huts along the street. Dogs were happy that their owners were treating them to the fresh air of the morning.

As she walked, she saw Junie, a little old man who gave the best shoe shines in town. "Hey, Junie. How you doin'? I see you have a line of people waiting to get one your famous shines. Do me a favor. Stop by the hotel next Thursday so we can talk about having you move your set-up into the hotel. It can be a very profitable thing for both you and the hotel."

Junie quickly agreed to be there bright and early next Thursday. She patted him on the shoulder and went on her way.

The mall was filled with shops to curb any shopper's craving. Robin had a shoe fetish, so whenever she shopped, she came home with at least two pairs. Today, though, she went and had her hair washed, conditioned, and bumped. Then she got a pedicure. While she was getting her manicure, her cell phone rang. It was Chanel, asking if she wanted to come to Kyle's basketball game.

"Sure. Who's going with us and where's the game?"

"It's at West End Middle School. We'll go together, and Todd will meet us there. Afterwards, we always take Kyle out to eat. You're more than welcome to come with us. Say yes. Please!"

"Chanel, be cool. I'll go. Pick me up at the hotel in an hour. I should be ready by then."

This should be exciting, she thought as she finished getting her manicure. As a teenager, she loved going to the games and hanging out with her friends. Night games were the best. That was when she could get out. A shiver came over her, and she stopped her little trip down memory lane before she hit any of her uglier memories.

As she was walking back to the hotel, she saw Sharon sitting outside one of the little pastry shops with a man. She appeared to be explaining something in a very dramatic way, occasionally wiping her eyes.

Robin walked over to the table to find that it was Nelson who was accompanying her. Not that it was a surprise or anything, but she didn't get the impression that they hung out together like that. Their relationship appeared more like a boss/employee relationship with a few perks here and there. Now they seemed a little too close.

I'm not liking this at all.

"What's happening, people? Sharon, what's going on? Why you so upset?"

Sharon looked up at Nelson as if to say, *Please ask her to stop talking so loud.* Nelson interceded, telling Robin that Cory had found the clothes and food that he gave Sharon.

"He destroyed the clothes with bleach and he threw out the food altogether. And as if that wasn't enough, he hauled off and punched Sharon in the mouth, knocking out her two front teeth, right in front of James."

"Oh damn. That's messed up. You ain't hit his ass back?"

"What?" Sharon got up. "You been talking shit since the day we met. What the fuck is your problem, bitch?"

Nelson just sat back, his hands locked behind his head and a toothpick hanging out of his mouth, watching as Sharon and Robin had words.

"You all tough and whatnot. You got your ass beat or did you beat his?" Robin taunted Sharon. She went to swing at Robin, but Nelson jumped up and grabbed her.

"Let me go, Nelson."

"Yeah, let her ass go so she can get her second ass whippin' for the day."

"Robin, you really need to go on to wherever it was that you were going," Nelson said as he held Sharon tighter.

"You right, Nelson. I probably should go before I knock the rest of her teeth out. Nah, Sharon, I'm just playing. That is messed up, though," she said then walked away.

"Robin, did you get my package?" Nelson yelled out to her.

"Yeah, I got your package." She rolled her eyes. "They ugly, but I'll wear them if it turns you on."

Sharon and Nelson looked at each other. Robin just turned around and started walking back to the hotel with a slight pimp stride.

He's cute. Whatchu gon' do with him?

Robin's cell phone rang.

"Yo."

"Yo? Okay, whatever! Where are you? I thought you were coming with us to the game." It was Chanel. She was at the hotel waiting impatiently for Robin.

"I'm coming. I'll be there in a few."

"Hurry up," Chanel said and hung up the phone.

Shortly thereafter, Robin came strolling down the street.

"Come on and get in, we're going to be late if we don't hurry up."

Robin hopped in the car and greeted them both like she was right on time. "What up, y'all?"

Kyle started laughing. Robin reached back and gave him some dap and snap.

"A'ight," Kyle said. "She's funny, Ma."

"Yeah, real funny," Chanel responded as she looked at Robin and wondered who she was trying to impress.

Robin flipped down the visor to checking out her hair. The girl who washed it was massaging her scalp something fierce. She was almost about to fall asleep in the chair. A little shake gave her hair a disheveled look, which accented how she was feeling—wild as all hell.

As they pulled into the parking lot of the gym, all the basketball players were huddled together, getting their talk on before the game. Kyle immediately jumped out of the car and left his bag for his mother to carry.

"Let me get that, boo," Robin said.

"Robin, you all right? You're talking really strange. That shampoo girl must have washed some of your brains out," Chanel said as she playfully mashed Robin in the back of her head.

"What? Oh yeah, girl. I'm fine"

"Kyle, honey, let's go." Chanel summoned him as she and Robin walked past him and his friends and into the gym.

"Fine-ass little homies out here," Robin said as she checked out the young boys standing next to Kyle.

"Let's go, Robin. You ought to be ashamed of yourself."

The game was going great, and everyone was having a good time except for the fact that Chanel was irritated that Todd was late. The last few games, he came right before the end, and it really upset Chanel. It was one thing to ignore her, but to not show up at Kyle's games really burned her ass.

This time, it was the second quarter when he came strolling in, wearing different clothes than he had on that morning. Right behind him was a woman following a little too closely. When he veered to the left, she headed to the right, but her hand slid slowly down his back.

He saw Chanel and Robin, waved to them, walked over to where they were and took a seat. The woman who came in behind him went to sit across the gym. When she saw Todd settle in next to Chanel, she stood up and blew a kiss to Todd. Chanel couldn't believe what she was seeing.

"What the hell is she doing here?" she asked. The woman was his ex-wife, Eryca.

"I don't know why she's here. Maybe she has a friend or family member playing. Don't start tripping out here in public, okay. I'm not in the mood for your shit."

"I don't care if you're in the mood or not. Why did you bring her here?"

"I didn't bring her here, Chanel. Why are you even acknowledging her?"

"You know, you're absolutely right," she responded. Deep down inside, Chanel knew exactly what was going on. For a long time now, she had a gut feeling that Todd was still involved with Eryca, but she could never prove it. Chanel tried not to get upset, but her pain showed on her face.

Robin caught a glimpse of this and looked across the court. When she spotted Eryca, she knew exactly why Chanel got quiet. Robin nudged her and shook her head.

"Chanel, this is not the place to address this issue," Robin said. "Don't worry about it. Deal with her later."

"You're right."

The crowd was going crazy, and just when the halftime buzzer went off, Kyle shot a three-pointer, putting his team two points in the lead. Robin, Chanel and Todd jumped up, clapping and yelling his name and number. Across the gym, so did Eryca.

After the game, Chanel, Todd and Robin got up to leave, but they didn't get far before Eryca approached them.

"How you doing, Todd?" she asked as she chewed her gum and twisted her hair.

Chanel and Robin looked at Todd.

"Answer the bitch," Robin said as she stood and waited for Eryca to jump.

"Reggie needs things, you know," Eryca said, referring to the child she had with Todd.

"Eryca, I'll call you," Todd said as he made his way off the bleachers. As hard as it was, Chanel kept herself composed as she quickly walked down the bleachers and out of the gym.

Robin waited behind. She slowly walked down the bleachers until she was right behind Eryca, practically breathing down her neck. "Boo!" Robin taunted. Eryca jumped and fell a few steps down the bleachers. Robin laughed as she made her way out of the gym.

Kyle managed to get Todd to take him out for a while, so Robin and Chanel went back to the hotel. They decided they would get cleaned up and meet back in the lobby later for a meal at Moments, the upscale restaurant that was also located in the hotel.

"Chanel, what was up with that?" Robin asked when they sat down in the restaurant.

"You know, I had a feeling that they were still in contact with each other when I was in the office one day and saw her name and number on the caller ID. I called her number back from the office phone. She picked up her phone and said, 'I'm waiting for you. Where you at?' Obviously she saw the office number on her caller ID and thought it was Todd calling her.

"Todd still denies any knowledge as to why she called. He just said that she likes to play those games sometimes. She was jealous that we were together and have things that they couldn't have together, and since Reggie pays her no mind, she has a lot of time on her hands."

"Well, I could see her calling to discuss Reggie, but why else would she call the office phone knowing that the possibility of you seeing it was, well, possible. She's probably just pulling your chain," Robin suggested.

"No. You know how you just know that something isn't right? That's exactly how I feel. But I don't feel enough jealousy to act on it. But on the other hand, I won't be disrespected in the presence of my son, regardless if he sees it or not, by anyone, especially that stank, trifling bitch. I'm a lady and will act as such, unlike her, but when it comes to Kyle, the gloves will come off.

"Imagine getting busted having sex in the parking lot of your job by your man," Chanel said. Robin gave her a quizzical look. "Yup. That's why she and Todd got a divorce. That was after he beat her ass, of course."

"Damn. If you're gonna be a tramp, be a tramp with class and get a room," Robin joked.

"I know. She is quite the stank ho."

"Yup. She playing with fire. And if that's the case, you need to check that bitch. I would if I were you."

Robin's language and attitude surprised Chanel. Not that she was offended, but it was just not like Robin. She was always so professional. It was actually good to see that she had a down to earth side about her.

After their meal, Robin went back to her place and got started on doing the summer to fall clothes transition. She was happy to be on vacation, and when she had nothing specific planned, she almost always got involved in domesticated things. Normally, housekeeping would change the themes and color schemes of the hotel, but Robin liked things her way, so she did her room herself.

It took the rest of Robin's vacation to get everything switched, from her clothes to the drapes, the place mats and the towels in the bathroom. Brown, green, soft gold, yellows and oranges surrounded the suite with the feeling of fall.

Chapter Eight

When Robin finished her vacation and went back to work on Thursday evening, there was an envelope waiting for her. She took it into the main office, closed the door and read the letter aloud.

"Rockin' Robin, if you can't follow basic instructions, we can't be partners. Call this number when you get this envelope."

Before she could even wonder what the letter meant, she heard a voice on the intercom.

"Robin, there's a call for you on line three."

She picked up the phone. "Robin speaking."

"Robin . . ." Her mother's voice sounded strange, like the unhappy bird voice Robin remembered hearing as a child.

"Ma? What's wrong?"

"Please come . . . soon as you can."

Robin didn't answer. She slammed the phone down and briefed the front desk employees on what was expected of them while she was out. She went to the parking garage, hopped in her 2002 Lexus ES 300 and sped to her mother's house.

Inside, she found her mother in a chair with her face in her hands. The house was a mess, and several large holes in the walls told Robin of the violence that had taken place here.

She lifted her mother's face to find her wearing two black eyes. Dark bruises covered her jaw, and when Robin's eyes traveled over her mother's body, she saw that the bruises seemed to be on every inch of exposed skin. When she caught her breath, she asked her mother, "What happened?"

Toscha was very weak, barely able to get the words out, but she struggled through her pain and managed to give Robin the story. "You were right . . . about Daddy. I told him . . . I knew . . . what he did . . . to you. He started yelling . . . then this happened." She looked around the room at the mess that surrounded them.

"When exactly did all this happen, Ma?"

"Last night."

"And you fucking just now calling us? Where is that blue-black motherfucka?"

"He left. I don't think he'll be coming back."

"You got that shit right. And the shit is on now." Robin looked into her mother's eyes and her insides felt like they were melting. Her eyes frowned, her lips tightened and her breathing was barely more than a pant. This was it for her, for them.

Oh hell, yeah. That bastard has raised his hands for the last time. Girl, you know what you gotta do.

"Stop it," Robin pleaded with the voice.

Ooooooooooh, you forgot to call Nelson.

"Shut up!" Robin yelled, startling her mother.

"Sorry, Ma. Come on and let's get you some clothes. I'm taking you to the hospital."

Yeah!

Robin helped her mother up from the chair and she let out a whimpering cry. She couldn't stand up straight. It was obvious that her ribs were broken. Robin called 911. The ambulance was at the house in a matter of minutes, and they took her mother to the hospital.

"Don't worry, Miss, we'll take good care of her," the EMT told Robin. "Will you be riding in the ambulance with her?"

"No, I'll be right behind you." Robin locked up the house and set the alarm, but not before she changed the code. This way, if her father came back, it would sound off and she would be paged.

As she drove nervously to the hospital, she dialed the number that had been on the letter she received at the hotel. She recognized Nelson's voice when he answered.

"Rockin', I'm disappointed. You got my first package a week ago and I never heard from you. You got this last envelope an hour ago, and you're just now calling me back. You gotta be on time if you want my time."

"Nelson, I'm not sure what the urgency was in calling you the moment I got your last message. I was going to call you back, but then I got an emergency phone call from my mother. She was bea—" Robin stopped herself before she started discussing her family issues with this man she barely knew. "She had an emergency and needed me to come to the house."

"I'll see you tomorrow, Rockin' Robin. Peace, baby." There was a click in her ear as Nelson hung up.

She pulled into the emergency room parking lot. The ambulance attendants had already brought her mother inside, and the doctors took her right away.

After Robin signed in and gave them her mother's insurance information, she went down to the waiting area. Just as she was about to plop down on the couch, she heard her name being paged to ER103.

She walked quickly to the room with an uneasy feeling. As she entered, she saw the nurse covering her mother's face with a white sheet. Chills raced through Robin's body, and she felt her knees get weak. A doctor approached and held her arm to keep her from falling to the floor.

Robin listened with tears in her eyes as he told her, "I'm sorry, but your mother didn't make it. Her injuries were too severe." He guided Robin to a quiet corner outside the room, where he helped her sit down. He explained the extent of damage Jiles had done to her mother.

"Ms. Sessoms, your mother suffered blows to her head that caused her brain to swell. She had two seizures and vomited in between them. All of her ribs were broken, and her lung was punctured. We were able to stabilize her breathing and get her on oxygen, but she was bleeding internally, and her body was too weak to overcome the extent of the injuries. I'm sorry for your loss."

Robin stood, wanting to go back in and see her mother again. The room started spinning, and her arms were too limp to reach out and stop it. Her legs collapsed and she fell to the floor. The doctors picked her up and laid her on a bed. They checked her vitals and covered her with a blanket.

The nurses searched Robin's pockets but found no identification. She had left the hotel in such a hurry that she was not carrying her purse or a wallet. The only clue they had was the name of the hotel embroidered on the lapel of her jacket. Assuming this was her work uniform, they phoned the hotel and asked to speak to a supervisor.

"Yes, she works here. Is there something wrong?" asked the employee who answered the phone.

The nurse explained what had happened to Robin and her mother. The employee rushed to find Chanel and put her on the phone. Chanel listened to the nurse then promised to be there right away to help her friend.

Chapter Nine

Robin was asleep for hours. Chanel had been by her side all night, and had fallen asleep in the lounge chair next to Robin's bed. When Robin finally awoke, she looked around the room and saw Chanel. As she realized where she was and remembered what had happened, she started to cry. Chanel heard her, and went to lay beside her.

"Chanel, she's dead. My father killed my mother."

"Robin, I'm so sorry." Chanel stroked Robin's hair gently to soothe her. "If there is anything that I can do, please, please let me know. I'm here for you, Robin, and don't you forget that." Tears ran down Chanel's face.

Robin began to cry uncontrollably, no longer able to speak. She curled into the fetal position and pulled the blanket over her face. Her eyes were swollen, and bags hid the long lashes that brightened her face. The usually put-together Robin was torn, minced inside.

"What time is it?" she asked Chanel.

"Quarter to five. Why?"

"I gotta go to my other job. If I don't leave now, I'm going to be late."

"You aren't serious, Robin. I can't let you do that. Your mother passed away last night, sweetheart. I think you must be in shock. I know this is hard for you, but you're in no shape to go empty anybody's damn garbage. Please be reasonable. I'm sure they'll understand."

"No. I have to go." She got up, went into the bathroom and washed her face with cold water. "I'm going back to the hotel to get a shower and change, then I'm going to work. I'll be in for my shift tonight."

"Robin, please," Chanel pleaded, but it fell on deaf ears. Robin was already out the door.

As Robin headed to the spot where Sharon would pick her up, she noticed she had a message on her cell phone. It was Ms. Grimes, telling Robin to stop by the truck yard. Sharon wasn't going to be in, and Robin would need to drive the truck by herself. Her CDL license would be in the glove box.

"CDL license," Robin said, wondering how they could have gotten her one without any kind of test.

Oooooh, I always wanted to drive a truck. You need to take mad classes and a road test to get a CDL. You got the hook-up, girl. I'm so excited.

"I can't drive a truck."

How hard can it be? You better learn real quick, chick.

Once Ms. Grimes gave Robin a quick lesson on driving the truck, Robin headed out on her route. She was still numb from the reality of her mother's death, and the stress of driving the big truck was actually a good distraction for her.

She did the run as she remembered. There were a few times where she momentarily lost control of the truck by cutting corners too short. Aside from a few mailboxes that she ran over, one or two mirrors that she tore off of cars and a few garbage cans that she knocked over, she managed to get through the neighborhood and make it to Nelson's. Although she was in a very shady state of mind, she didn't forget her sunglasses, and that was sure to please Nelson.

She backed up, put the truck in park and walked into the back yard. Black and White stood their ground, proud and silent.

"Rockin' Robin, scan and come in," a voice over a small intercom announced.

She did as she was told, entering through the double sliding doors and sitting at a table. An assortment of cheeses and fruits and a bottle of Tequila awaited her arrival.

"I don't have house champagne. I Hope Jose will do the job. I see you remembered your glasses," Nelson said as he came into the room and poured a shot for Robin.

Unresponsive, Robin reached for the shot glass and downed it. "How about another one, this time in a bigger glass?" she asked.

"I'm sorry to hear about your loss."

Robin looked up at Nelson through her dark glasses and wondered how he knew about her mother.

"Rockin', hear and remember this. Good news travels fast, but bad news travels faster."

Slumped across the table, Robin didn't say anything.

Nelson pulled up a chair and sat next to her. He didn't want her to feel uncomfortable, so he didn't touch her. Instead he pulled out some paperwork to make a proposal he had been planning for quite some time.

In the beginning, Nelson wasn't sure of Robin's courage and capabilities. He would come in on Wednesday nights and sit at a table in a dark corner of the bar, having drinks and observing her behavior. Even from a distance, he could tell there was something special about Robin. Something he could use to his advantage.

He had Dr. Christopher meet him there to observe her as well. Nelson paid Dr. Christopher well, so Dr. Christopher followed his orders without question or complaint. He was to get to know Chanel, gain her trust then convince her to recommend his services to Robin. The plan had worked without a hitch.

After Robin's sessions with Dr. Christopher, the therapist would feed information to Nelson, who was starting to feel confident that Robin was the person he needed. Finally, when he found her prints on his gun, he had no more doubts about her courage. It took a lot of nerve to handle someone else's property, especially a weapon, and act like it was nothing. By the time Robin was on her way to the interview with Ms. Grimes, Nelson had already paid her to give Robin the job and assign her to the route that passed his house.

"What is this?" Robin asked, pointing to the paperwork in front of her.

"Rockin', I know you're wondering what exactly it is that I do. I'm home all day, chillin' in a mansion in middle suburbia. I know everything about you. By the way, how's your counseling going?"

"Dr. Christopher says that I'm doing well," Robin answered, still slumped over the table. She was too shell-shocked from the recent events to even wonder how Nelson knew about Dr. Christopher.

"Let me guess. Your mother finally confronted your father about how he treated you. She probably told him what a pig he was and that she wanted him out. He got mad because she spoke out of her place, and in an uncontrollable frenzy, he beat her basically to death."

Robin's body jerked as she cried.

"Rockin' Robin, what do you want to do about this? Tell me. If you want to walk away and let him get away with it, then I'll respect that. But if you want to avenge your mother's death and your life, then I can help you with that as well. I tell you what. You think about it and let me know.

"In the meantime, you can go in the shed and pick up my garbage. It's not shredded paper this time, and it is a bit heavier. If your strength isn't up to it, you can come and get it next week. What's it gonna be?" Nelson asked.

"I'm here already, so I'll take it now."

"Okay, cool. Now, you won't be dumping it at the regular dumpsite. There's a special site especially for garbage like this. It has to be properly handled so that it doesn't smell."

Nelson led the way to the shed. Black and White backed off. He opened the shed. Inside was a metal garbage can with a top that had been welded onto it. He pulled the can out onto the grass.

Robin took it from him, and although it was too heavy to lift, she dragged it to the truck. Nelson followed her and watched as she struggled.

"Can you help me?" Robin asked, trying not to breathe too deeply because the garbage smelled so bad.

They picked up the garbage can and put it in the back of the truck. As she was leaving, Nelson told her that he was going to call her in a few minutes to tell her the location of the special dumping site.

She raised her hand, acknowledging that she heard him. As soon as she reached the end of the street, her phone rang. It was Nelson.

He gave her the driving directions then said, "Two guys will be there to assist you. Just let them have the trashcan and you can be on your way. Be sure you call me as soon as you're back en route to return the truck." There was a click in her ear.

That damn Nelson never says good-bye before he hangs up.

Chapter Ten

"Congratulations, you've just completed your first run," Neslon said to Robin when she completed the drop-off.

"Excuse me? The fuck you talkin' 'bout?"

"Rockin', you know what I'm talking about. Sharon and I have become very close. When Cory did that to her and to the things that I gave her son, I couldn't just sit on that. She didn't even tell you everything that happened. That scumbag raped her in front of James. And as little as he is, all he could do was watch his mommy be violated. Fuck that. She's my girl. I got a lot of love for her, and you know I love the kids."

"Yo, bro, that's what's up, nigga," Robin said, understanding what Nelson was referring to. That was no ordinary can of garbage she dumped for him at the special site. "I'm wit' ya on dat shit. So, who the fuck is next?"

Nelson dismissed Robin's response. "Just go home and handle the arrangements for your mother's burial," he said then hung up.

Robin, we rockin' now. I thought I was the only one who had urges like that. Glad to see you're stepping up in the world.

"What? Who are you?" she yelled as she began banging on the steering wheel.

Robin's cell phone rang again. "What?" she screamed when she hit the talk button.

It was Dr. Christopher, wondering why she had missed her two appointments last week. She didn't show nor did she call.

"Yeah, well, I've been busy!"

"Are you okay, Robin?"

"Yeah. Damn, man."

"Your next appointment is scheduled for next Tuesday at noon. Will you be there?" Dr. Christopher wanted to confirm.

"I said yeah!" Robin hung up the phone.

Dr. Christopher was satisfied with Robin's response. It was typical of people with multiple personality disorder to forget their normal routines and sometimes not be able to account for the time missed. However, her unruliness troubled him.

It was decided that because of the extent of the damages to Toscha's body, she would be cremated. Chanel was an enormous help with the arrangements, and she even let Robin have the memorial service and brunch at the hotel. Many people came to pay their respects, including a detective who was assigned to handle the case. He approached Robin and expressed his condolences.

"Thank you," she said as she shook his hand. She was still unaware that he was a homicide detective, and he didn't feel it was appropriate to discuss the details of the investigation under these circumstances. He had no choice, however, when she asked, "How did you know my mother?"

"Actually, I'm Detective Fama, homicide division."

"Oh? And what do you know about my mother's death? You know my father killed her, right? He beat her to death." Tears welled up in Robin's eyes.

"I can tell you that we questioned him, and he said that he was out playing cards and hadn't been home the evening of the beating. And although we have confirmations of his alibi, he was informed that he's a suspect. We took prints from the house, but since your parents still lived together, his prints aren't enough for evidence. We need more, and I assure you that we will continue to search and keep our ears to the ground, but at this time, they have to treat it as a break-in homicide until we get a viable lead."

"I appreciate that very much, Detective. Please keep me posted. You can reach me at the hotel."

The little bit of information that Detective Fama shared with Robin wasn't good enough. Her father killed her mother and they were waiting for leads. She saw that she would have to handle this herself. Then again, Nelson had offered to help, and now she was giving his proposition some serious thought.

As she mingled with people she didn't know, Robin saw her father walk in. He browsed about the room then walked over and sat at an empty table. With his hands folded and his pimp-looking hat slanted to the side, he lit a cigar and sat back in the chair. Robin immediately approached him.

"You have a lot of nerve showing your face here, dressed like somebody's sugar daddy. You still reek of the piss that you sat in at the hospital."

He blew circles with his cigar smoke directly in her face then gave a nod to someone across the room.

Punch the shit out of him, Robin. What the fuck you waiting for? He more than deserves it.

"You have five minutes to get out."

As she started to walk away, Nelson came over and shook her father's hand. Robin was dumbfounded. She watched Nelson with a frown.

"Jiles, it's good to see you. Sorry to hear about your wife. If you need anything, let me know," Nelson said. "I'll see you at next week's card game."

"Card game?" Robin questioned. "You play cards with—" She pointed to her father and said his name like it was poison. "*Him?* You know my father?"

"Yeah. Me and old Jiles go way back. Right, Jiles?"

Again he nodded and blew more circles. Robin walked away, trying her hardest not to cry. When he said that he knew everything about her, Nelson failed to mention that included knowing her father, the bastard.

This is what I'm talking about. If he knew everything about you, don't you think he knew your father? You act so simple sometimes.

A few minutes later, Nelson approached her. "Can I speak to you?"

As much as she wanted to curse him out, she was at her mother's memorial service, so she left the room calmly with him. They went to talk in an empty coatroom.

"What the hell was that all about?" she demanded.

"Rockin' Robin, I told you before that I know everything. My resources are unlimited. I've been playing cards with your father for some time now on Thursday nights. Don't worry. I took care of it. I had someone give him an alibi so that he can stay out of jail. It would be that much harder to get to him if he was locked up. We need him on the outside in order to get him. You have to trust me."

A skeptical look masked Robin's face, but she listened intently to Nelson.

"Look, Rockin'. You have to let me set this up so that if and when the time comes that you want to handle this, everything will fit perfectly. I have people in the police department who will aid me in this. Just say yes or no, and we can go from there."

"Nelson, I can't believe you sent me to that disposal site. When did you kill Cory? Where was Sharon? Does she even know?" Robin asked, changing the subject because she was not ready to deal with Nelson's proposal. As much as she hated her father, she wasn't quite ready to start thinking of herself as a murderer.

"Yes, Robin, she knows. Who do you think did it? I'm out of the business of committing the actual act. I give the resources and make sure you're ready mentally, and once you do it, I make sure you have representation should you go to trial and/or jail. If not, you will at the very least be prepped by a lawyer friend of mine should anyone ask you any questions."

"How do you know all of these people? And how do you know that you can trust them?"

"I'm a lawyer. Well, I'm retired, and these people have been my clients at one time or another, or they've helped me with my cases in the past. We've developed a relationship where we help each other." He rubbed his hands together.

Robin had to get back to her guests, and she needed time away from Nelson to digest all that he had just told her. Despite everything, she was very intrigued.

When she got back to the room, most of the people had left, including her father. Only Chanel, Todd, Kyle and a few of her mother's neighbors who were finding it hard to let go remained. Robin made a general announcement, telling them that they could help themselves to the flowers, and if they wanted any food, take-home containers were on each of the buffet tables for their convenience.

She went over to Chanel. "Thank you so much for everything. Just put the bill in my mailbox and I'll take care of it immediately."

"Sweetheart, there is no bill. It's already been taken care of by that gentleman over there." Chanel pointed to Nelson. "And Robin, I'm so sorry." Todd, who stood next to Chanel, was quiet as usual, and he didn't bother to express his condolences.

"Well," Robin said, "I better start cleaning up, then."

"That's been taken care of too. That man hired a cleaning crew that should be here soon to get rid of the mess."

Robin excused herself and went over to Nelson to thank him for his generosity. She was unsure why he took an interest in her from the beginning, but she was sure glad to have him around now. She would've needed a third job to repay Chanel for the presentation she gave on behalf of her mother.

Robin was ready to go to her suite to be alone. First, she went to the front desk to check for any messages. There was an envelope for her, containing a condolence card from Nelson. At the bottom, it read: *P.S. You're welcome.*

Exhausted, she made her way up to her suite and lay across her bed, remembering her mother. She thought about how Toscha's smile could light up a whole room.

When Robin was little and she laughed with her mother, she would get goose bumps. Toscha's voice was like a bird's voice, full of tranquility. Her heart was full of love that she shared with everyone. And now she was gone at the hands of her husband. There was no way Robin could let her father get away with it.

Chapter Eleven

Dr. Christopher entered the office and sat across from Robin. It had been two weeks since their last session, and Robin was tired and overwhelmed.

"The last time I was here, you said that I spoke about someone else. What did I say?"

"Well, you mentioned the name Chrissy, and you sounded like you knew this person. I'll put you under, and we can touch on that today."

"No. I don't want to go under. I want to talk about my mother, and I would rather be awake. I buried my mother this past Sunday. She died from injuries caused by my father. He beat her so bad that he broke all of her ribs, gave her two black eyes, and fractured her jaw."

"Oh, Robin, I'm so sorry."

"A few days before that, I told my mother about all of the sexual and emotional abuse that my father used to subject me to when she'd leave the house. She denied it ever happened and told me I was delusional. But I guess when she got home and thought about how I used to go straight to my room after school, how I didn't tell her when I first got my period and how I never had any boyfriends, it prompted her to confront him. He obviously denied it and started to beat her. He killed my mother!" Robin started to cry.

"Robin, how often did your father sexually abuse you?"

"Man, that motherfucka, every chance he got to do it to me, he did. It was never enough. He wanted my little ass more than he wanted my mother's. When I started telling him no and shit, he went out and got himself in trouble. He messed around with a girl at my school. She told and he went to jail. Good for his dirty ass."

Jiles had actually gone to jail for three years behind that crime. That was why Robin couldn't understand that her mother wouldn't believe her when she said her father had raped her too. How could she be in such deep denial, Robin often wondered.

Dr. Christopher had never heard Robin speak with such an edge. He prodded her even more to see where it was coming from.

"Robin, your father is a sick man, and I completely understand how you feel."

"You know how I feel? Well, tell me, Dr. Christopher, how would you feel having an uncircumcised stubby piece of meat shoved into you? Bet you wouldn't like it, you being a man and all," Robin said, slapping her knee and letting out a loud laugh.

"Robin, had you ever told your mother before?"

"No."

"Why not?"

"I tried to tell her, but she would always say that it wasn't a good time."

"Would you wait until it was just you and her?"

"That's a dumb-ass question. No, I tried to tell her when my father's dick was inside of me and I was watching Woody Wood Pecker on television. What do you think?"

"Robin, as an adult, had you ever brought this to your mother's attention prior to a few weeks ago?"

"We wanted to tell her and shit, but that old bastard told me that he would have to put it in my butt if I did. Why you keep calling me Robin?"

"Well, that is your name. Isn't it?

There was silence. Dr. Christopher sat and watched Robin's body language change from ladylike to a thug-like demeanor that matched her new, harsher speech. She fell back into the chair, her head was tilted to the side and she had a smirk on her face. She sat and said nothing.

Dr. Christopher was sure this was another personality that had surfaced, and it was the person who Robin had referred to in their previous sessions. He proceeded carefully.

"Okay. If you're not Robin, then who are you?"

"I'm who and whatever she needs me to be. I say and do what she can't say or do. I'm what she ain't strong enough to be."

"And what is that? Because the Robin I know has held her own through this whole dilemma. Why is it now that you choose to show your face, or should I say speak up?"

"Because I felt like it. I don't work on other people's schedules. I do as I please, and what Robin really pleases. She thinks it, and I say and do it. So what's the topic of discussion today?"

"Well, Robin wanted to talk about the abuse that she suffered at the hands of her father, Jiles, and how her mother denied it up until just recently. Did you know that her mother died last week?"

"Yeah, I knew. That's why when I wanted to come out on Sunday, she told me it wasn't the time. Normally, she don't put up a fight. But I understood why. The old lady's husband finally pulled her number."

Dr. Christopher was amazed at how when it came to Robin, this person appeared to talk with respect and caring.

"Where is Robin?"

"She in the corner. Leave her alone. She loved her mother very much, and it's because of that love that she didn't say anything earlier. And now that she said something, her mother is gone. Is there something you want me to tell her?"

"Let her know that it's okay. We'll work it out. Before you go, though, can I ask what your name is?" Dr. Christopher asked calmly, wanting to appear to be unconcerned and accepting of this presence.

"My name is Chrissy."

"Thank you, Chrissy. Tell Robin I'm waiting for her."

Dr. Christopher sat back and waited. His heart went out to Robin. Out of all of his patients, she was one of the few that he took a real liking to. Her personality was vibrant, and she tried really hard during her sessions to confront her issues.

Robin remained laid back and quiet. She looked around the room and showed no emotions. Dr. Christopher's eyes didn't move off of her. He wanted to see the transition from Chrissy back to Robin.

After about fifteen minutes of staring at each other, Robin began to rub her hands together then held them under her chin. She closed her eyes. Her lip began to quiver, followed by a silent and much needed cry. She fell to her side on the couch and hid her face. Dr. Christopher went to her and put his arms around her, lifting her back into an upright position.

"It's okay, Robin. Feel what you need to feel, and don't be ashamed. I know this a very difficult time for you." He held her until their session was over.

Chapter Twelve

"What do you mean I should understand?" Chanel asked Todd. "Why should I have to put up with her not wanting to accept our marriage? It's been fourteen years now. The bitch should be used to it by now. She wouldn't be acting like this if you weren't either filling her head with stuff or sleeping with her. So, which is it?"

"Chanel, I told you that I'm not sleeping with her. You know she not wrapped too tight. Any time she sees a window to cause trouble between you and me, she's gonna climb in. And the only way she can do that is if you acknowledge her actions. If you ignore her, she'll eventually get tired and stop all of this nonsense. You really need to have a little bit more faith in us."

"Oh, yeah. I should, right?" Chanel answered sarcastically. "Please, Todd. In order to have faith in us, you have to be honest with me. Are you being honest with me?"

"Yes. Yes, I am. Now get off of my back, bitch!" he yelled.

Chanel stood speechless for a moment. Kyle was in the other room, and she didn't want him to hear or see what was going on. She grabbed her purse and stormed out the door, but not before whispering harshly, "Go fuck yourself."

In the lobby, Chanel tried to get herself together. Robin noticed that her friend looked distressed.

"Hey, girl. What's the matter?" Robin asked in a very tired voice.

"Robin, I'm fucking telling you, Todd is a lying bastard. I know he's still seeing Eryca because bitches don't trip unless something is still going on. You know what I mean?"

"I hear you. Come on. Let's go for a ride. I'll drive. I just need to run up to my room for a minute and I'll be right back down."

Robin went to her suite, washed up quickly and changed her clothes. Her message light was blinking, but she needed to get back to Chanel. The message could wait.

They drove around aimlessly until Robin's cell phone rang. It was Nelson, and he wanted her to stop by his house for a drink.

"I'm not alone."

"So, come anyway, Rockin'."

Robin convinced Chanel to go with her, and they headed to Nelson's house. Robin had never been to his house at night. Recessed lighting lined the cobblestone walkway, which led to a three-inch thick, pewter-trimmed glass door. A waterfall at the left of the house was lit with hues of green and yellow. Robin rang the bell, and Black and White came running to the door, barking wildly.

Nelson entered the foyer and called the dogs to him. They ran to his side, and he pressed a remote control button to unlock the door. Robin and Chanel went in and headed for the living room, where Nelson had already gone.

Nelson was sitting on his sage-colored Italian leather sectional, which took up three of the room's four walls. Soft jazz came from the speakers that surrounded the room. Fruit, cheeses, sushi, and vegetables were displayed elegantly on the dining room table.

"What's the reason for all of this? Are you expecting more company than Chanel and me?"

"Actually, Sharon is coming over, and Lewis is already here. Lewis is the attorney that you'll need to get to know on a very personal basis. I told you before, we have to make sure our shit is in check so we don't get checked. Rockin', how did your session go today?"

"How do you know that I had a session with Dr. Christopher today?"

"I told you I know everything. And Chanel, for the record, your husband is still sleeping with his ex-wife," Nelson said as he sipped his drink.

Chanel introduced herself, remaining surprisingly calm. "I'm sorry. We met for a moment during the services for Mrs. Sessoms. I'm Chanel Kendricks."

"I know, boo. No need to be formal. I know you and your poor-ass excuse for a husband, Todd. You better go with your gut instinct because if it was ever right, it's right now."

"Excuse me?"

"Mr. and Mrs. Todd Kendricks . . ." Nelson began telling Chanel what he knew. "He's a part-time student and a full-time addict who's still sleeping with his addict ex-wife. You have your degree in social services from the University of Pennsylvania, but you aren't actually using it. You own the hotel, and you're doing a nice job, I might add. Eryca Kendricks, the other woman he was married to, is the mother of his oldest son, Reggie, and you have his youngest, Kyle. They're divorced, yes, but he still sees her. She has drug dealers for boyfriends, which is right up Todd's alley, and if you're not careful, your son will be brought into that lifestyle as well."

Chanel's mouth dropped open. She looked quickly at Robin as if to ask, *Who is this man, and why did you bring me here?*

"How do you know so much about me?"

"Sweetheart, ask your friend. She'll confirm that I know everything. I am—or was—a lawyer licensed in the states of New Jersey, Pennsylvania, New York and Connecticut. I have represented the best of the best and the scum of the earth, suffering only one loss, which I will explain to you later. But the bottom line is that I no longer practice law like everybody else does.

"If you've ever had any dealings with courts, whether you were the defendant or the plaintiff, you probably felt that the decision wasn't fair, that other information should've been taken into consideration, or that telling the truth just isn't good enough. I know this to be true because that's how I felt." He pointed to his chest.

Nelson paused to refill his glass, asking if anyone else wanted a drink. As he was pouring, the doorbell rang and Sharon walked in.

"Ah, just in time. We were sharing," Nelson said as he lifted his glass to her.

Sharon greeted everyone with a smile on her face. She wore a red-and-brown pinstriped suit. A Coach bag complemented her white crepe shirt and brown wing-tipped loafers. She looked like she had just stepped out of photo shoot.

Here comes the bitch.

"Stop," Robin whispered as she began to rub her hands together. Everyone looked curiously at Robin.

Black and White were stressed out when Sharon came in. The last time they saw her, she was moving hurriedly and showing a lot of excitement. They sniffed around her feet and smelled her hand, and that seemed to calm them. They weren't feeling anxiety from her this time, so they warmed up to her, allowed her to pet them then went back to their master's side.

Once everyone had a filled glass, Nelson formally introduced Lewis Weinstock, his right-hand man. A tiny man, he stood only five feet tall and weighed 110 pounds. Lewis was single with no children. He had his own home nearby but spent ninety percent of his time at Nelson's house. He too was licensed to practice law in New Jersey, Pennsylvania, New York and Connecticut. In addition, he was licensed in Washington State and California.

His intelligence far outweighed that of any law professional. His years of studying allowed him to find, examine, and master the loopholes of any and every law. Lewis could find a solution for any problem.

"I'm feel really weird about all of this. How does he know everything about me?" Chanel whispered to Robin, who was too busy watching other things to respond.

Sharon was in the corner talking with Nelson. He was rubbing her back in a comforting way, and she was still smiling.

Ay yo, she moving in on your man! You gonna let that happen? I'm coming through, I'm telling you.

Robin leaned back.

"All right, everyone is here, so let's all have a seat and have good conversation. Like I told you a few minutes ago, and Sharon, you have had the pleasure of meeting and speaking with Lewis already, Lewis is your best friend from here on out. There will be no secrets—not that there could be—held from him, and as long as we're all honest, everything will go smoothly. I must say to you, though, if you're feeling a little bit uncomfortable or unsure that you won't be able to uphold our nondisclosure clause, you should leave now. I should tell you, however, that it's really too late."

"With all due respect, I didn't ask to come here, so I'm not digging your threat of it being too late to leave," Chanel announced. "I don't know you, despite the fact that you seem to know a lot about me, and don't think I belong here."

"You know, I think you're right. So, if you want to leave knowing that your husband is still fucking his ex-wife, tells you he's going one place when in fact he's at her house getting high, takes money from the business to support both his and her drug addictions, which will eventually lead to a foreclosure on your home—you know the one you rent out for double the mortgage payment so that you can have pocket money—then you're free to go. You didn't ask to be here, and you can leave without being in contempt," Nelson responded.

When Chanel stood speechless before him, he added, "Just see Lewis on your way out for the foreclosure paperwork that will be sent out to you next week from the mortgage company."

Chanel was so confused, she didn't know what to do other than go to the desk where Lewis was sitting. In front of him sat a file with her name on it. He opened it and showed her a pile of documents stating that she was six months past due on her mortgage, showing a figure of $8,900.00 delinquent. The word "foreclosure" was stamped in big red letters on the first page.

She went to reach for it, but Lewis, with hands as quick as his mind, closed the folder and shook his head. He advised her, "Taking this folder and reading its contents will confirm that you agree to the terms in our verbal understanding."

"What fucking understanding?" Chanel shouted, placing her hands on her hips.

"Baby girl, chill. It's not that serious yet. Lewis, take her in the back and show her the rest. That's her business, and she may not want to share with us."

"Mr. Bray," Lewis said, "whatever you say."

Chanel glared at Robin while she followed Lewis into the back of the house. Robin shrugged her shoulders because she too was taken by surprise by all the events that were unfolding.

"Rockin' Robin, it's all good. I know you didn't expect for her to be called to the floor, but this is what I do." Nelson said.

"What you do . . . What exactly is it that you do, because I have yet to figure it out."

"When Lewis is done in a few, I'll explain to you how I got into the business."

While they were waiting for Chanel and Lewis to return, Nelson, Sharon, and Robin talked. Nelson could sense some tension between Robin and Sharon.

"Look, I don't know how you two got off on the wrong foot, but it stops here. I can't have this nonsense going on."

"Nelson, you know me. I don't bother anybody. She started with her mouth the first day," Sharon said.

"I started with my mouth? Bitch, you're the one who was bragging about how all these rich folks, including you, Nelson." Robin poked her finger in his chest. "Be taking care of you all whatever," Robin belted.

"I don't care. Squash it." Nelson's voice was stern.

After about a half-hour, Chanel returned to the room. It was obvious she had been crying, but appeared to have it together now.

"Hey, Chanel. What's the problem?" Robin asked.

"Don't ask her that," Nelson said. "If she wants you to know, she'll tell you in private. You don't pull cards around here. Do you understand?" He was shouting now.

I know you not gonna let him talk to you like that for a second time. His house is nice and shit, and he look like he is rollin' in dough, but fuck that. He ain't gonna be talking to you like that. If you don't say something, I will.

Robin rubbed her temples and began to rub her hands again.

"Yo, Nelson."

"Not now, Rockin'. We have some things to talk about."

"Go away," Robin said softly.

Nope.

Nelson continued his story. "Now, I believed at some point in my life that justice was served in the court of law, which was fair and unbiased. I grew up in Hillside, New Jersey with a brother named Byron, and both my parents were in the home. I graduated high school and went to college on an academic scholarship."

Nelson got up and stood in front of Chanel, Sharon and Robin as if he was conducting a class.

He was.

They all listened intently. Sharon leaned over the arm of the couch with her feet bent behind her thighs. Chanel sat cross-legged, and Robin sat back on the couch with her head tilted, still rubbing her hands as Nelson continued.

"I graduated from Trenton State University, first in my class, and decided that I wanted to be a lawyer. After completing three years of law school, I passed the Bar exam on the first try then took the exams for the tri-state area.

"I met Lewis at Trenton State. He was a year behind me but we kept in touch. When he graduated, passed the Bar and became certified to practice law, we joined forces and opened our own office, Weinstock and Bray. You may have heard of it."

"I have," Chanel stated.

"After being in business for three years, we got so busy that we had to hire another lawyer to work on the small cases. Veronica Jordan came aboard full of go get 'em and ready to work. She started the day after we interviewed her, and things were going great. She was handling her business, came home with many wins and was potential partner material.

"After we did a background check on her, we found out that in her high school days she was involved in some illegal activity and decided that making her a partner wasn't in the best interests of the firm. We told her, and she was okay with it. She just wanted to know that she wouldn't be fired behind it. We assured her that as long as she didn't participate in that type of activity any longer and it wouldn't come back to haunt her and or involve the firm, she had job security. So, everybody was happy.

"I was attracted to her from the start, and since she wasn't going to become a partner, I was even more attracted to her. We started going out, and the flow was smooth. We dated for about six months and then I asked her to marry me."

"After six months? Damn, brother, her shit must have been tight," Robin blurted out. Chanel, Sharon, Nelson and Lewis just looked at her.

Nelson continued. "We moved into a condo right away and bought a house a year later. She got pregnant with my son, Dannon, and a few years later, my twin daughters, Neeah and Naohme, were born.

After the kids were born, things were still good. It's when I was putting many hours in at work and most of my free time into the children that things did a 180-degree turn."

"Wow, Nelson. You never mentioned that you had children," Sharon said.

"Up until now, it was none of anyone's business."

"Why you worried about his kids?" Robin demanded to know.

"Robin!" Chanel exclaimed.

"Is there a problem, Robin?" Sharon asked as she stood up.

"You want one?" Robin asked as she got up and moved toward Sharon.

Sharon got up. Chanel went to grab Robin, but Robin swung her hand off. As she walked past Nelson, he grabbed her arm.

"Don't you see me talking? Sit down, Sharon."

Sharon did as she was told. Robin slowly looked over at Nelson.

"I like that. Get rougher."

"Save it, Rockin'." Nelson let go of her arm.

Robin walked backwards to her seat, blew Sharon a kiss and winked at her. Nelson continued once everyone was seated again.

"She started shoving me whenever I gave her an answer she didn't want to hear. The shoving went to slapping and cursing me out in front of the kids. I tried to talk to her about stopping that behavior in front of the kids, but she didn't listen." Nelson's voice was becoming louder as he spoke. It trembled when he spoke specifically of his children, as if he might cry.

"After months of therapy and counseling, she up and walked out of a session that in my opinion was going well, and told me that I was the one with the problem. She wasn't going to participate any longer. I stayed. I was very upset and hurt. I loved my family more than life itself and made sure they had everything they wanted and needed. When I got home from the session, she came at me with a hammer, missing my head but hitting my shoulder and dislocating it totally. And this was done in front of my kids."

Lewis shifted in his seat. He was obviously disapproving of Nelson's openness.

"I went and filed for a restraining order, but since we were still married and not separated, I had to make a choice. I had to leave and try from the outside to make it work, or stay there and possibly do something in self-defense that I would regret for the rest of my life. She wasn't going to stop, and if I had stayed, I would've killed her. I love my children too much to take away their mother. I'd rather see them when they want to come here than put them through any more emotional distress."

"Nelson," Lewis called, "that's enough. Let's get to the point."

"Okay, ladies."

"Ladies. Yeah, right. These bitches are sitting here looking at you and listening to your sob story. You ain't had no abuse until you had—" Robin was interrupted.

"Ay, Rockin'," Nelson interrupted, "hold that thought."

"Chanel and Sharon, why don't you go into the other room and help yourself to some food? I need to talk to Rockin' for a minute."

Chanel and Sharon went into the dining room, where a spread fit for kings decorated the huge dining room table. A crystal chandelier reflected light over the table, making it look like a kaleidoscope.

Nelson sat next to Robin, who by that point had switched her position, sitting back with one leg crossed over the other.

"How long are you going to leave him or her, whatever he or she is, locked up inside you?" he asked.

"What the fuck you talkin' 'bout? You kind of cute. Come here, baby."

Nelson peered at Robin, tilting his head to one side. "You know just what I'm talking about. Who the hell are you? I know you're not Robin. She's too womanly. So?"

"Please. She's just a scared little girl who lets everybody walk all over her and talk to her however they want. She don't know how to handle her business, and when she punks out, I step up to the plate. Got beef, nigga?"

"No. No beef here. I just want to know who I'm talking to. What's your name again?"

"I didn't tell you my name yet. But I see you really want to know, so I'll tell you now. My name is Chrissy. I ain't no boy and I ain't no girl."

"Where do you come from? Or should I say, how long have you been with Robin?"

"I've been with her from day one, Mr. Nelson Bray. I was with her in the womb. That rat-bastard bird dog father of hers just cultivated my existence and anger by doing what he did to her and my—I mean *her* mother. How did you know I was here?"

"Oh," Nelson said as he nodded his head and cupped his chin. "I see now. Your mannerisms are rougher. You, as opposed to Robin . . . I hate to put it this way, but you are foul."

"Well, I gotta tell you, Robin always ran and hid from the spitting in her face, the locking in the closet, and the foul sex that her father used to give her. She was dying. I had to step up. For her own sake, I came out and represented."

"Represented?"

"Yeah. I'm the one who put a stop to all of that bullshit when I bit the shit out of his dick. The day I did that was the last day he put that thick-skinned black thing he call a dick in me . . . or her... Well, the fucking both of us."

Nelson sat in amazement. How could such a beautiful, intelligent woman like Robin be in such pain and still appear to be somewhat normal? He knew she had issues, but had no idea that she fit the bill like she did. He thought he was going to have to groom her, but this other person was ready and would be the one. If he could keep Rockin' focused, he could get her to kill Veronica and get custody of his children.

"I like Rockin' Robin. When you call her that, man, I just want to shine out loud. Let me shine, let me shine, let me shine. Oh, ohhhhhhhh," Rockin' sang.

"She don't know that, though. I usually come out when someone is talking about some foul shit that really pisses me off. She has pretty good control, but I'm feeling strong right about now, yo. Real strong. How's about me and you—"

"Rockin' Robin, huh?" Nelson asked.

"Yeah," Rockin' said smirking.

Nelson got up and said, "You let me know when you're in effect. You can use Rockin' Robin as your way of letting me know, but you have to know that that's my name for her, for Robin. You're only borrowing it."

They gave each other some dap and went in to get something to eat.

Chapter Thirteen

Robin sat in the lobby and waited for Dr. Christopher to finish up with another patient. She was trying to remember what time she got home last night, and wondering why she woke up dressed in what she considered "club clothes." Her black tank top, jeans and "do me" pink stilettos were hardly appropriate for going to work at the hotel. All she could remember was going into Nelson's house and sitting next to Sharon and Chanel. The rest was a complete blur.

Pamphlets and articles lay on the coffee table in front of the couch where she sat. They depicted domestic violence victims and survivors and promoted medicines to help them cope. One in particular, entitled "Raped and Ruined", touched every bruised and violated part of her body and mind. It had a picture of a young girl peering out from behind a partially closed door. Rockin' picked it up and looked at it.

"You ain't the only one, girl. I feel your pain," Rockin' said as she tossed the pamphlet back on the table

The door opened and Dr. Christopher invited her in.

"So, Robin, when you were here on Tuesday, we had a visitor," he said.

"Ta-dah! I'm still here. Robin is away right now."

"Chrissy. What a pleasure. Say, is Robin okay?"

"Yeah. She's fine. I got her under cover. You know, you're a cutie pie too. You and Nelson are yummy," Rockin' said as she licked her lips.

Dr. Christopher was caught off guard. He wasn't expecting Chrissy to come into the office. He had planned the session with the hopes of talking to Robin about why Chrissy was even in existence, but who better to ask than Chrissy?

"Why, thank you. Chrissy, I'm going to be honest with you. I started seeing Robin a few months ago. Why are you just coming out now? What draws you to the surface?"

"Robin seems to have all of you fooled. She demonstrates great control. However, she depends on me to get her through each day. She shines on the outside, but inside, she still that scared little girl who really don't want to exist. I keep her going. I'm that energy that people see and when it gets too much for her, I come out totally."

Dr. Christopher pushed the button on his digital recorder and placed it in the middle of the table. Chrissy looked at it with disapproval but then smiled as if the spotlight were on her.

"Again, Chrissy, how do we know when you're present? Is it a head movement? A smirk or certain laugh? What?"

"She knows me as Chrissy, but you can call me Rockin' Robin. And you will know it's me by how I speak."

"Which is?"

"Uncensored."

"Okay. I understand that. Let's move on."

It was obvious to him that Robin—or Rockin' Robin, as Chrissy wished to be referred to as—suffered from disassociative personality disorder or a split personality. Chrissy took over as a defense mechanism when Robin's emotions collided with anything that posed a threat to her physical or mental state. It was safe to assume the disorder had developed as a result of the abuse she suffered at the hands of her father.

Somehow, this personality had remained relatively dormant for years, allowing Robin to live a somewhat normal life. Now, however, Chrissy seemed to be appearing more often and becoming more aggressive. He suspected this was the explanation for the recent sessions Robin had missed. She was out of her space, and Rockin' Robin was in action.

After the hour-long session was over, Dr. Christopher made it a point to formally welcome Rockin' Robin to the sessions. If he befriended her, she might be willing to be more open with him.

"Oh, thank you. I like this shit. Holding all that mess inside was giving me the bubbles. I get real nervous, and when I have to come out, I don't ever know what I'm gonna do or say. I'm quite entertaining if I really think about it," she said with a wink as she walked out the door.

It was time for Robin to be at work at the hotel. She walked into the lobby with a robust attitude. There was no one at the front desk, so she wandered into Breezes, where she saw Chanel and Todd arguing.

"Fuck you," Todd shouted at Chanel.

"No, fuck you. You stank ball, no-stroke-having, sorry-ass excuse of a man. You ain't shit, and that so-called ex-ho wife of yours ain't shit either. I'm tired of yo' bullshit, and she can have your loser ass back because I'm done with you." Chanel wiped her hands in the air.

Todd stuck his middle finger up at Chanel and started to walk out of the lounge. He walked right into the girl he knew as Robin.

Rockin' Robin grabbed him by the neck with every ounce of strength she had. He yelped as loud as two dogs getting hot water poured on them.

Chanel stood still. Again, she had never seen Robin act like this, but with the way Robin was handling Todd, she wasn't going to interfere. Rockin' continued to squeeze with one hand, grabbing his left arm and turning it up behind his back with the other.

"What it be like, girl? I see you got some trouble here. Who's this cat?"

"Robin, that's Todd."

Rockin' peered at him, shrugged her shoulders then pushed him down on the floor. He went down, grabbing the back of his neck and breathing like a wild animal.

Chanel didn't run to him. She was too mesmerized with the look in Robin's eyes. They were laughing, but she wasn't. It was almost like she was someone else.

"Okay. Okay, Robin." Chanel put her hands up in a sign of surrender. "It's cool. Thank you. Your timing couldn't have been better."

"Why you calling me that? My name is Rockin' Robin. Get used to it, chick."

Rockin' walked out. Chanel grabbed her bag and went over to Todd, who was still squirming on the floor. She kicked him in the ribs and told him "This is not over, Todd. You'll hear from my lawyer."

She ran after Rockin', who was on her way up to her suite. Chanel caught the elevator just in time. She hopped on and heard Rockin' singing "I Am Number One" by Nellie. Chanel remembered that when they were on their way to Kyle's basketball game, she had seen that same look on Robin's face.

She waved her hand in front of Rockin's face, but she just continued to sing. The elevator stopped on the fifth floor. Rockin' started to get off, and Chanel called out to her.

"Robin . . . Rockin' Robin! Whatever the hell your name is, this isn't your floor. You're on the fourth floor."

Robin turned around and looked at Chanel then at the number above the elevator.

"What am I doing up here?" she asked, her voice sounding calmer, more like the Robin that Chanel knew. "I never come here unless I'm getting something from you or Todd. And why are you all out of breath?"

"Robin, come inside with me. I want to talk to you." Chanel took her arm and pulled her into her suite.

Robin sat at the edge of the couch while Chanel poured them drinks. She had her usual white wine spritzer, and Robin had a double shot of tequila. Chanel sat next to her.

"Robin. What's going on with you? You haven't been yourself lately. It's almost like you're someone else sometimes. The things that come out of your mouth just don't sound like you. Are you tired? Maybe these two jobs are too much for you. Is there anything I can do to help you?"

"I don't know what's wrong. I wake up feeling like myself, and the next minute I feel anxiety. I feel like there's someone else inside of me. I hear a voice, and I look to see who's talking to me, and there's no one around me.

"I used to see, or thought I saw someone in the corner of my eyes when I was little. And it still comes and goes, but ever since I've been in counseling, I've been hearing the voice again. I can hear the voice loud and clear. It's always there, telling me that everything will be okay or asking me 'why this' and 'why that.' "

"Have you talked to Dr. Christopher about this, Robin?"

Robin shrugged and fell back onto the couch.

Chapter Fourteen

"Mr. Bray, this is Dr. Christopher."

"Dr. Christopher," Nelson said when he answered his phone. "How are you doing today?"

"Fine, thank you. I wanted to give you a call. I had Robin in this morning. After carefully observing her movements and change in attitude this last session, I have to say that she definitely suffers from DPD. You may know it as split personality. Initially, the other personality called itself Chrissy. But she now chooses to be called Rockin' Robin."

"Really? And you know this for sure?" Neslon was pleased.

"Yes. And Rockin' Robin has lived within Robin for many years, more than likely from the day she was first sexually abused. Strong is an understatement for her personality. She seems determined to be the prominent identity, and will show her face at the slightest mention of abuse, very foul language, or if Robin herself feels an enormous amount of anxiety. I haven't, however, had the opportunity to determine whether she is harmful to Robin or anyone else. But if I had to say anything at this time, I would say that she's no one to fool around with or taunt with idle threats. If you say something to her, be prepared to follow through."

"Bet. You keep referring to Rockin' Robin as 'she' or 'her.' Did she tell you, out of curiosity, that she is definitely female?" Nelson asked.

"She said she's neither, so I respectfully refer to her that way because she is physically a woman. Whether or not she wants to identify with that has yet to be seen, but the fact that she wants to be referred to as Rockin' Robin leads me to believe that her personality is of feminine gender."

"I appreciate you calling me," Nelson said. "Robin has become a very dear friend of mine, and I want to know exactly what I'm dealing with when it comes to her. I can call you if I need you in the future."

Dr. Christopher paused briefly then said, "Why do you have such an interest in Robin, if you don't mind my asking?"

"I do mind you asking." Nelson wasn't about to disclose the truth to Dr. Christopher. That would be too much information. The doctor was willing to share this information for the right price, but if he knew what Nelson planned to have Rockin' do to his ex-wife, he might suddenly have an attack of conscience.

"So, I can call you if I need you, right?"

"Of course you can, Nelson. Call me anytime. Good day." Dr. Christopher knew not to push.

"I will. And your check is in the mail. Good day to you."

Nelson hung up the phone then turned around in his oversized leather swivel chair. He opened the phone book on his silver-and-black cherry Corian desk, dialed a number and waited for an answer.

"Jiles. Nelson here. I understand you're hosting the card game tonight. What should I bring?"

"Young brother, just bring yourself. I stepped into a little bit of money and I'm handling everything. Even gonna have a few girls here for *whatever* is your *pleeeeasure*," Jiles answered, purposely emphasizing the last phrase.

Nelson had a smile on his face when he ended the conversation, leaning back in his chair and putting his feet on the desk. Black and White sat with reverence, one on each side of the desk. He smoothed their soft fur, remembering when he adopted the two loyal pets.

The day he left his wife, his life was in utter disarray. Granted, he had money in the bank, but he no longer had his family. His self-esteem was low, especially since Veronica had been awarded custody of the children in spite of her history of irate behavior and daily mood swings.

In the judge's opinion, nothing Nelson said could gray the area of her competence as a mother. The judge wasn't willing to consider any of Nelson's allegations because the children appeared to be sound in mind and in body. Interviews with them concluded that they loved both their mother and father, and although they verified that they had witnessed their mother as the aggressor in the marriage, she was awarded full custodial and legal custody. It was simple. It was black or white, no in-between.

As he drove home from the courthouse that day, Nelson stopped at a coffee shop. He ordered a café latte and a few almond biscuits then sat at a small table in the corner. Someone had left a newspaper there, so he opened it and began to read.

The local community section of the *Asbury Park Press* often listed yard sales, current musical events and an Adopt-A-Pet of the week. Nelson chuckled, thinking maybe a pet was what he needed to fill his suddenly empty life. He noticed the photo of this week's pet, or rather two pets, one black and one white Akita. He read the information on the dogs. They were dropped off at the Adopt-A-Pet center, severely battered and not immunized. The center nursed them to wellness, and now they were up for adoption. Something about the photo made Nelson seriously consider adopting the two dogs.

After he finished his coffee, he went down to the center. They welcomed him eagerly because he was the only person to come in to see these specific dogs. There had been phone inquiries, but because of their history, people would shy away, thinking the abused dogs would have problems in the home.

When Nelson went into the kennel where they sat caged, they wagged their tails happily. Their front legs were intertwined, almost like they were waiting together, paw in paw, for a new home.

That was it for Nelson. He was hooked. He paid for their shots, had the center give them a thorough cleaning, which included cleaning their teeth, cutting their nails and cleaning their ears, and he took them home with him that same day.

They took to Nelson immediately. Black was subtle in his demeanor, and White was brisk and good-natured. They sniffed and grunted until they found a spot where they felt comfortable, then sat at his feet and whimpered. They could tell he needed love just like they did, and they had been inseparable ever since. Their names were obvious, as with everything else in Nelson's life—Black and White, with no in between.

As he looked at his loyal companions, he thought about his later card game with Jiles Sessoms, and he thought about Jiles' daughter. If things went according to Nelson's plan, Rockin' Robin would become another loyal companion.

Back at the hotel, Robin was too intoxicated to go downstairs and work her shift, so Chanel went down and made sure things were going smooth with the few people she had working that night. Periodically, she would check in on Robin.

The next morning, Robin was up bright and early. She had a headache, and her mouth was as dry as cotton, but she still got up to do her trash route. Sharon picked her up at the usual place, and they headed out on their Friday morning run.

At the end of the route, Sharon and Rockin' pulled up to Nelson's house. He was out on the patio, reading through documents while Lewis typed on his laptop. Black and White sat under the table at Nelson's feet.

"Rockin' Robin," Nelson called out as he made his way to the backyard. "Why don't you stay here for a while? I'll send for your car. Don't worry about clothes."

Sharon looked over at Nelson.

"Is there a problem, Sharon?"

"Nelson," Sharon stood with one hand on her hip and one pointing at Robin. "You're just going to invite her to stay over here?"

"It's my house, Sharon."

"And? You two got something going on, Nelson?"

"Sharon . . ." Robin began to speak.

"Bitch, I'm not talking to you." Spit flung from Sharon's mouth onto Robin's face. Nelson's eyes were locked on Rockin'. He knew Sharon had just invited her to shine.

With no warning, Rockin' grabbed Sharon and head-butted her, breaking her nose. As Sharon grabbed her face, Rockin' punched her in the throat. With labored breathing, Sharon tried to run.

Rockin' looked around the backyard and spotted a piece of wood with rusted nails about three feet away. As she followed Sharon to the truck, she picked it up and with enormous force, swung at the back of Sharon's head. Sharon fell to the ground instantly.

Nelson came off of the back porch and stood behind Rockin' as she continued to beat Sharon over the head with the piece of wood.

Stop!

Rockin' ignored Robin's cry from the inside. She kept swinging until Sharon lay lifeless on the ground in a pool of blood.

"Now you can call me a bitch." Just as Rockin' was about to swing again, a clicking sound interrupted her flow.

"I think that's enough," Nelson said, standing with the barrel of his gun against Rockin's left temple.

She tossed the wood to the side. "You know this shit turns me on, Nelson.

"Is that right? Well, that may be, but I can't let you do this."

Rockin' turned to face him. She took the barrel of the gun into her mouth and sucked it.

"You are seriously—"

"Don't," Rockin' warned him. "You'll be sorry. You'll be just like Jiles."

Rockin' backed away slowly, no longer finding humor in Nelson's position. She grabbed the garbage, made the drop, brought the truck back to the depot then returned to his house as Nelson had requested.

It was dark, and as she walked to the back, she smelled the scent of a cigar. Nelson was on the back porch with Black and White.

He looked up at her. "Why?"

"Why what?"

"Why did you do that to Sharon?"

"She talked too damn much. Just because she worked for you, Nelson, don't give her the right to run her mouth like that to me. She don't know me. She was talking like we had something going on, you know."

"Yeah, I guess you're right. Let's go inside." Rockin' followed Nelson into the house.

"Do we, Nelson? Do we got something going on?" Rockin' asked as she attempted to grab his butt. He pushed her away.

"Nah. You can take a shower and I'll meet you in the den."

Rockin' went into the guest bathroom and took a long, hot shower. As she washed her hair, Robin had a few words for her.

You know that was so wrong.

"I'm so tired of your scary ass. You would've just let Sharon walk all over you and talk any kinda way to you. That's the difference between you and me. And you know what? Nelson is fine as hell. If you could, would you do him? That chick Sharon said they didn't have anything going on, but I heard y'all talking the first day you met. He just gives her stuff for nothing? Yeah, right." Rockin' lathered her body with soap.

No. I'm not that way and you know it.

"Figures. Well, I'm gonna try and get me some. Watch. And anybody standing in my way is gonna get it for real!"

Rockin' stepped out of the shower and dried off then walked into the den wrapped only in a towel. Nelson had turned on some music and brought out two bottles of beer. He patted the seat next to him. "Come sit."

Rockin' sat next to Nelson. He handed her a beer and she turned it up to her mouth. After she finished more than half, she burped loudly.

That's not ladylike.

"Where do you see a lady in this piece?" Rockin' asked as she stood up and held her hands out by her side. Nelson watched silently.

You're just like him.

"Agghhhh!" Rockin' waved her hand in the air and sat back down.

"So, Nelson, what we gonna do tonight?"

"What do you want to do, Rockin'?"

She looked down and pointed at Nelson's penis.

"Nah. I told you we're not doing that."

"Why not?"

"It just wouldn't be right."

Rockin' got up and dropped her towel. She walked backwards and did a little spin.

"You no like what you see?" she sang.

"It's not that. We're partners, and partners should never mix business with pleasure.

She moved closer, gently fondling her breasts. Nelson was becoming aroused but maintained his focus.

Rockin' sat on Nelson's lap and grabbed her beer. She poured some onto her breasts. Nelson watched, becoming increasingly turned on by Rockin's movements against his crotch.

"Ooops, what's this?" Rockin' asked as she touched his hard penis.

Nelson gently pushed her off and got up. Rockin' sat on the couch with no emotions on her face, staring at Nelson like he was crazy.

"It's not happening, Rockin'. I'm not interested in having that type of relationship with you. I told you it's strictly business."

The look in Rockin's eyes made it clear that she was upset. She jumped up and went into the guest bedroom. A few moments later, she came out, fully dressed.

"Rockin', maybe someday. Just not today," he lied.

"You better believe it," she said.

Chapter Fifteen

The next morning, Rockin' lay in bed and thought about the night before. The ring of the phone startled her.

"Rockin' Robin," Nelson stated.

"At your motherfuckin' service."

"Come on over. I want to talk." He hung up the phone.

An hour later, Rockin' was at Nelson's house, still wearing the outfit she had changed into at his house the previous night.

"So, what's this about?"

"I wanted to talk to you about yesterday. I couldn't imagine that you planned on hurting Sharon like you did, did you?"

"No, but you know what? I'm not Robin. Nobody's gonna talk to me like that. Haven't you noticed I ain't wrapped too tight?"

"Okay, I feel that. But you didn't give anybody the opportunity to explain why Sharon might have felt threatened by your presence. You just up and got crazy."

"And your point is?"

"Just listen to me."

Nelson guided Rockin' to the bar in the living room, where they sat while he told her the story behind the day she had seen him and Sharon at the mall. He was excited to tell her how it all went down.

"After I left Sharon that afternoon, I paid Cory a visit. He was skeptical when I approached him, but I started talking to him in the homey talk. I played it off by asking him where he could get the purest of the purest heroin in the area. Cory, as crooked and conniving as he was, knew exactly where to get it. Little did he know that I also knew where to find it because I know all the dealers and swingers in the neighborhood. I either defended them at one time or used them in the past for other hits I did. That's how I knew, when he told me what it would cost, that Cory added twenty percent as a finder's fee."

Nelson looked across the room at White, who was jumping around in the corner, chasing his tail. Black sat quietly by Nelson's side. He rubbed Black's head as he continued the story.

When Cory returned with the drugs, Nelson convinced him to ride with him to his house to get the money. During the drive, Nelson was silently fuming. Not only was he already pissed about what Cory had done to Sharon, now he was even more upset that he had tried to get over with the finder's fee. But that was okay, because Cory was one dumb fool, and he was about to get his.

At the house, Nelson left Cory alone in the living room for a while. Cory laid the dope out on the table and waited patiently for Nelson to come back with the money. He was so intent on getting paid that he hadn't even noticed the dealer he got the heroin from didn't ask for money. Anyone with half a brain would have known right then and there that something foul was going on.

Cory, however, had no clue that he'd been set up, so he was taken completely by surprise when he stood up to admire the living room and Nelson grabbed him in a chokehold from behind. When Sharon walked in with a rope in her hand, Cory's face was a mixture of confusion and panic.

Nelson gave Sharon a nod and told her to go ahead and do what she had to do. She knew that if she didn't handle him now, the next time he beat her, he would kill her. She walked toward him slowly, pulling the rope taut in her hands.

Nelson slammed him down into a chair. Cory tried to scuffle, but Nelson's hold was too tight. As she put the rope around his neck, Sharon looked in his eyes and gracefully said good-bye to him. Nelson let go completely and stood close by as she tightened her grip.

Cory's feet were going in all kinds of directions, but his upper body was tight. She pulled tighter. The veins in his neck protruded. He grinded his teeth as he tried to pull the rope away from his neck and struggled to breathe. Sharon still wasn't strong enough to cut off his breathing completely, and Nelson saw that she wasn't going to be able to do him. He got behind and pulled with her.

Within minutes, Cory's feet stopped moving. His hands remained at his neck, and his body became limp. They held on for a few minutes more, just to be sure his ass was pronounced.

Rockin' paced around the room. "Pronounced what?" she asked.

"Hit, Rockin'. Dude was hit."

Her mouth was wide open. She was fascinated at how he masterminded this whole thing. And he showed no worries about being caught. She knew that when it was her turn, it would be even better.

"You know you need to talk to Chanel about what you do for a living. She got some serious issues with her asshole husband. He doin' her real wrong. Want me to get her to talk to you?"

"Oh no, I'm not worried about her coming and talking to me. It's just a matter of time before she asks you for more information about me, and that's when you bring her to see me."

"Word. That's what up."

Nelson went to his safe, located under one of the couch cushions, the one that only he sat on. He lifted and pulled out a black box, the same box Robin had held for him while he stayed at the hotel. He carried it over to her and slowly opened it. Its contents sparkled.

She picked it up and held it in front of her face, admiring every part of it. She looked in his mirrored glass curio and pointed the gun. Her stance was tight. Nelson was impressed at how she handled it—like she was a pro.

When she had opened it at the hotel, she didn't know there was a hidden camera in the box. Nelson watched her from his room through a mini surveillance system that he traveled with.

He remembered how she wasn't afraid to handle a gun at the hotel, and as he watched her now, he felt confident that she could pull off any job without hesitation.

"I think I'm going to pay old Jiles Sessoms a visit. We need to say some things," Rockin' said as she admired her reflection.

"Is this for me?" she asked as she put it back in the box.

"For sure. Just take it home, put it in a safe place and we'll talk about it later."

Rockin' started to walk out the door, but stopped when Robin had a question.

Ask him about Sharon's son. Is he okay?

"What about her son? She . . . " Rockin' pointed to her chest. "wants to know."

"Ay, it's the nature of the game. He ain't been right since that day." Nelson shrugged.

Why didn't he stop us from killing Sharon?

"What was Sharon's problem with you asking me to chill here for a few?" Rockin' asked Nelson.

He was silent.

"You fucked her, didn't you?"

"No."

"Yeah, you did it to her." Rockin' laughed. "What did you do with her body?"

"What makes you think she's dead?"

Rockin' was silent.

"Do you regret what you did, Rockin'?"

I do, Robin said as if Nelson could hear her.

Rockin' shook her head. "No." She left the house, got in her car and drove off.

Chapter Sixteen

Chanel sat on the edge of her bed, holding a picture of her and Todd on their wedding day. How she could have been so stupid to think an obnoxious, self-centered asshole like him could ever love anyone but himself was beyond her.

A few days before their wedding, his now deceased father asked her if she was sure she wanted to marry Todd. Now that she looked back on it, it was a warning in disguise. Nobody knows you like your family, and no matter how you disguise your true self, it will come to light, the foulness that lies within.

To everybody else, Todd appeared to be this wonderful man, but behind closed doors, he was altogether different. He was messy, dug up his nose without tissue then rolled up whatever booger he found in his fingers and flicked it, scratched his balls and smelled his fingers, and was just disgusting in many other ways.

Fortunately, their son took after Chanel. He was very neat, mentally all together, and had excellent personal hygiene. He was sincere and honest, unlike his father.

She poured herself a drink and wondered how she could bust him in the act of cheating or doing drugs, something that would give her grounds for divorce and guarantee her full custody of Kyle. Who could she trust?

"Robin," she said out loud. She was working that night. Maybe she could get someone to cover for her, and together they could put together a surveillance operation of their own, Chanel planned.

Rockin' walked into the hotel and straight to the desk, expecting a letter from Nelson. Instead, there were three certified mail envelopes and one regular envelope waiting for her. She took them and went up to her suite. She walked into her bedroom to change her clothes, but after she really looked at herself in the mirror, turning around and admiring her outfit, she said, "Ol' Nelson got taste and shit. These threads is happening."

She plopped on her couch, set her newly polished 9-millimeter next to her, and opened the envelope labeled "read me first." It was from Nelson.

Rockin' Robin,

I just wanted to drop you a few lines. I learned some interesting information from your father at our last card game. He was bragging about how he stepped into some money. After getting him a little saucy, I was able to get him to tell me exactly where he got this money—a $250,000 insurance policy he purchased six months before her death. He was able to collect on the policy as soon as the police ruled him out as a suspect in your mother's homicide.

I have sent you three things I thought you might be interested in. Included in envelope number one is the final autopsy report, detailing the extent of your mother's injuries. Envelope number two has a copy of the insurance policy and cashed check that was sent to your father. In the package with envelope number three is a tape of the conversation during the card game last night. I'm sure you'll find your father's "confession" and his tone, which verges on some warped sort of pride, rather interesting.

Give me a call when you get settled.

Already hyped, she hesitated before opening the packages in their numbered order. The autopsy was graphic, and she couldn't even bear to finish reading it. She threw it to the side. The insurance policy was basic, and was paid up for a year.

"This motherfucka planned to kill her," she said out loud.

She dropped the policy on the floor and went for package number three. The tape was titled "No Turning Back Now." She put it in the stereo cassette player and sat in the middle of the floor. While she listened to the slurred and hateful voice of her father, she loaded her pistol.

"Simple cunt bitch wasn't worth shit but rubbing my knob, and she ain't even do that good. I made her. She wasn't shit without me. Thought by holding out on a brother when I so-called pissed her off and shit was hurting me, but I just went for the little cunt whore that she had. And I saw that it ran in the family. Neither was a good fuck," Jiles said, sounding amused by his own story.

"Don't you know that hussy knew I was fucking her daughter? And she ain't even say nothing to me 'bout it for all them years. Had the nerve to bring that shit up that night. Man, she wouldn't shut the fuck up. I told her, 'So what? Don't be mad now. The little bitch ain't here with us no more. Tired-ass ho. Get out my face.'

"She kept coming in my face, so I beat her stinking ass. Beatin' on that bitch made me hot, so I made her blow me, but her damned teeth were all fucked up from when I punched her. So, I gave her one last good, hard fuck right up her ass, then stuck it in her dirty pussy. I pulled out at the last minute and left my wad all over that worthless cunt.

"What a sight, man. Woulda liked to have a picture of that for the photo album . . . Yes, sir. Women just love that shit. Ask that cunt daughter of hers. Always beggin' for her big daddy to take her to heaven.

"She started crying and shit, so I kicked her. Mm-hmm. I bet you I did! Tried to block her face, but I still punched the shit outta her. I swear, man, these bitches these days just think they can control a man.

"She went to call the cops, and then I punched her in the mouth. She shut up then, stupid bitch." He stopped talking only long enough to laugh maniacally.

"She fell to the floor and I kicked her one more time. Knew I musta broke some a those ribs. Grabbed my coat and left. My job there was done a long time ago, when that bitch didn't give me a son."

There was a knock at the door. Rockin' shut off the tape but remained seated until she heard the knock again. This time she got up and answered the door. Chanel was leaning against the door frame with a drink in her hand.

"You busy?"

"Nah, come on in."

Rockin' walked with a little pimp to the couch. Chanel noticed that her demeanor was different. She knew that Rockin' was in rare form.

"Robin. What is that?" she asked, eyeing the gun Rockin' had just picked up.

"That's *Rockin'* Robin, and don't forget it. And what the hell does it look like? Duh!" She waved the gun in the air.

"Why do you have it, Rockin'? You're going to hurt somebody with that."

"That's the point," Rockin' responded as she slid the gun into the waistband at the back of her pants.

"Okay, Rockin' Robin," Chanel said, treading carefully around this strange new side of Robin. "I'm feeling you. Can we talk? I have a problem and I need your help. I know for sure that Todd has been hanging around Eryca and getting high. I have a feeling that he takes Kyle with him, and I'm tired of his shit. I want to catch him and—"

"And what?" Rockin' interrupted impatiently. "It ain't like you gonna put his lights out or something."

Chanel stood quietly and sipped her drink, her eyes on Rockin's gun.

"Oh . . . Oh! You do want his dumb ass dead? Oh, hell yeah! I should have snapped his neck that day in the lounge. I would've loved to, you know. Maybe we need to go see Nelson."

"I was hoping you'd say that. And so I guess you won't be working tonight," Chanel said in a conspiratorial tone.

"Fuck no. In fact, I need some time off 'n shit. I got personal things I gotta tend to. Is that gonna be a problem?"

"No. I don't see a problem, Rob—I mean Rockin'. Rockin' Robin," Chanel repeated.

"Good. Git yo' shit and let's roll to Nelson's."

Chapter Seventeen

"So, whatchu gonna do now? That motherfucka killed your mother. And from the looks of it, he planned the shit. Girl, I'm telling you I'm so ready to cancel Christmas fo' his ass. I'm so fucking pissed off. You know what? We gon' get his raggedy ass. Trust me when I tell you. And you can sit in the corner if you want to, or you can come out and play with me. Either way, his days are so numbered. So, what's it gon' be?" Rockin' asked Robin.

"Yo, Rockin'!" Nelson yelled. "Brandy or gin?"

"Chill, motherfucka. I heard you. Hit me off with a double shot of Remy, a'ight. And don't be yelling at me unless you're telling me to bend over and grab my ankles. Like this." Rockin' demonstrated.

"Nelson," Chanel said, "she's been this way since I came to her room a few hours ago. It's like she's two different people sometimes. You know, I think she has multiple personalities. It's not my field of expertise, but I touched upon it in school."

"She does," Nelson answered matter-of-factly. "She's a little girl who is so scared to come out for fear of being violated, so she got Rockin' Robin, who takes care of all of her issues for her."

"How do you know this?" Chanel moved closer to Nelson. Rockin' watched as she did so.

"Doll, I told you I know everything. Dr. Christopher, you're familiar with him, right?" Chanel nodded. "Well, he and I are old acquaintances. He treated me while I was going through therapy. I wasn't always the cool, calm, collected person that you and everybody else sees. Abuse of any kind can destroy a person completely. Dr. Christopher helped me get myself back together. But I was hardly as bad off as she is. I got a feeling that Robin is tucked away somewhere, maybe for good."

While Chanel and Nelson talked, Rockin' Robin remained bent over, grabbing her ankles. When she noticed that neither Chanel nor Nelson were paying her any attention, she stood up and walked over to them.

"I thought that was funny. Y'all so corny."

"So, Rockin'," Nelson said. "Whatchu gonna do?"

"Pick his punk ass off is what I'm gonna do."

Nelson already knew what her answer would be, so he had taken the liberty of setting up an appointment for Rockin' Robin to go to the shooting range. All three of them got into Chanel's car. As they drove down Main Street, Rockin' yelled, "Ay yo, Chanel! Ain't that yo' husband and shit? What he doin' down here? This the hot spot for the junkies and shit. Yo, you got a junkie for a husband for real? Oh man, this is too wild."

Chanel looked in the direction where Rockin' was pointing, and she saw Todd sitting on a broken bench, looking around nervously. Chanel slowed down, and as they rode past, she saw Eryca emerge from the bushes, wiping her mouth. Some dude stood up with her and zipped his pants. He handed something to Todd, then Eryca and Todd headed quickly into the woods.

Chanel couldn't believe what she was seeing, but the view would only get worse. At the end of the street, she saw a basketball court full of kids shooting hoops. That was when her biggest fear came true. She drove past slowly and spotted their son, Kyle, playing ball not less than 50 yards away from where his junkie father was getting high with his ex-wife.

Chanel stopped the car and threw the gear in reverse. Nelson turned around to face Chanel. Rockin' Robin had already popped her head between them.

"Let me take that pussy right here," Rockin' said. "Right here, right here!"

"No, I don't think so. Chanel needs to decide exactly what it is that she wants to do with him," Nelson suggested. "Chanel, look."

He pointed into the woods, where they could see Todd and Eryca sitting on the ground, shooting up. Todd slowly fell back while Eryca shot up again. Chanel stepped on the brakes, her body full of tension.

"This isn't the time, Chanel. Just say that you want to take care of it, and you know we can hook it up," Nelson said in a calm voice, hoping to pacify her.

Chanel started to sob. Between her sniffling, coughing, and blowing of her nose, she managed to say, "I'm so tired of his lies and deceit. He has my son out here in the streets while he ruins his life. I want him taken care of."

"Oh, hell yeah!" Rockin' screamed so loud that Eryca turned her head in the direction of the car.

"Down," Nelson whispered. Chanel, Nelson and Rockin', with a huge smile on her face, ducked in their seats. They waited a few minutes before Nelson sat up and looked around. He watched Todd and Eryca come out of the woods, walk to the basketball court to get Kyle then climb into Eryca's car.

Nelson was able to convince Chanel that there was no need to follow them. There was nothing they could do to Todd in front of Kyle anyway. Todd would be taken care of soon enough. In the meantime, they resumed their trip to the shooting range.

Nelson sat back while the range instructor guided Rockin' in the handling of her gun. Chanel sat quietly to the side, deep in thought about how she was going to handle Todd. She was too numb to cry anymore.

"And to think that I stayed loyal to this asshole all this time while he fucked around right under my nose."

"You say something?" Nelson asked.

She shook her head, got up and walked outside. Nelson followed her. Rockin' watched from the reflection inside her glasses.

"Ay, Chanel, hold up." He ran to catch up to her. When he reached her, he said, "I'm going to plan a get-together at my house. I'll let you know the day. To the guests, it will be a men's night out thing. I'll have a card game going, some food, drinks, maybe some strippers and his favorite, heroin. If I'm correct, he'll probably want to bring his get-high partner, right?"

"Yeah, he'll probably bring that bitch," Chanel said sadly.

"Okay. That's cool. I got something for his ass. Chanel, it's uncut and well, let's just say he'll be high for the last time once he takes a hit of this. I'm telling you, he'll be done." His tone became ominous. "But you would have to administer the dose. I'll get them real high ahead of time so that there will be little if any struggle, and then you just give him his last hit." He rubbed Chanel's back. Rockin' was still watching.

"You want me to give it to him? What about Eryca?"

"Don't worry 'bout her. I got her taken care of. I'll have her in the other room giving head, thinking that she's gonna get high as payment. She's nothing to worry about."

Chanel nodded in agreement. She had to admit that the mere thought of Todd not being around to cause her any more pain was lovely. She quickly dismissed any uncertainty and went back inside with Nelson.

"Oh, man. Yo, this is the shit," Rockin' said after she shot off over a hundred rounds. She decided to pretend like she didn't see Nelson and Chanel a little too close for her comfort.

"You got a professional here, Bray. Better not let her out of your sight. She's tight," the instructor commented.

"Thanks. And send the bill, right?"

"You got it."

When they arrived back at Nelson's house, Chanel let him out, and Rockin' Robin jumped in the front.

"Ladies, it was a nice evening. I'll be in touch."

As soon as Chanel drove away, Rockin' asked, "Ain't you excited 'n shit?"

"Excited? No. I don't know. I feel strange. I didn't know I was capable of feeling so much hatred for the father of my son, my husband. His abuse has gotten to be too much. I can handle me, and he can destroy his life all he wants, but I can't have him dragging Kyle into his mess. I just can't."

"Then you know what the hell you gotta do, be-yatch. Don't think about the shit too much. Just do the damn thing. You like Nelson?"

"What?" Chanel questioned.

"You feeling ol' boy? Come on, you can tell me."

"No. And if I was?" Chanel said with a laugh.

"He's taken. That's my man." Rockin's voice was dead serious.

"Oh, all right. Whatever." Chanel had bigger things on her mind at that point. "What are you about to do?"

"I'm 'bout to step out for a bit. And no, you ain't coming. I need some me time."

Chanel drove to the hotel in silence.

"Remember. He's mine, Chanel," Rockin' said when she stepped out of the car.

Chanel felt uncomfortable with Rockin's comment, but left it alone for now. She went inside the hotel, and Rockin' headed for her own car. She popped in a 50 Cent CD and stepped on the gas, tires squealing as she fishtailed out of the parking garage and off into the night.

Where are we going?

"Why? Just sit yo' ass in the corner where you been. I got this."

Chapter Eighteen

Freshly painted walls and brand new carpet complemented the furniture Jiles Sessoms had ordered for his totally renovated house. All the family pictures that once graced the walls were thrown out. Most of the things that belonged to Mrs. Sessoms were put on the curb for vagrants and passersby to pick through. As for the rest, Jiles spent Saturday evenings in his backyard, drinking heavily and dancing around a bonfire, throwing in little bits of his life with his wife and daughter, giving him the satisfied feeling that he was free of them forever.

Since his wife's death, he had acquired a new set of friends who knew nothing of his vile personality. They were hoodwinked by the charming smile and overlooked that most certain vibe of untrustworthiness. When the sole purpose of getting together was to drink and party until they slurred snores in a drunken sleep, who cared about how one felt about the next person?

His home, the house where Robin grew up, became the chapel for little girls and cheap whores, and the playground for games of craps, blackjack and poker. Hundreds of dollars were brought in and exchanged by both winners and losers, mostly the latter.

It was 6 o'clock, and Jiles smelled of his favorite cologne, Obsession. Marla, one of his youngest pieces of ass, had arrived early as she always did. She was in her early teens and was already a gold-digging ho. He knew that, but he was fascinated with her childlike demeanor and her body, which had barely entered puberty. She would wear her schoolgirl outfit for him and let him spank her, and in exchange, he would give her a couple hundred dollars.

She skipped up to the door. "Daddy, I been a bad girl."

"Well, come on up here and let Daddy spank ya."

Robin sat in her car across the street, looking at the household items strewn about the sidewalk where she used to sit as a child, watching cars go by. Stray dogs pissed on the very same couch she'd slept on every Saturday night when she fell asleep watching *The Brady Bunch.* Cats pounced on the hats her mother wore to Sunday service.

She put on a pair of black leather gloves while she stepped out of the car, then walked across the street and stood directly in front of the house she once called home. She could hear the cooing and teasing going on inside.

"Dirty motherfucka," she cursed.

Oh, no. Why are we here?

"I thought I told you to go some fucking where. You breaking my concentration."

Please. Please. Don't go up there. He's gonna do it again.

"He ain't doing shit to me. Besides, I just want to say hi to the motherfucka." Rockin' Robin felt for her gun in the back of her pants and walked up to the door. She knocked three times.

"All right now. Alllll right! Got damn. Let's get this party started," Jiles yelled as he opened the door. When he saw who was there, he had to squint to be sure that he saw correctly. He tried to shut the door shut in her face, but she stopped him by kicking the door open. It hit him in the forehead as it swung open.

"What the hell are you doing here? You ain't no longer welcome in my house," he said, rubbing the welt on his forehead.

"Fuck you and get the hell out of my way." She pushed him aside and barged in.

"I see you got some new ass. She looks older than let's say, seven."

"Excuse me?" the girl protested.

"Shut up, bitch. This ain't got shit to do with you."

"I'm outta here, Jiles."

"Here. Let me help yo' dumb ass." Rockin' grabbed Marla's purse and Marla and tossed them both out the door, slamming it shut with her foot.

Jiles grabbed her and they fell to the floor. He punched her like she was a man on the street, and she punched him right back like the punk ass that he was.

"That's all you got, chump? You punch like a bitch!" she said as she pulled out her gun and stuck it in his balls.

She grabbed his shirt tightly around his neck, pulled him up and sat him on a chair. Straddled across him, she forced his mouth open and put the gun in.

Beads of sweat dripped from Rockin' Robin's face onto her father's chin as she examined the face she had hated for so long. Scraggly hairs coiled from his face. His eyes were permanently bloodshot from his routine drinking. His salt and pepper eyebrows had become one, and finalized his raggedy troll look.

"Ain't got nothin' to say, Jiles?" She took the gun out just enough for him to say something.

"You one crazy bitch." He was trying to mask his fear, but his voice was breathless.

"You ain't seen shit yet. Why you kill my mother? You wasn't satisfied with sticking your dick inside of me every day, huh? She tried to be the best mother to me and wife to yo' sorry ass, and she tried to protect me from you. How would you like it if somebody stuck their dick or something else inside of you? Huh? Huh?

"It's because of you that she couldn't sit with me and do my hair. Tuck me in at night 'n shit. And forget about teaching me how to take care of my private parts. You did that! And you right, I'm one crazy bitch. I hate life and I hate you. And I'm cummin' as I'm sitting on top of you ready to put one in yo' head."

A smile came over her face. Her father, knowing his end was near, managed to part his lips just enough to let her salty beads of sweat ooze into his mouth. He sucked his lips.

"You still taste like shit."

She shoved the gun into his mouth with all her might, knocking out his loose molars. He tried to scream, but she got up off of him and kicked him in his balls, silencing him completely. He fell off the chair and onto the floor, one hand grabbing his jaw, the other grabbing his throbbing crotch.

"Why God even blessed you with a child is beyond me. We didn't have a chance to speak to him before we were born, otherwise we would have asked for a background check. And if we knew what we know now, we would have begged for another bird daddy. Oh, my bad. Bird dog. Where are your wings anyway?" she asked him, swinging her gun in the air.

Blood bubbles slid from his mouth onto the new carpet until he was finally unconscious. Rockin' walked back into the bedroom that once belonged to her mother. It was totally redecorated. It was obvious that her father went to great lengths to make sure there were no traces of her memory in the house. She turned and walked out of the room. The door to her bedroom was closed.

I don't want to go in there!

"You ain't got no fucking choice. I told you. I'm running this here show."

Rockin' Robin slowly pushed the door open. It squeaked as it did when her father used to open it and sneak into her room late at night to do it to her. This was Robin's cue to go into her corner and let Rockin' handle what her father used to do to her. As she entered the room, flashes of her father's grizzly grin danced around her mind.

Ahhhhh!

"Shut up! The fuck you screaming for? Can't nobody hear you anyway. Damn, you a tart!" Rockin' fussed at Robin

She looked around the room and noticed that parts of it remained the same as she had left it. Many things were different, though—a new radio, new clothes and new hair accessories. The bed was new, and made up with pretty, feminine linens.

"What the hell? Why does he need new clothes and hair shit? Must be for Marla," Rockin' said out loud.

Okay. I'm scared.

"Yeah well, what's new? Do you recognize any of the shit that's in here?

Mm-hmm. A few things. But I don't see my Brenda doll. I want her. We held each other tight when he used to stick his thing in me. Please find her. Maybe he packed her away. Go into the closet and see if she's there.

Rockin' Robin walked over to the closet and opened the door. On the floor she found boxes of new girls' underwear, sweaters, jeans and shoes. On the shelf, all of Robin's stuffed animals were stacked neatly.

Rockin' looked them over, thinking they looked weird. They looked angry.

They just watched him. What could they do?

A pair of eyes looked at Rockin' from behind a stuffed bear. Clearly, it wasn't another stuffed animal because she could see that the face was hard and ashy.

Ooooh, there she is. Brenda! Get her, Chrissy!

"What did you call me? My name ain't Chrissy no more. Didn't I tell you that my name is Rockin' Robin? Don't let me have to tell you that shit again. And you ain't gotta yell."

Rockin' pulled the doll from behind the stuffed animals. She looked at it with a frown on her face. The doll's hair was all over the place and it had no clothes. The plastic arms, legs and head were held together by a stuffed piece of cloth. "X" marked the location of her private parts.

"Okay. Now what the hell do you want me to do with her?"

Just take her with us. We can't leave her here.

"I ain't walking around with a doll baby, okay!" There was a moment of silence between Rockin' and Robin.

"Ohhhhhhhhh, okay!" she finally yelled. Rockin' sat on the bed and took in the full view of the room while she held Brenda. She lay across the bed and stared blankly at the wall, holding Brenda close.

Remember now?

"Yeah," Rockin' responded in a low and solemn voice. A flash from one of Robin's episodes with her father played with both Rockin' and Robin. They remembered one day when after dinner, her mother wasn't feeling well and went to bed early. Robin must have been around 9 years old. Her father was acting in a way that was rare and scary. He was in a good mood.

After he was sure Toscha had fallen asleep, he asked Robin if she wanted some ice cream. Robin thought that maybe if she accepted his offer, that night might be different. Maybe that night would be the night he'd realize that she was his little girl, and even though she wasn't a boy, she needed love, and he would love her. He would leave her alone from that night forward.

They ate their ice cream and watched television. It was about 9 o'clock when her father said that it was time for her to go to bed. "But first come over here and give me a kiss goodnight," he said.

Foolishly, Robin thought he would have mercy on her little body and leave her alone. When she went to give him a kiss on his cheek, he turned his head and she ended up kissing him on his lips. Robin slowly pulled away and looked into his eyes, which had lost any and all false emotion. They were reduced to little dots surrounded by what looked to be tiny ants.

He pulled her to him and set her on his lap. "Did you like what just happened?" he asked. Afraid to say either yes or no, she just sat on his lap and held Brenda tightly.

Jiles lifted her up a little bit, unzipped his pants, pulled up her nightgown and moved her panties to one side. The pain was excruciating as he eagerly and aggressively moved her up and down on his penis. At first glance, someone might have thought this was an innocent scene, a child having fun bouncing on her daddy's lap. But if they took the time to look at her face, they would see a damaged child, numb to all reality.

Jiles moved quickly and roughly, like he was bouncing a rag doll on his lap. When he was finished having anal sex with Robin, he pushed her onto the floor and put his penis back into his pants without wiping himself.

Robin, who was in excruciating pain and bleeding profusely, walked away slowly, with her butt cheeks as tight as she could so that the blood wouldn't drip on the floor. She dragged her Brenda doll, who was staring at Jiles' cowardly yet satisfied grin as her head bumped every so often on the carpeted hallway. Robin went into her room and closed the door.

Robin sat in the middle of her bed and allowed herself to bleed, hoping that it would get all of him out of her. When she thought she was done, she took off her panties and nightgown. She removed her sheets and wrapped them around her soiled clothes then cried herself to sleep.

In the morning on her way to school, she dumped the sheets in a brook that rapidly flowed away from her house. For days after that, her panties had red dots in them. When her mother asked her what had happened, Robin wouldn't answer. Toscha's denial of the horror that was happening to her daughter forced her to create her own excuses. Robin must have hurt herself while she was riding her bike or climbing a tree, Toscha decided. It was never spoken of from that day forward.

Rockin' lay on the bed, one hand holding the Brenda doll and the other cupping her vagina. Her nerves had her body jolting, and her jaw was clenched tight.

A noisy thud yanked Rockin' out of her daze. She jumped up and ran into the front room, holding her gun close to her side but still gripping Brenda.

Jiles had managed to drag himself to the counter, and as he reached for the phone, it fell on the floor. Rockin' Robin slowly walked to where he lay. She grabbed the phone and yanked it out of the wall.

"Who you think you calling? Don't worry. Your company will be here soon. They'll find you, and you'll be a'ight. But you see, I'll still be fucked up. You'll spit out a few teeth that you losing anyway, and your balls will be blue for a minute, but I still gotta live with the demons that rent space in my head for the rest of my life because of you and your dirty dick, you and your demented definition of fatherhood, you and this phone stuck up your black, dingle-berried ass!"

Rockin' Robin turned him over and started to pull off his pants. An idea came to her, so she hit him in the head to keep him still while she went outside. From the sidewalk, she grabbed one of her mother's hats. As she was going back up the stairs into the house, she heard something rustle in the bushes. She looked over and saw Marla squatting and quivering, soaked with tears like a leaf on a rainy fall day.

Rockin' stopped for a minute and pointed the gun at Marla's head. She twisted her lips as if she were rubbing Vaseline into them.

"How old are you, ho?"

"Thirteen," Marla nervously answered.

Rockin' looked at her and frowned. She could care less how this little girl got mixed up with her father. She was more concerned with the fact that Marla could identify her.

"Let's go," Rockin' instructed Marla, swinging her gun toward the door. Marla scurried up the stairs and into the house. Rockin' was right behind her. She closed the door and locked it.

Jiles was still lying on the floor, but he was awake. He looked at Marla then at the girl who he knew as Robin, his meek and unwanted daughter. The Robin he knew couldn't and wouldn't have the nerve to act out like this woman in front of him now.

He gurgled his words and asked, "Who the fuck are you? Toscha, is that you coming back to haunt me? 'Cause if it is, you can carry yo' ass back where I sent cha." He was laughing at himself. "Or are you that screwed up child of your mother's that was supposed to be a son for me? You were supposed to be my son!" At this point, he was screaming at the top of his lungs. He managed to spit on her feet with a bottom jaw that protruded from the swelling and snapped back and forth when he spoke. Rockin' was satisfied that she had broken his jaw, just like he had done to Toscha.

Marla started to sob loudly.

"Shut up! Shut yo' fucking mouth! I ain't gon' tell you again. Ay! You heard me, right?" Rockin' warned. Marla's cry went to a soft whimper.

Rockin' Robin's cell phone rang. She pulled it out of her jacket and looked at the caller ID. It was Chanel, but Rockin' was in no position to talk with her now. A situation that needed to be thought out carefully was on her hands.

She instructed Marla to pick up her father and lay him across the couch on his stomach, and to pull his pants down totally. As little as she was, Marla's fear gave her the strength to drag him up to the couch. He huffed and puffed at her handling of him, and shot looks of disgust at Rockin' Robin.

A beeping sound indicated that Chanel had left a message, but Rockin' was too involved, and Chanel would just have to wait. It was almost 8 o'clock, and his card party was about to start.

Rockin' instructed Marla to pick up the phone and set it on the counter. She also had her open the door to see if anyone was pulling up. Having her do these things put her prints in the house, since Rockin' was unsure how many times, if any, she had actually been there.

"You got a cell phone, little chick?" Rockin' asked Marla. Marla reached into her purse and handed Rockin' her cell phone without a word.

"Just remember, ho, that my resources are unlimited. If you breathe a word of this to anyone, I will be back to see you. You can believe that! Now, get the fuck out of here." Marla ran for the door instantly.

Rockin' held her cell phone and kneeled down next to Jiles. He looked at her with such resentment, but his trembling lips told Rockin' that she had his undivided attention. She made her departing message very clear to him.

"We'll hook up again some day soon, bitch nigga. And trust me. When we do, it will be your last day on this earth." She set a red hat with multi-colored flowers on top of his head.

"Now, don't you look pretty? Not!"

She picked up the cell phone that Marla had given her, spread his cheeks and shoved the phone right up his stinking ass, savoring the sound of his agonized screams.

"Let's see you make a phone call now," she said with a wicked laugh, then strolled out, leaving the door wide open.

Chapter Nineteen

Why didn't you just kill him?

Not yet.

I just want it over.

"And it will be," Rockin' said as she retrieved the messages on her cell phone.

"Robin, Todd and Eryca got pulled over by the cops because they were speeding. Needless to say, they were high. Kyle was in the back sleeping when they did a search and found needles, residue and other stuff under the driver's seat. I have to go down to the police station and get Kyle. Please meet me down there."

Rockin' Robin hurried down to the station. As she pulled up, she saw Chanel walking out with Kyle. He was a minor and obviously had nothing to do with the drug possession charges that were filed against his father and Eryca, so she was able to take him. They, on the other hand, were being held on $50,000 bail each.

"What happened?" Rockin' asked.

"Come on and follow me back to the hotel. I don't want to talk here."

When they arrived at the hotel, there were two messages. One from Nelson for Rockin', and one from Junie for Robin. Junie, the shoeshine man, wanted to know if Robin's offer still stood for him to move his business inside.

"Who's Junie?" she asked Chanel.

"Robin? Or . . . ? Well, anyway, he's the little old man that you always talk to when you go down to the mall. He called last week about you asking him to move his setup into the hotel as a joint business venture. I told him that I didn't see any problems, but if he spoke to you then he should verify it with you. But since you'll be off of work for a while, just leave me the message and I'll be sure to get him in this week. I know you guys are cool and you care about him a lot."

She's right. I love little Junie.

"That's my friend?"

"That's Robin's friend," Chanel clarified.

"Junie? He's old and we have to look out for him? He's a good guy? Yeah, a'ight. We can do that."

They went up to Chanel's suite. Chanel made sure Kyle got to bed okay, then she made a drink for herself and Rockin'.

"I went to see that old bastard today."

"Who? Your father?"

"No. Jiles Sessoms. He was supposed to have his card game tonight. Don't you know that this motherfucka threw out all of my—her mother's furniture. All of her clothes, pictures, and Sunday hats. He has some fucking nerve. I tried to talk to him, but he pushed my buttons, and well, to make a long story short, I guess I'm no longer welcome in his house. That be a'ight with me."

"Wow. That must have been very difficult for you."

"Nah. Not for me, but Robin kept whining. She be trying to play me out because now I have to keep this Brenda doll of hers." Rockin' pulled the doll out of her jacket. Chanel took it from her.

Get it back.

"Chill. It's only Chanel."

"What?" Chanel asked.

"Nothing. She don't want nobody touching her. She said something about it being the only doll that she held close to her when her father would be doing it to her."

"Rockin', is Robin okay?"

An uncertain and tired look came over Rockin' Robin. She downed the rest of her drink and collapsed into a chair. "Yup. She ain't coming back, though. Since I took over the show, she's taken refuge in the corners of our soul. She feels safe. Probably the safest she ever felt. We talk, but that be about it. So, here's looking at me, kid." She raised her drink in the air then took a long swallow.

"But enough about us. What the hell is the deal with your punk-ass husband? When you gonna handle his dumb ass?"

Chanel sat on the edge of the chair, shaking her leg and biting her nails as she contemplated her answer. Todd had done it. Kyle had told her this was not the first time Todd had left him at that basketball court while he went off with Eryca. Not only was he blatantly cheating, he was putting their son in extreme danger by bringing him on his get-high trips. Chanel knew something had to be done.

Chapter Twenty

Nelson noticed Jiles' front door was wide open as he pulled up in his Excursion. He got out, armed his vehicle and slowly walked up to the door, diligently removing his gun from its side holster. He carefully and quietly went into the house.

Blood stained the new carpet, and the house smelled of sweat and shit. He followed the stench, walking into the kitchen, back into the living room and down the hall to the bathroom, where he found Jiles on the floor. He was half-naked, covered in his own feces. Nelson's mouth dropped open.

"Yo. What up, Jiles?" Nelson asked in a cautious tone.

Too weak to answer from trying to push and/or pull Marla's cell phone out of his ass, Jiles just lay there. He had crawled into the bathroom, intending to make it there before he shit all over himself. Obviously, he hadn't made it.

His jaw was now twice its normal size. His foot bled where he had stepped on one of the teeth he spit out onto the bathroom floor. The others remained in his mouth, hanging by the strings of his diseased gums.

Nelson took off his jacket and put away his piece. He stood in a Sean Jean turtleneck sweater and jeans, and a pair of Ferragamo shoes, in total contrast to the broken, shit-covered man before him. He shook his head in awe of the scene.

Trying not to vomit from the smell, he helped Jiles up and into the shower. The steam from the hot water magnified the smell of the soiled floor, so Nelson went into the kitchen pantry and got a bucket, mop and some ammonia. As he came out of the kitchen, Jiles' guests arrived. Nelson placed the cleaning supplies down and hurried to open the front door.

"What's up, man? Sorry, but the game, man, had to be cancelled. Ol' Jiles drank one too many too early and got himself sick. But check it out. Next week, it's gonna be on at my place. I'll leave the details with Jiles, and all the bros can come and chill. I'll have it all set up."

Aside from making cracks about the smell, they pretty much accepted Nelson's explanation. Before they left, they guaranteed Nelson that they would be at his house next week.

Nelson grabbed the mop and supplies and took several deep breaths before he re-entered the bathroom, where shit was smeared all over the floor and walls. He looked under the bathroom sink and found a pair of rubber gloves. Nelson began to fill the bucket with hot water and ammonia.

The shower stopped, but the door remained closed. Jiles stood in utter silence and humiliation. That was fine with Nelson, as he would rather be out of the bathroom when Jiles came out of the shower. He worked as quickly as he could, placing the broken teeth and the disgusting cell phone into a plastic bag, and cleaning the floor and walls twice to be sure he got everything. When he was done, he let Jiles know.

"Okay, man. I'll be out in the living room working on those blood stains," he said as he left the bathroom and closed the door.

After he heard Nelson fumbling around in the kitchen, Jiles pulled back the shower door and slowly stepped out. He wiped the steamy mirror over the sink. Because he was unable to move his jaw, he couldn't cry as powerfully as his heart and ego wanted him to. So, he watched the tears slide down his now burnt-brownie-looking skin onto his choppy mustache, then onto his swollen stomach.

He reached for a towel hanging on the back of the bathroom door and gingerly dried himself. As he bent down to dry his feet, tightness in his rectum prevented him from standing back to an upright position, so he sat on the toilet. It felt like something wasn't allowing his butt cheeks to come together. He carefully stood, reached under the sink for the handheld mirror, pulled his leg up and rested it on the sink. He lowered the mirror to view the problem and nearly fainted when he saw his backside.

Blood and vein-filled hemorrhoids lined the outside of his butt. It looked like someone had taken about ten purple grapes and hot-glued them to the crack of his ass. He slowly put his leg back down and wrapped himself in the towel. He put on his robe and walked out into the living room.

Nelson had cleaned up the blood with some Goo Gone he found in the kitchen cabinet. While Jiles was in the bathroom, Nelson put water on the stove for a cup of tea.

"Damn, man. What happened to you?" Nelson asked as he handed Jiles a cup. Painfully, Jiles responded.

"That cunt bitch," Jiles mumbled through his swollen lips. "She came here . . . did this."

"Who? Who you talkin' 'bout, man?"

Jiles looked at Nelson, his voice shaking as he said, "Robin."

"Robin? Your daughter?"

He nodded.

Nelson tried to ignore the spit that dribbled out of Jiles' mouth onto the table, and watched him as he slowly got up and went for a bottle of liquor.

"I want that bitch dead," Jiles demanded.

"Come again?"

"I'll pay you . . . Send her . . .with . . . her momma." The sentence seemed to take every bit of Jiles' strength.

Nelson wasn't certain what Jiles was suggesting, since he didn't think Jiles knew what it was he did for a living. To be sure, he repeated what he thought he'd heard.

"So, let me get this right. You want me to put a hit out on your daughter, Robin. You want her dead, out of your life for good?"

Jiles nodded slowly.

"Let me ask you something. I can look around here and see that you've been spending your money freely. I've also seen you lose thousands at your card games. My question is, how can I be sure that you're going to pay me?"

Jiles went to a drawer beneath the counter. He pulled out a pile of papers and handed them to Nelson. They were papers describing the life insurance policy Jiles had taken out on his daughter. It was even larger than the one on Toscha. Robin was worth half a million dollars to Jiles if she was dead. After seeing her strength and fury that night, he knew he would have to enlist some help to get rid of her, and he was willing to pay well for that.

"How much you want?" Jiles asked through his swollen jaw.

Nelson's lips became firm and his jaws locked as if he had dumped an entire box of Lemonhead candies in his mouth.

"All right, Jiles. I understand," he said, ignoring Jiles' last question. "Let me get out of here. Oh, and the rest of your guests came for the card party, but I told them that you weren't feeling well and that next week, it's on me. The card party will be at my house. Is that cool?"

Jiles nodded. "Yeah. And think about . . . what I said."

"Oh, brotha, for sure. I sure will."

As soon as he got in the truck, Nelson called Rockin'. "Yo. We need to hook up. Where are you?" After he heard her reply, he said, "I'll be right there."

Chapter Twenty-one

When Nelson arrived at the hotel, the lobby was humming with late-nighters who gathered to have a nightcap. Paula was manning the front desk.

"How are you, miss? Can you buzz Robin for me?"

"Sure. And who should I tell her is here?"

"Nelson."

Paula buzzed Robin's suite and got no answer, but she had seen her come in with Chanel, so she called up to Chanel's suite. They were there, and told her to send Nelson up.

Chanel and Rockin' Robin were still up talking about Todd and Eryca. It was 12:30, and they were too hyped to be tired. When she let him in, Rockin' offered Nelson a drink and turned on the radio. Chanel was curled up with a blanket on the couch, sipping on her drink.

"What's up, ladies? Up kind of late."

Chanel explained what had happened with Todd and Eryca, and how they had Kyle with them when it all went down. From the sound of her voice, it was obvious she was in a different space.

"So, you're about ready then, right?"

"Yeah, that bitch is ready. She better hope that I don't get to his ass first," Rockin' answered.

You can be so rude sometimes.

"And your point is?"

But I love you anyway.

"Yeah. I love you too."

Nelson and Chanel looked at Rockin'. They had seen this behavior often enough now to know that she was talking to Robin. Her face was still, her eyes were wide, and her mouth was in a half-smile. They watched her and waited patiently, knowing that Rockin' Robin openly communicated with Robin and they needed to respect that this was how it was going to be.

It saddened them that she was in such pain, put upon her by her father. They were concerned about her, but knew if they tried to get into Rockin's space any more than she opened the door for them to get in, she wouldn't be happy at all.

"Um, Rockin'," Nelson said after a while, "I went to your father's house for our weekly card game. I don't really know specifically what went down when you were there, but humiliated is an understatement as to how he is feeling, and—"

Nelson became silent as Rockin' got up and made herself another drink. She didn't offer anyone else a refill. "And?" she asked.

"And he wants you dead. He asked me to pull some strings and put a hit out on you. In fact, I think he wants me to do it myself."

"Is that right? So, whatchu gonna do, Nelson?" Rockin' raised her arms to the side as if to say, T*ake your best shot, motherfucka.*

Nelson laughed. "You be bugging, girl. This is how it's gonna go down. Next Thursday, the card party will be at my place at around 7 o'clock. Chanel, when Todd gets out, I'm going to conveniently run into him and invite him over for sort of like a relax and chill thing for him. I'm sure that he'll bring Eryca. Now, you can't get all crazy, because you'll be in the back room, and I need you to stay there until it's time.

"Rockin', your pops is going to come, too, and all I need you to do is listen. The room that you're going be in is my control room. It's located in the basement, and it contains my state of the art surveillance and monitoring system, which will allow you to see and hear everything. You can't be trippin' either, okay?"

Both women nodded.

"Now, we'll let them drink and get their eat on. Have them relax a little, get high off of some cheap shit, and then I'll tell Todd that I have something special for him to take his mind off of things. I'll bring him to one of the back rooms, and that's when Chanel will, you know, come in and give him a dose of heroin that will keep his lids closed for good."

"What about Eryca?" Chanel asked again.

"I haven't quite figured that out just yet, but by Thursday I will."

Chanel's phone rang. It was Reggie, Todd and Eryca's son, calling to ask if Chanel had seen his mother or father. He was at a friend's house and needed a ride. Unfortunately, Chanel had never developed a relationship with him because of the animosity between her and Eryca, so she didn't feel obligated to offer to pick him up. She simply said that she didn't know where either of them were and hung up the phone.

"Well, I don't know about y'all, but I'm excited." Rockin' announced.

"It's settled," Chanel responded.

They sat around and talked more until Chanel and Rockin' Robin drifted off to sleep. Nelson sat and watched them while he had a few more drinks and thought about his children. He hadn't heard from them in a while. As much as he wanted to reach out to them, go pick them up and take them out shopping or to the movies, the thought of calling and hearing his ex-wife's voice gave him anxiety. The truth is, he loved her unconditionally for as long as he could, but now he hated her. He wondered how he could have loved someone who beat him.

He missed the soft kisses Neeah and Naohme used to give him, and how he used to play football with Dannon in the backyard. Tears welled in his eyes. For the first time, he was allowing himself to break down and release the feelings that shackled his heart for years.

Rockin' was stretched out on the chaise lounge on her stomach. She had woken up when she heard Nelson crying softly, but dared not let him know that she saw him. She closed her eyes and talked to Robin.

"You up?" Rockin' asked Robin quietly.

Yup. What's wrong with Nelson?

"I don't know, but if I had to guess, I bet he misses his kids. I want kids."

Yeah, right. What would you do with a kid? It's not like you know how to raise one. You can thank my father for that. Or should I say our *father? I don't want any. I'm scared that I'll abuse them like he abused us.*

"Where are your wings? You were supposed to be able to fly, and maybe we wouldn't be in this fucked up situation if you could fly."

Rockin', I saw you fall to the side when you jumped and you didn't have your wings. I reached for you, but your body got washed away. Don't feel bad because when I came here, I didn't have my wings either. That's when I knew I was in trouble, but I was comforted because I took your soul with me on my way down. I'm sorry that it had to be this way and you didn't have a chance to be normal, but I'm not sorry that I have you here with me.

"So you know I gotta take care of him, right? I ain't sure how you feel about that, but I really don't care. I knew you weren't strong enough to handle the way he did you, and I'm sorry that you're stuck in that corner now, but I'm not sorry for bringing us this far. We gonna make it. Don't worry."

Nelson heard Rockin' mumbling. He got up, kissed her and Chanel on the cheek and left without saying a word. Rockin' and Robin talked into the wee hours of the morning.

Chapter Twenty-two

"Okay, Junie, we'll see you on Monday. Your stand will be right next to the men's sauna." Chanel told him over the phone the next day. "Thank you. You have a nice day as well."

Chanel hung up the phone and went to check on Kyle in his bedroom. He was watching television. She wanted to ask him so many questions, but hated to put pressure on him like that. It was obvious, though, that he knew exactly why his father wasn't there now.

"I'm sorry, Mom. I tried to tell them to bring me home. They kept pulling over and shooting up, so I just finally cried myself to sleep. I hate him, and I hate her too."

"Oh, sweetie." Chanel fought back tears. "You don't have to apologize for anything. You didn't do anything wrong." She rubbed his hair and took him in her arms. "You can't blame yourself for your father's actions, and you can't right his wrongs. Just learn from this, honey, that doing drugs can ruin your life and in some instances, kill you. I'm so sorry that you had to go through that ordeal but don't worry, you won't have to go through that again. I promise."

"Yo. Where's the grub? I'm hungry as hell," Rockin' yelled from the living room. Chanel and Kyle went into the kitchen, where Chanel prepared pancakes, eggs, bacon and fresh squeezed orange juice. They enjoyed breakfast and idle chit chat, not once speaking of what happened the night before.

When Todd was arraigned later that day, Chanel sat with Kyle in the courtroom. At first she thought it wouldn't be wise to take Kyle to court with her, but then she decided to let him see firsthand what would happen to him if he chose to live the life that his father did.

"Veronica Jordan for the defendant, Your Honor," Todd's lawyer announced as she stood up and fixed her suit jacket.

"How does your client plead, counselor?"

"Guilty, Your Honor."

"Thank you, Ms. Jordan. On the charges of possession of heroin, since this is your first offense, I'm imposing a fine of one thousand dollars and forty hours of community service."

Todd sat in silence, still high, while the Judge continued.

"For the charge of endangering a minor, I'm imposing an additional fine of five thousand dollars to be made payable to the local homeless shelter, and you will not be allowed supervised visitation with your son until a twelve-step program is completed. Do you understand, Mr. Kendricks?"

"My client understands, Your Honor, and thank you for your leniency," Veronica replied.

"Veronica Jordan. That name sounds familiar," Chanel whispered as she and Kyle left the courtroom. Kyle asked if he could go out to the car and wait because he didn't want to see his father.

Down the hall, Eryca sat with a public defender. She got off easy because she was just a passenger. The judge handed her a $500 fine and a mandate to complete a twelve-step program.

Eryca saw that Chanel was staring at her, so she stared back. Todd came out of the courtroom and went straight to Eryca. Shocked, Chanel waited patiently to see if he even had any intention of talking to her.

When he was finished talking to Eryca, Todd finally approached Chanel.

"I'm catching a ride with Eryca. Do you have any money on you?"

Chanel slapped Todd and walked out. She got in the car with Kyle and drove off.

"What's going to happen now, Mom?" he asked.

Chanel took a deep breath and answered, "Your father will be away for a while, and you and I will start to rebuild our lives and spend more quality time together. How does that sound?"

"Great, Mom," he answered. Kyle loved his mother. In the mornings before he went off to school, he would find her in the hotel to give her a kiss goodbye. Whether she was in a meeting, on the phone with an important client or stressed out because people called out sick and left her high and dry with no staff, she always dropped everything to show him love and affection. They had a close relationship, and he knew that she was his backbone, his strength, and his example of what he wanted in a wife when and if he ever decided to get married.

Rockin' sat on Nelson's couch and watched a movie. Black and White sat at Nelson's feet with allegiance, waiting for any orders their master might have.

Why are we just sitting here? Robin wanted to know.

"Well, what do you want to do? I'm perfectly fine here, sitting on my ass."

Let's go out for a while. Spend some time alone, just me and you.

"Can we go to a movie?"

Robin laughed. *Of course.*

"Bro, we going out for a while. You need anything? You lookin' kinda sad. Is there anything you want to talk about? You know I'm here for you, boobie. What's today?"

"I'm good, thanks. And today is Thursday, Rockin'."

"I'll be home later, so give me a call."

Rockin' gave Nelson some dap and was on her way. The phone rang.

"Nelson, hi. Is Robin over there?" Chanel asked.

"No. She just left. What's going on?"

"Nothing much. Kyle and I are going out shopping for the day and maybe catch a movie. Spend some quality time together. Know what I mean?"

"Hmm. I used to."

Nelson's response set off a bell in Chanel's head. He was clearly thinking about his kids and his hated ex-wife. Now Chanel knew where she'd heard the name Veronica Jordan before today. She was Nelson's ex-wife. He had mentioned her that night he'd told them his life story. He already sounded upset, so Chanel thought it better not to say anything about Veronica now.

Instead, she tried to cheer him up. "If you're not busy, you're welcome to come with us."

"Thanks, but you guys go and have a good time. Tell little man I said peace."

"I will. Take it easy." Chanel hung up the phone. As worried as she had become about Nelson, she didn't want to let it ruin the time with Kyle. She did promise herself, though, that she would call and check on him later.

Monmouth Raceway Mall was Kyle's favorite place to shop. They had lots of sneaker and hat stores, and those were his favorite things to buy. While he shopped for those things, Chanel went to the Nine West store and did some window-shopping. They met a half-hour later at the food court and had lunch.

Once they finished lunch, they were tired of being inside, so they went to a local skate park and watched the skateboarders and roller bladers hop and jump all over the place. That got old after a while, so they decided to take in a movie.

The theater wasn't too crowded, maybe fifty people or so, but a group of rowdy teenagers was there. When the movie started, they just wouldn't be quiet. Chanel tried to ignore it for a while, but when she got tired of their noise, she went out to the manager's office and had them removed.

About halfway through the movie, Chanel heard more talking. She turned around to look for the offending person, thinking she could ask politely for some quiet. When she couldn't find the talker, she decided to get up and follow the voice.

It was coming from the back. As she got closer, she recognized the voice.

"Rockin', is that you?"

"Word. What it be like, girl? Who you here wit'? It bet' not be ol' boy. Ooohhh, please tell me you ain't here with that muthafucka."

"No. Be quiet. I'm here with Kyle. Are you alone?"

"Who the hell else would I be with? Me and Robin, we chillin'. Well, us and this Brenda doll. Still can't get over that I got to carry this shit around," she said, laughing and shaking her head.

"Okay. You want to come and sit with us?"

"No. Like you, we spendin' some quality time together."

Chanel looked at Rockin', concerned that she was alone, but she knew it was no use trying to convince her to move. She left Rockin' and went back to sit with Kyle. When the movie was over, Chanel watched Rockin' get in her car safely and decided to follow her home. Little did she know, home wasn't where she was going.

Rockin' drove a few miles and ended up down the street from Robin's father's house. She parked across from a stream that flowed away from the town. Rockin' got out of the car as Chanel watched.

"A'ight. We going back to kick his ass? You know he want you dead, right?"

So I heard. And no, we aren't going to kick his ass, Robin answered. *I want to see if he's home, and if he isn't, then I want to go into the house and see if we can find my mother's ashes. I never got them from when she was cremated.*

"I see his car in the driveway. He home. Where he gonna go with a tore up butt hole?"

That was brilliant. They laughed together. *You got your gun just in case? Brenda doll?*

"Don't leave home without it. And yeah, damn! Fucking doll."

You're mean.

"Whatever, man."

Rockin' opened the car door, pitched the Brenda doll into the back seat and withdrew her gun from the back of her pants. She walked slowly, looking around the neighborhood as she approached the house. As she walked up the stairs, Chanel called out to her.

"Hey, Rockin'!" Chanel called as she stepped out of her car. "What are you doing here, girl? I see you have your, you know, gun with you. Is everything okay?"

She stepped between Rockin' and the front door of the house.

"The question, homey, is whatchu doin' here? Didn't think that your definition of spending quality time was following me. We here to get her mother's ashes. You cool wit' that?"

"Yeah. But why don't you go back to your car and let me see if I can get them for you? How's that?" Chanel felt it was necessary to handle Rockin' with kid gloves, fully aware that she was further gone than either she or Nelson had thought.

Rockin' agreed to let her knock and see if he would hand over the ashes, but she refused to go back to her car. Instead, she defiantly waited on the side of the house, behind some bushes. Chanel put her finger up to her mouth, warning Rockin' to be quiet.

"Just knock already," Rockin' whispered.

Hesitantly, Chanel lifted the knocker and dropped it against the door. There was no answer. She waited a few moments then knocked again, but to no avail. As she started to walk back down the stairs, she heard the blinds moving on the window.

"What the hell do you want?" Jiles growled from inside.

"I'm here to see if I could get Robin's mother's ashes. She—" Chanel looked out of the corner of her eyes at Rockin'. "She wasn't able to come and ask you herself because she's sick, so she asked me, and well, here I am," she said with an uneasy smile on her face.

Jiles left the blinds crooked and hurriedly opened the door. "You tell that bitch that I said fuck her. After what she did to me, she better start looking for something for her ashes to go in."

Chanel stood her ground, though his hot breath in her face was disgusting.

"Now, you get the hell off my property before you need something for your ashes too, bitch."

Now I see why Robin hates your guts, she thought as she turned around and walked to her car.

Rockin' heard the entire altercation, and it was taking everything for her not to go in there and blow his brains out. Chanel knew that was what Rockin' had in mind, and she didn't want it happening now, not with her son in the car. Even after being treated like she was scum of the earth by this man, she was about to stop his murder. She waved her hand to Rockin', urging her to come away from the house.

Rockin' scurried out from the bushes, keeping her eyes on Robin's foul father, who remained in the doorway, wrapped in a worn-out yellow robe, black torn slippers and white socks.

How's that ass of yours?" she taunted, swaying her gun back and forth, daring him to say or do anything.

Rockin' and Chanel got into their cars and drove off. When the house was no longer in sight, Rockin' pulled up to a stop sign and waved for Chanel to pull up beside her. Kyle quietly sat in the front seat while Rockin' and Chanel exchanged words.

"You should have just let me handle this. Now that his dumb ass knows that I want the ashes, who knows what he'll do with them."

"Rockin', please, not in front of Kyle. And put that damn thing away. What are your plans for the night? Are you going right home?"

"No!"

Chanel drove off, taking Rockin's blunt response as another way of saying "Leave me alone!" As she drove, she called Nelson and told him what had happened. He asked her to come over, and she agreed that she would be there as soon as she dropped off her son. The poor child had seen enough craziness for one night.

"Kyle, sweetie," she said when they pulled in front of the hotel. "When you get in, please go by the men's sauna area and give a message to the man shining shoes. Today was his first day. Tell him I'm busy tonight, but I'd like him to stop by tomorrow so we can discuss how his first day of business went." Even in the midst of all the drama going on in her life, Chanel still had a hotel to run.

Kyle gave his mother a kiss and went inside to do what he was asked to do.

Chapter Twenty-three

Eryca and Todd sat in his hotel suite, unconcerned with the fact that not only were they getting high in Chanel's home, but at that very moment, Kyle was heading toward the shoe shine station, where he would find Junie knocked unconscious.

When they left the courthouse, Todd and Eryca scraped their pockets but didn't come up with enough money to go out and buy a few hits. So, when they returned to the hotel and found Junie alone, cleaning up his workstation, Todd hit him over the head with a pipe and robbed him. Junie and had been lying on the floor ever since. When Kyle found him, he immediately called his mother then 911.

Chanel turned her car around and made her way back to the hotel. As the medics put Junie in the back of the ambulance, Chanel came up beside Junie and rubbed his cheek. He still hadn't regained consciousness.

"Everything is going to be okay, Junie," she told him.

Chanel went to the front desk and asked if anyone had seen or heard anything unusual, but no one had. The officers needed to fill out a report, so Chanel encouraged Kyle to tell them everything he knew while she continued to question the people at the front desk.

"Well, has Todd been here today?" she asked.

Paula had seen him come in a few hours ago and head toward the area where Junie was working, but then he came back and hurried upstairs. Chanel immediately knew it was likely that he was responsible for what happened to Junie. The problem she faced was how she was going to tell Rockin' about this.

Junie was meek and unkempt most of the time, but Rockin' took to him since he was a good friend of Robin's. When she first met him, Robin felt sorry for him because he had no family and lived in a one-room apartment downtown. A part of her was intrigued, though, that he never had to complain of a nagging wife or bad children, and often acted as if he was just as happy not having any family. His lonely world may have been that, but she was certain that it was far better than the world she grew up in.

Chanel called Nelson and told him what had happened. Stunned, he asked her if she had told Rockin' yet.

"No, but we can't keep this from her. She has to know, and you know she's gonna trip. Speaking of which, I still can't believe the way she acted in front of her father's house tonight."

"Where is Rockin' now?"

"She went her own way after we left her father's house, and I'm really concerned. That's why I was on my way to talk to you. She's gone, man. She's really messed up."

Nelson sat in silence for a moment. "I know. I know. Dr. Christopher called me wondering if I had seen her because she missed another appointment. I'm not too worried about that. She may be to out there, yeah, but we'll go through with what we had planned. The card party is on Thursday. I'll be able to assess her behavior and we can go from there."

When Chanel hung up the phone, she saw Todd and Eryca and another woman leaving the hotel. Their eyes were darting all over the place, looking guilty as hell, just as Chanel had expected they would. She wasn't sure who the second woman was.

She waited until they left before she went upstairs to see what mess they had left, and sent Kyle to the restaurant to order dinner for them. When she walked into the suite, everything looked in place. Well, she supposed there was only so much mess they could make with a spoon, some type of tourniquet and a needle. Nonetheless, she wanted to make sure that everything was cool before Kyle came up.

She went in the bathroom and found their paraphernalia, swiped it in the garbage, picked up the phone and called housekeeping. She requested a crew with at least three of their biggest linen carts. After she hung up the phone, she went in the bedroom and gathered all of Todd's belongings, bringing them into the living room. She heard a knock at the door as she set Todd's belongings on the floor.

"Bring them in and start putting these things into them please," she instructed the maids who were at the door. They knew better than to question Chanel, so they did as they were told.

Chanel went into the bedroom again and returned with all of his toiletries and neckties. She grabbed one of the linen carts and wheeled it into their bedroom, where she put all of his shoes, sweaters, tennis rackets, basketballs, books and notebooks from school, colognes, and anything else that was his, into the cart. Then she wheeled it back out to them and told them to take his things and put them outside the kitchen's back door.

"And when you get down there, please send maintenance up. I need these locks changed. Now!"

One of the maids pressed the button for the elevator. When it arrived at the floor, the doors opened and Kyle stepped off, holding his mother's dinner in his hand. He recognized the clothes in the carts. A feeling of relief came over him.

For as long as Kyle could remember, his father was everything but a father. He smiled for the customers, portraying a false picture of a dedicated husband and father, while feeding an addiction to heroin and cheating on his wife. Kyle had absolutely no emotional ties to his father. He didn't voice his issues, only because he knew how his mother felt about Todd at one time. To save her feelings, he concealed the hatred he felt for the man he called Dad, hoping that his mother would one day feel the same way.

As he watched his father's belongings carted off, Chanel called out to him. "Come on, baby," she said with arms held straight out, reaching for him. As he walked toward her, tears welled up in her eyes. Despite the dysfunction that she had allowed in his life, he still grew up a nice young man, maintaining grades that kept him on the honor roll. She shook her head slowly, still reaching for him, her hands pulling for him to hurry into her arms.

His stride was confident and strong and to Chanel, not fast enough. He looked at his mother and wished that she didn't have to endure the pain and humiliation that his father had put her through. Her eyes, still bright even after many sleepless nights and hours upon hours of crying and searching for answers, were warm and welcoming. He took his mother in his arms and held her tight as she collapsed, submitting to the end of a more than difficult tribulation in her life.

Kyle took his mother inside, where he helped her sit down on the couch. While she cried softly, he set two place settings, poured some Sunny Delight, his favorite drink, into their glasses, and set their food in the middle of the table. He led his mother to the table, and they had dinner the way it would be from that day forward— just the two of them.

Chapter Twenty-four

Rockin' went into Jack's Bar and Grill. She had never been there before and was amused by all the college students congregated there, even on a school night. She sat at the bar and ordered a rack of Jack's famous barbecued ribs.

"Yeah, can I get a double shot of Jack Daniel's and an Amstel light?"

She perused the bar, noting black men with white women, white men with black women, boys with other boys and girls with other girls. Gender and race was of no significance there.

Rockin', why did you bring us here?

"I don't know. Felt like doing something different, really different. Besides, a bar is a bar is a bar."

Well that drink you ordered is going to have you seeing triple if you're not careful.

The bartender brought out the drinks that Rockin' had ordered. She downed the double shot and chased it with a gulp of Amstel light. She ordered another double shot while she waited for her ribs to come out.

"Chill. It's gon' be all right," she assured Robin as she downed her second double shot. Just as she acknowledged the burning sensation in her chest, rounding her lips as if she was blowing smoke circles, a man sat beside her. She reached behind and felt her pants to make sure that her gun was close by should she have to pull it.

"Man, I have never seen a woman handle a double shot of . . ." He gestured toward her shot glass, inquiring what she was drinking.

"Jack Daniel's," she said in answer to his question.

"Is anyone sitting here?" he asked, pointing to the empty barstool.

"The stool is empty. You got next."

"Damn, girl." He motioned for the bartender to bring her another round, while unfolding nothing but hundred dollar bills. Rockin', who was starting to feel the effects of her drinks, looked over at him then at his stash. He stood about five feet, with a low cut and pork chop sideburns that collided with a full goatee. His build was medium, and his hands were huge.

She bent over to see what kind of shoes he was wearing. Seeing Nelson in Ferragamos every day set her standard of shoe etiquette, and anything less was a no-no.

"What kind of shoes are those?" she asked.

"That's a weird question. Normally the first thing someone asks is 'What's your name?' or 'Are you married?' or 'Haven't I seen you somewhere before?' But you want to know what kind of shoes I have on. Well, let's see." He got up off the stool and took off his shoe, setting it on the bar in front of Rockin'. She examined it then burst into laughter. The shoes were Steve Maddens.

"Um, I ain't gonna say nothing," she slurred then took another sip of beer.

"So, what's your name? Where are you from?" the man asked as he put his shoe on again.

"My name is Rockin' Robin. Tweet-tweedle-la-deet. Oh man, I crack myself up," she joked as she downed her third double shot of Jack Daniel's.

"All right. My name is Marcus Penley. Nice to meet you." He held out his hand. Rockin' shook it, noticing how soft, yet strong his hand was.

She turned back to her beer. They sat for a moment without saying anything.

"Watch this. I'ma fuck his mind up," she mumbled under her breath for Robin's benefit. Then she turned to the man and asked, "Wanna fuck?"

Oh, no you didn't. Robin was appalled.

"Excuse me?" Marcus said.

"I'm just playing," she said, laughing hysterically. She totally caught him off guard, and that tickled her.

"What is this, happy hour or something? All of these college kids are in here getting fucked up, knowing full well that they got tests in the morning. College was never for me. I would have been a total fuck up if I went."

"That's not a positive thing to say. I'm sure you're being a bit hard on yourself," said Marcus, thinking flattery might help him at least get her number. "You appear to be intelligent, you're dressed nice, and—"

"And things are not always what they appear to be," she finished his thought for him.

Marcus looked at her as her friendly face took on a hard look. The girl he had just met obviously had some serious issues, he decided. Then again, he was just looking for a good time, so her problems really didn't concern him.

He ordered a beer and asked Rockin', "Can I get you anything else?"

"Nope. I'm just waiting for my rack of ribs. Can I get you anything else?"

"If you're not gonna share your ribs, then yeah. Order me some."

She whistled to the bartender and added another order of ribs. Not long after, the bartender brought their food. They ate and talked about general things and ordered more rounds of Jack Daniel's and beer. By 10 o'clock, they were both toasted and feeling very attracted to each other. Rockin's cell phone rang, but she turned it off without answering.

"You want to go somewhere quiet?" Rockin' asked Marcus.

"Yeah, that would be cool. Where do you want to go?"

"How about yo' spot?"

Marcus looked at Rockin', surprised by her boldness. He couldn't help but be turned on by how her lips hugged the spout of her beer bottle. When she took a sip, her tongue went slightly into the bottle, creating a funnel for the beer to flow through. Maybe she would hit on him and mean it this time. If nothing else, he could get his dick sucked.

They both went into their pockets to pay their tabs. Marcus thought he was being a gentleman by offering to pay her bill. When Rockin' shut him down and suggested that he worry about his and only his, he knew that even a dick suck was hardly possible.

The air was warm and the autumn leaves shimmied as the wind blew softly. They were both intoxicated and luckily, Marcus had a place nearby. As they walked, they talked about what he did for a living. He was a professional masseuse.

"That must be cool as hell, rubbing up on people for a living," Rockin' commented. "And it must be nice to pay for someone to rub you 'n shit."

"Have you ever had a massage?"

"Nah, bro. Not my kind of thing. I do other things to relax and occupy myself."

Yeah, well I would like one, so go ahead and ask him if we can go to his office.

"Unh-uh."

Please.

"Aaaalllllllll right! You get on my damn nerves," Rockin' yelled out loud.

"What?" Marcus stopped in his tracks and stared at her. Even as drunk as he was, he knew something was off about this woman.

"No. Yes." Rockin' answered quickly. "Can we go to your massage place and . . ." She paused. "Can a sistah get some rubbin'?"

"You know, you're a character," Marcus joked.

"You have no idea," Rockin' responded.

Marcus' Miracle Massages was not too far. The bright neon blue sign sat in the palm of two huge hands. He unlocked the door, turned off the alarm and turned on the lights then invited Rockin' in. Plush couches with pewter and glass tables warmed the reception area. Pictures of hands massaging shoulders, backs, legs and feet hung on the walls in the hallway leading to the massage rooms. Each of the three rooms had a massage table covered with a terry cloth sheet. White towels were stacked neatly below a shelf that held exotic oils and fragranced beads.

"Yo, this is the bomb," Rockin' cheered.

"You like it? It's nice. Three years of masseuse school and a couple dollars that I saved up allowed me to open this place. I already had my clientele because before this, I did it on the side. So, do you want a massage?"

Rockin' looked wearily at Marcus. She couldn't remember ever being touched by a man other than Jiles Sessoms. She didn't know a touch that wasn't a demeaning touch, a touch that didn't make her feel shitty afterwards, or a touch that wasn't forced upon her. Her defenses climbed as she closed her coat across her chest.

"Okay," she finally said quietly. Rockin' figured she could handle Marcus if anything got out of line.

"Was that a yes?"

"Sure. Where do I get changed?" she asked, gaining a little confidence.

Marcus directed her to a dressing room down the hall. The shelves inside the large room were stacked with huge, cottony soft towels, and a collection of the same oils that were in the reception area. Bonsai trees were elegantly set on wrought iron and bamboo tables, and one actually had a stream running through it. Rockin' picked a massage oil made with avocado and cucumber.

"He don't have no chicken and biscuits oils or lotions in this piece. I bet most of his customers are white."

You are not right, girl. Be quiet and go get us a massage. Even Robin was feeling confident enough to go through with this.

When Rockin' came out, she was dressed in a white robe with only her underwear underneath. Her gun was in her panties, just in case. She walked into the room where Marcus had turned on a CD of tropical rain forest sounds. He had changed into a white T-shirt and white sweat pants and was washing his hands in the sink.

She stood in the doorway, twisting her unpainted toes and biting her lip, unsure if she was ready for this. He turned as he was drying his hands and gestured for her to lie on the table.

"I won't bite. I promise," Marcus teased.

"I'm not sure I won't, though," she responded.

Marcus walked over, took her hand and led her to the table. He left the room so that she could take off her robe and cover herself with the white sheet. As she lay there waiting for him to return, she had to admit that the ambiance of the room was helping her relax.

He returned a moment later and began the massage at Rockin's feet. "Okay. Have you ever had a pedicure?

Say yes, Robin told her.

"Yes. Mm-hmm."

"Then me touching your feet won't tickle you and make you laugh." He lightly twisted the bridge of her foot then moved up to her calves. They were full of tension. He lifted the sheet to the bottom of her butt. This made Rockin' close her eyes and wonder if she had made a mistake. Inside, Robin was also praying for what should have been a relaxing experience to be over.

Rockin' covered her face with her hands as he lowered the sheet back over her thighs and pulled it away from her back. He guided her head down so that the nape of her neck was accessible. With two fingers, he gently massaged the back of her neck then moved her bra straps so that he could massage her shoulders. Rockin' was getting nervous and could feel herself losing the relaxed feeling that had eased its way into her body.

Marcus moved lower to the ball of her back. She clenched her teeth as he massaged her, moving his hands freely over her body as if he knew every inch of it.

Oooooh. That feels good, Robin moaned, surprising Rockin'.

Nah, fuck that. Don't you see what he's doing? Rockin' thought.

No he isn't. It's not the same, Robin protested.

How the fuck do you know? You didn't speak up then, so I don't expect you to speak up now!

Rockin' and Robin argued internally until Rockin' just couldn't take it anymore. She jumped off the table and pulled her gun out from her crotch area. Pointing directly at Marcus, she stood, stance firm, and looked into his eyes. Marcus stood with his hands in the air, a dumbfounded look on his face, unaware that he had crossed the line that only Rockin' and Robin knew.

"Robin? What's up?"

"Don't you move your ass. Let's go and get my clothes." She whisked the gun toward the door, indicating to Marcus that she was no longer interested in any services he offered and wanted to leave. He led the way to the dressing area, and Rockin' followed him. She didn't take her eyes off of him once.

You ruined it! Robin complained.

I said shut the fuck up!

Marcus remained quiet as they entered the room. Rockin' told him to sit while she got dressed. She grabbed her bag and bid him goodbye.

"You better be careful who you take home, brotha. Christmas could have been cancelled for you." She backed out of the room and closed the door behind her. She ran to her car, which was only a few blocks away, got into it and sped off.

Chapter Twenty-five

"Where have you been?" Chanel asked Rockin' as she came into the hotel. Her clothes were disheveled and she was fired up.

"Dayum, can't a sistah have some private time? Pffffff!" Rockin' headed to the bar. Chanel followed her.

It was 12:30 and Breezes was still humming with the idle chit chat of people who were buzzed and engrossed in flirtatious smiles and "Let's go get a room" eyes. Rockin' continued on with her double shots of Jack Daniel's kick while Chanel ordered her favorite, a white wine spritzer.

"So, Rockin', how was your day?"

"Ai'ight. Yours?"

"Well, I have something to tell you," Chanel said, wishing she didn't. "You know Junie started today."

"Right. How was Junie's first day?" Rockin' asked not noticing the sadness in Chanel's voice.

"Rockin' . . . um, Junie was robbed tonight. Kyle went to check on him when we got back this evening and found him knocked out beside his station. The ambulance took him down to the hospital. I just got off the phone with the attending physician. She said that he regained consciousness and was a little shaken, but would be okay. He does have a huge lump on his head, but that should go down in a couple of days."

Rockin' looked at Chanel with an emotionless stare.

"Who the fuck did it? Did anyone see anything or anybody?"

"The people at the reservation desk said they saw Todd go back there and then a few minutes later he came rushing through the lobby and went up to his room. After they took Junie away in the ambulance, I saw him come downstairs with Eryca and some other woman." She sighed heavily. "Todd asked me for some money earlier but I didn't give it to him. I believe he robbed Junie to get high. I'm so sorry, Rockin'."

"What the fuck for? Your loser of a husband just gave *me* a reason to want his junkie ass hit. You better hope I don't get to him before you do what you supposed to do. Comprende?"

Rockin' slammed her glass on the bar and ordered another. She and Chanel stayed at the bar until closing time.

Nelson sat in his library and looked through photo albums of his kids. There were pictures of each of their births, first birthdays, first day of pre-school, and first camping trips with Girls Scouts and Boys Scouts. The pictures of Veronica had been removed before Nelson got them from Dannon. It had been over three years since he divorced her, and over six months since the kids called and asked if they could come over.

Veronica was a very spiteful woman. She abused Nelson to no end and when he left, she tried to make the kids believe that Nelson was the one who abused her. She even went so far as to tell them their father had an affair that led to their divorce. But they saw. They saw their mother throw things, spit ugly words out at him and rant and rave around the house when things didn't go her way.

In the beginning, she abided by the order for set visitation, but it irritated her to see her children show any happiness about going to see Nelson. When Nelson started dating, it gave her an excuse to put the brakes on the visitation arrangement. She told him that if he was going to have another woman in the house when her children were there, that they wouldn't be there. She had the woman's background checked and confronted her about what she learned.

Nelson's new girlfriend, Crystal, was a stripper at one time and was picked up during a raid at the club where she worked. While Veronica pointed her fingers and waved Crystal's minor rap sheet in her face, she warned her that if she heard Crystal was ever around her children, she'd be sorry. Veronica would see to it that she would never again swing on anybody's dick, let alone a pole, then she called her a porch monkey and dismissed her.

Needless to say, Crystal left Nelson alone after that. Since Veronica made it perfectly clear that Nelson wouldn't stand a chance at being happy with any other woman, especially if he intended on spending time with his children, he decided to forego any significant other in his life. The trouble and aggravation wasn't worth it.

Even after he gave in to her demands, though, she still didn't allow him to see his kids. After months of calling and getting hung up on or cursed out, Nelson gave up trying to be the father that he should be to his children. He submitted to the fact that Veronica would rather die than let him be happy. Now all he had left were photos of his children and memories that were becoming too distant.

Black and White were asleep at his feet. The house was quiet. Nelson sat back in his chair and thought about calling Veronica's house and trying to talk to the kids. He picked up the receiver then put it back down, telling himself she wouldn't answer the phone so late at night. But he missed his children desperately.

"Fuck it. I'm calling."

He picked up the phone, dialed Veronica's number and listened while it rang. After five rings, Dannon picked up the phone.

"Dannon, it's me, Dad."

"What's up, Dad? How have you been?"

The mere fact that he asked how he'd been told Nelson that Dannon missed him just as much as he missed Dannon.

"Neeah, Naohme, it's Dad. Pick up the phone!" Dannon yelled out.

"Hi, Daddy," the girls said in unison. "When are you coming to pick us up? Are you okay?"

"Yes, babies. I'm fine. I'll come and get you whenever you want to come. Just let me know and I'll be right there."

"You could come now."

"No. I think that would upset your mother if I came to the house at this time of the night. Maybe I can get you tomorrow. How does that sound?"

"She doesn't care. She's not here anyway," Dannon said to his father.

"What do you mean she's not there? Where is she? Who's home with you?"

"Cella," Neeah responded.

"Cella, huh? Okay. Cella is good peoples. Is Cella asleep?"

"Yeah, Daddy. You coming to get us?" Naohme asked.

"Yes I am, lovey. How does 2 o'clock tomorrow sound?"

"All right," Dannon said.

"Oooooo, okay, Daddy. We love you," Neeah and Naohme shouted with excitement.

"I love you." He hung up the phone before he broke down and cried like a baby. His children were his life.

He had been trying to hold on and be strong for them. Speaking to them after such a long time reminded him just how much he loved them.

Are you okay, Daddy? Nelson thought he heard a voice.

He looked around the room and dried his eyes. "Lewis?"

Black was on his back with his legs in the air, and White was wrestling with his tail. They both scurried to their feet when Nelson got up and walked into the foyer. Black and White didn't follow as usual. They stayed in the library, growling and showing their teeth.

The grandfather clock recessed into one of the walls in the sitting room struck 1 o'clock. Nelson walked back in and stood in the middle of the room. All of a sudden he felt a sharp pain in his arm. He grabbed it as he fell to the floor. Black and White came sniffing, still growling, but remained a distance away from him. Nelson felt dizzy and squinted to see where Black and White, his protectors, were.

"Black. White. Come to me." Nelson was still on the floor, grabbing his arm. They pounced around in place, and it wasn't until Nelson looked into their eyes that they knew he needed them.

"Okay. Come on now. I'm okay." They obeyed Nelson and came to his side. He leaned on them to get up on his feet, and all three of them retreated to his bedroom.

The hot water felt good on Nelson's body. As he washed, he rubbed the scar he'd had ever since Veronica shot him in the arm. He remembered the day it happened.

That day, he wanted to take the kids out for breakfast, but she wanted to cook. The children were already dressed and ready to go, but she didn't allow him to take them. He gathered them anyway, but when he was about to walk out the door, she shot him in his left arm.

Dannon called the cops. She was arrested but later released because he didn't press charges. In fact, she even talked her lawyer talk and they ended up giving her back her gun. Thinking that she was in total control now, she let the gun lay around the house even when the kids were around. That became another reason for Veronica and Nelson to argue, until one day Neeah found it and started to play with it.

Dannon just happened to be coming into the living room where Neeah was and called frantically to his father. Nelson came running into the room and grabbed the gun from Neeah. He immediately hid it from the kids and Veronica. Later that evening, he told her what had happened and told her that he put it away, but wouldn't tell her where. To this day, she had no idea where Nelson hid it.

After he got out of the shower, he dried off and put on his flannel Ralph Lauren pajamas. He got in the bed and patted the mattress for Black and White to join him. They jumped up and took their places at the foot of the bed, where they would stay until he woke.

The next morning, Lewis buzzed Nelson on the intercom. It was 9:30 and Nelson still wasn't up. Normally he was up, dressed, and would have eaten by 7:00, especially on Fridays. He never missed a beat, and Lewis could usually set a watch to his routine. When he didn't answer, Lewis went to Nelson's bedroom door and knocked softly.

"Nelson? NB?"

Nelson still didn't answer. Lewis knocked again, this time a little harder. He bent down and looked under the door. Black and White stood in position, waiting for Lewis to open the door.

"Black, White. It's me, Lewis," he announced. Though they knew him quite well, they were completely loyal to Nelson, and would attack if Lewis didn't first put them at ease. He put his hand under the door so that they could smell him. They fell back and allowed him to open the door.

As Lewis entered, the dogs jumped back on the bed where Nelson remained asleep. Lewis looked around the room. Nothing seemed to be out of place, until he noticed that the glass that usually sat on the nightstand was not there. Nelson always had a nightcap, so for the glass to be missing was strange. It was equally unsettling that the television was off, since he always fell asleep and left it on all night.

"Nelson." Lewis shook him gently. "Nelson. Wake up. Are you okay, man?" He drew the heavy drapes that cloaked the double bay window then opened the window so that the fall air would help Nelson wake up. Nelson was awakened by the sun.

"Oh, man. I slept hard. And still I feel so spent. What time is it?"

"Around quarter to ten on a beautiful Friday morning," Lewis responded, still a little concerned with Nelson's change in habit. "Did you have a late night? Did some partying maybe?" Lewis hoped his answer would be yes.

"No. Not really. I . . ." Nelson paused. "I called the kids and talked with them for a while."

"Is that right?"

"Yes, and they wanted to know when I was going to come and pick them up. In fact, they wanted me to go there last night and get them. Dannon said that Veronica wasn't there, but Cella was there with them.

That was around 12:30 or so. That's all I remember. I can't believe I slept this long and I still feel tired." He grabbed his arm.

Lewis observed Nelson while he looked at the calendar and reminded him that the dumpsite needed to be "cleaned." This meant that all of the sealed garbage cans at the special dump site had to be moved to an incinerator. Lewis needed Nelson to sign off on the papers to get the ball rolling before the inspectors came in. This was done on an annual basis near the end of October.

"Lewis, you need to go ahead and handle that for me. I told the kids I would pick them up today, and that's what I'm going to do. Please hand me the phone."

"Are you sure you don't want me to call?"

"No. Enough is enough. She won't keep me away from my kids any longer." As Nelson spoke, the doorbell rang.

Lewis went to get the door and Nelson proceeded to make his telephone call.

"Hello," Veronica answered in a sharp manner.

"May I speak to the kids? Please?"

"That's right! You better call here correct," Veronica snapped. "And make it snappy, nappy!"

"Hi, Daddy. So you coming to get us?" Neeah and Naohme were already on the phone and heard what their mother had said to their father. Veronica hung up her extension.

"Neeah and Naohme, if you want me to come and get you, I will. Where's Dannon?"

"He's in his room getting ready for you to pick us up 'cause you said that you were coming at two."

Nelson could hear Veronica in the background. "Y'all ain't going nowhere!"

"Daddy, we told Mommy that you called, and she got real mad."

"That's okay, baby girl. I figured she would. I'll be there at two o'clock. I promise. Bye, baby."

Nelson swung his legs over the side of the bed. He had anticipated that Veronica would act up when she heard that he was coming. For her to act any different would mean she actually grew up.

He washed his face and brushed his teeth then went into the kitchen where Lewis was getting his breakfast in order.

"Come on, Lewis. You don't have to do all that. I slept late. I didn't get amnesia and forget how to get my own breakfast. Who was at the door?"

Lewis pointed to a dozen yellow roses on the dining room table. Nelson walked over, pulled the card and read it out loud.

"Whatchu crying for? Yo' shit can't be as bad as mine. Bro, we see ya later. Rockin' . . . oh, and Chanel."

"They're crazy as hell. Those are my home girls," Nelson said as he sat at the table next to Lewis.

"What are they for?" Lewis asked.

"I guess they saw me—" He stopped himself before admitting he had broken down the night before. "I don't know." Nelson knew that Rockin' had seen him cry that evening in Chanel's hotel room, but he didn't dare let Lewis know that he was letting his emotions get the best of him.

"Lewis, pull the court order for my visitation with the kids. And call Judge Haskins and put her on call should I need her. I'm picking my kids up at two."

"You got it, boss."

Chapter Twenty-six

"Yeah. Can I get Junie's room?"

"I'm sorry, ma'am. I need the patient's last name," the nurse responded.

"Bitch, the little old man who was brought in last night. He was hit over the head. Are you a blonde?"

"Hold on, please."

Do you have to be so rude? Robin asked Rockin'.

Rockin' polished her gun while she waited for Junie to pick up the phone. Her gut feeling was telling her that she was going to have to cancel Todd's ass before Chanel could on Thursday.

"If Junie tells me that Todd was the one who robbed him, that's fuckin' it. He's all mine, and that diarrhea that you got about Thursday can be done," she said as if Chanel were in the room to hear her.

"Ay, ah, hello?"

Rockin' was silent.

"Hello. Who's there?"

"Junie! What's up? What's this I hear about you gettin' violated on your first night at the hotel?" Robin asked.

"Oh, Robin, I'm too old for this. One minute I was bent over my shoe shine kit packing up, and the next minute some man asked me if I could spare some change. I turned around, and before I could even answer, I saw him raise his arm and then the lights went out. And then I woke up here."

Ask him, Robin insisted.

"Junie, I want to be real clear on this. Did you see who it was that did this to you? And before you answer, think real hard."

"Well, yes. I mean, I know what he looks like, Robin."

"Okay. I'm listening."

Junie described the man who had robbed him. As Rockin' suspected, Todd had beat Robin's old friend for everything he had earned on his first day at the hotel—only $27.

"I just can't do it, Robin. I hope you understand that I'll be going back to the mall if they'll take me back. They're releasing me tomorrow then I'll go talk to the mall manager."

"Junie, of course not, yo. I understand, and I'm sure they'll take you back. I'll pick you up and take you home tomorrow." Rockin' spat on the barrel of her gun.

After Junie thanked her, they hung up. Rockin' went into her bedroom, put on her black velour sweat suit and a pair of red Timberlands. She pulled her hair back and put on a baseball cap then went into the bathroom and grabbed a pair of rubber gloves. She went into the kitchen and poured some orange juice, champagne and pineapple chunks into the blender. She was a little hung over from the night before and needed something to buzz her just enough to get rid of the headache that was dancing on her forehead. As she drank, she called Chanel.

"'Sup?"

"Rockin', is that you?" Chanel asked.

"Yup. Whatchu doin'?"

"Sleeping."

"That's new. Normally yo' bitch-ass husband would be demanding breakfast right about now."

"That bastard is downstairs in the steam room. Fuck him. He can get that crack ho Eryca to cook his breakfast."

"Ooooh, I like how ya talkin'. I'll catch up with you later."

Rockin' gulped the last of her breakfast drink. As she took the elevator down to the main floor, she adjusted the gun belt hidden under her oversized sweat suit.

She walked nonchalantly past the front desk into the sauna area. When she peeked in the little window on the door, she saw Eryca sucking Todd's dick while he was shooting up. She looked around to see be sure the coast was clear then slowly and quietly opened the door and slid in. She put on her gloves.

The lights were dim and the steam formed a cloud-like wall between them. Eryca was so busy and Todd was so high that neither one noticed Rockin' come in. She stood there for a moment and watched Eryca spin on his dick head. Todd's head was tilted back, and he was flying high.

When Rockin' moved, Eryca noticed the motion out of the corner of her eye. She stopped sucking Todd's dick and stood up to look around the foggy room.

"Who's that?" she asked, trying to wave away the steam with one hand while still fondling Todd's dick with the other.

"It's me, baby." Rockin' tried to sound like Chanel. Todd lifted his head, and Rockin' stepped further away into the steam.

"Shut up. There ain't nobody there," Todd hissed at Eryca as he let his head fall back again.

Eryca tried to brush off the eerie feeling, taking the needle from Todd and shooting the heroin into her arm. Rockin' watched as the money they took from Junie flowed through their veins and straight to their brains. Once she saw that Eryca was as high as Todd was, she floated through the steam that separated them.

Eryca, who was now hunched over Todd's lap, sat up and reached out to Rockin' as if she were pushing her out of the way.

"What are you doing?" Eryca asked.

Rockin' pulled her gun and said, "Take it." At first Eryca refused, but when Rockin' cocked the chamber, Eryca did as she was told.

"Point it to his head."

Eryca attempted to point the gun to Todd's head, but when her hand kept shaking, Rockin' grew very impatient. She snatched the gun from Eryca's hand, pointed it at Todd's face at point blank range and said, "Wake his dumb ass up. You let him cum in your mouth? You a nasty bitch."

"Todd! Todd! We fucking got company. Todd!" she yelled.

"Got damn, bitch. What you—oh, shit. Robin? What the fuck you in here for?" he asked, trying to put away his shriveled up ding-a-ling.

"Bro, I'm here to collect on a debt. I think you owe my buddy Junie some cheddar."

Rockin', please don't, Robin pleaded.

"Yeah, okay. Picture me walking away from this," Rockin' said out loud.

"Oh shit." Eryca sighed. "Who is she talking to? This is some good dope."

"You fucking crazy freak bitch," Todd said as he tried to stand up.

Pap! Pap! Pap! Rockin' shot Todd in his chest and his stomach. Then she looked at Eryca.

"Open your mouth, bitch." Eryca slowly did as Rockin' demanded.

Pap! One shot into Eryca's mouth then she looked back at Todd. *Pap!* One bullet to his head splattered his brains onto the tile. Gray matter slid down his neck, onto his shoulders and fell between the cracks of the wooden bench and onto the floor.

Oh, Rockin', Robin said, *let's go! I feel sick.*

Rockin' put the gun in Eryca's hand, turned around, walked out of the sauna, and started back up to her room. This time, she took the stairs. They seemed endless. As she walked up the stairwell, her legs felt like they were weighted down by cinder blocks. The rails waved at her as she tried to grab hold of them. She wanted to vomit but refused. Her survival instincts allowed her to swallow the lump of pineapple that clogged her throat, and the sting of the acid from the orange juice and champagne made her eyes burn and her mouth water.

Breathe, Rockin' told herself, *just like we used to. Take deep breaths.*

When she finally reached her floor, Rockin' walked down the hall with one hand on the wall. She unlocked the door, went into her suite, and closed the door behind her.

A trail of boots, gloves, sweat suit, socks and underwear led the way to the bathroom. The water in the shower felt frigid because her body temperature had risen to exceed the normal degree of the human body. She sat in her tub while the water coated then beaded on her body. Flashes of her father's face, yelling at her, spit flying in her face and into her eyes, bounced around in her mind. *Smack!* Every time she looked him in the eye, he would knock the living hell out of her.

She fell back into the shower, where she and Robin sat quietly.

Chapter Twenty-seven

Rockin's telephone call had woken Chanel, so after she took her shower and got dressed, she went into the kitchen and put on some coffee. She sat at the table and thought about the plan for Thursday.

"Okay. It is what it is," she said to herself.

"Hey, Ma."

"Hey, honeybunch. I thought you were 'sleep."

"I was, but you woke me when you tried to close the door quietly and didn't," Kyle said jokingly.

"So, what do you want to do today?"

"What's today, Saturday?"

"All day!"

"You know what? I think I just need to chill out. I really don't want to do anything. Have you heard anything about Mr. Junie?"

"No. Not yet. I'll call him in a little bit. Want some breakfast?"

"Nah. Ma, can I talk to you?"

"Yes, baby. Sit down."

"I know you love my father, or you did at some point, but I never felt close to him. For a long time now, you know, I understood exactly what's been going on. There were days when I came home from school and he and Eryca were up here getting high, and her son was here with them. I would just go in my room and close the door.

"I only called him Daddy because it made you happy, not because I felt he loved me like a daddy should love his son. He never knew how to be a father. You want to know something? They used to try to get him to use too."

"Who?" Chanel asked.

"Their son, Reggie. I don't know if he ever did, but that's why I didn't want to be bothered with him. I wasn't going to voluntarily put myself in a position where Dad thought that I was down with that.

"I remember when you used to ask him if he was still dealing with her. Pffffff, man, he never left her alone. You and I were always second. Trust me! I hate his guts for what he's done to you and hasn't done for us. So, please don't feel like you have to stay in this situation on account of me, because personally, I think we're better off without him."

"Wow, I never knew you felt that way. I've always tried to hide our problems from you, but I guess I didn't do a good job, huh? And you're right. I loved your father at one time. But now, I can honestly say that I have no love for him whatsoever. He has been everything but a husband and father. He has put us in tremendous debt while he fed his addiction, an addiction that will eventually kill him. So I understand and appreciate how you feel.

"You're a smart kid, and I know that you've seen and heard things that you would rather have not, but think about it; having heard and seen these ugly things, I guarantee you that you'll make some girl a sincere and loving husband," she said as she rubbed his hair.

"I love you. Words aren't enough to make you understand how much you mean to me and how sorry I am that you've had to deal with this. We will be okay. I promise you that."

She hugged him then stood up from the table. "Now, I have to go downstairs and check on things. What are you about to do?"

"Play some video games."

"Okay. Give me a kiss and let's meet downstairs at noon for lunch."

"Bet!"

Chanel poured more coffee into a mug and headed for the door. She stopped when she heard a cell phone ringing. She went into her bedroom and saw that it was Todd's phone.

She opened the phone but didn't say hello. She didn't have to, because the person on the other end started speaking immediately.

"Todd, it's Veronica. Last night was tight!" Chanel heard her sniffing on the other end. "You still having a set today? I got some good shit."

Chanel remained quiet.

"Hello?" When she didn't get an answer, Veronica obviously understood that it might not be Todd on the phone. She immediately hung up.

Chanel stared at the phone when she heard the call disconnect. "Oh my God! Nelson's ex-wife is one of Todd's get-high hoochies. I swear you can't put a suit on just anybody. Wait until Nelson hears about this."

Just as she put down the phone, it started to ring again. This time Chanel answered it and spoke.

"Hello?"

"Hello, this is Veronica Jordan, Todd's attorney. Is he available?"

"No, I'm sorry, he isn't at the moment, but he asked me to tell you that it's still on. Give him a call in about an hour and he'll tell you where and what time you guys can get together to discuss... well, you know."

"Right. Yes, that will be fine. Thank you, and you have a nice day."

Yeah, bitch, and you do the same, Chanel thought before she said, "You do the same, Mrs. Bray—ah, I mean Jordan." She hurriedly hung up the phone and immediately called Nelson.

"Chanel, what's up?"

"Nelson, you wouldn't believe who just called on Todd's cell phone."

"Who?"

"Veronica, your ex-wife. And the first time she called, she started to talk before I even said anything. I guess she thought Todd answered the phone, but he's not here. Anyhow, so she came right out and asked if he was still having a set and said that she had some good stuff. I didn't say anything because I was totally floored, and so she hung up. A few minutes later, she called back, and this time I said hello. She announced herself, trying to sound all professional, and asked if he was in. I told her no, but then I said that he told me to tell her that yeah, it's still on but to call back in an hour and he'll let her know what time they can get together. She sounded all happy with that news. What's up with that? She uses?"

"I don't know. She didn't as far as I know. Oh man, this ain't cool. Last night I called the kids."

"Aw, Nelson, that's nice! How are they?"

"They were real happy to hear from me. They wanted me to pick them up last night, but I told them no because I didn't want to start any trouble. Dannon said that she wouldn't care because she wasn't there anyway. She must've been out with them."

"Oh my God. I think I might have seen her last night." Chanel went on to explain what had happened to Junie, and how she had seen Todd leave the hotel with Eryca and another woman she didn't recognize. "Could it have been her?"

"Could be. At this point, I wouldn't put it past her. This morning when I called the kids again to let them know that I was going to pick them up around two, she was running her trap in the background, talking about they're not going anywhere. She a trifling bitch sometimes. Excuse my language."

"Just tell me you don't say that in front of the kids."

"Nah. Never that. Whew, man. So, now I'm waiting for Lewis to tell me that the judge is standing by if Veronica gives me a hard time."

"Want me to come with you?"

"That's cool. I got this, though. I don't need anymore drama. She would trip if I brought you with me to get the kids. Lewis will be there with me. Thanks, though, boo."

"Yeah, right. You're always trying to act like you don't need anybody."

"It's all love, baby. Come by later, you and Rockin'. I want you to meet my kids. Oh, and thanks for the flowers. That was sweet."

"What flowers?"

"I got some flowers today from you and Rockin'."

"Ah, you're welcome. See you later. Bye."

How long are we going to sit here? Robin asked Rockin'.

Rockin' shrugged her shoulders and continued to let the water run on her body.

I'm cold. Enough of this already.

Rockin' sat up and turned off the water. She sat in the tub for a moment then said, "You right. It's done and over with. Nobody saw me. I'm cool."

She got up and out of the bath, grabbed her oversized towel and wrapped herself up. She put her face as close to the mirror as she could and smiled.

What are you smiling at?

"Just say cheese."

Cheeeeeessssssseeeeeee!

"A'ight. So, what we got planned for the day? I wonder if Nelson got my flowers."

You mean the flowers from you and Chanel. You're a trip. Why don't you call him?

"Whatever! That's my boo," Rockin' said as she dropped her towel. She walked butt naked, stopping to do a little dance before she went into the living room and picked up the phone to call Nelson. She heard a knock at the door and went to open it.

Excuse me! Aren't you going to cover us up?

"I ain't," Rockn' refused as she opened the door for Chanel.

"Look at you, opening the door in your bare ass," Chanel said as she laughed and walked in. "Why are you in here naked? Are you expecting some company or something?"

"No. But if you must know, I just got out the bath. You never seen tits and a cooch before?" Rockin' asked as she pointed at her vagina and squeezed one of her breasts.

Yeah. And now I think I have a cold, Robin added.

"Oh, quit your whining."

"Tell Robin I said hi and that I miss her. And you are not right."

"Oh, you not liking my company, heifer?"

"Of course, but I still miss her. My front desk has been a mess since she's been gone. It's not like you're down there handling all of the business," Chanel said jokingly. "You hungry? I'm meeting Kyle at noon for lunch. Come with us."

"Okay. I'm hungry. Just let me throw some threads on."

"You need to clean up all these wet clothes. What, did you take a shower in them?"

Rockin' ignored Chanel as she picked up her stuff. She went into the bedroom, put on a pair of bootleg jeans, a black-and-pink tank top and a pair of pink pumps. She put on a hat and was ready to go.

"Um, I'm not saying nothing," Chanel commented when she saw the outfit.

"Let's be out," Rockin' said.

As they got off of the elevator, they saw Kyle leaning on the reservation counter, talking to one of the clerks.

"Look at my baby. Ain't he handsome?"

"Mm-hmm. Just yummy!"

Chanel nudged Rockin' with her elbow as they approached the desk. "Hi, Tara," she greeted the clerk.

"Hi, Mrs. Kendricks. How are you today?"

"I'm fine, thank you. Everything okay?" Tara nodded. "Kyle, are you ready to eat?"

"Actually, Ma, I was talking to Tara, and when she told me she was eating lunch alone, I sort of invited myself to join her. Do you mind? I know we planned—"

"Sweetheart, no. Go and enjoy yourself and I'll take a rain check on our date."

"Well, can we go? 'Cause you know a sistah is hungry."

Man, you can be so obnoxious, Robin said. Rockin' started doing her little dance.

"What is wrong with you?" Chanel asked. "You're mighty hyper today."

They started making their way toward Breezes when they noticed a commotion at the door of the sauna room. Chanel made her way through the crowd.

"Excuse me. Can I get through? I own this hotel. What seems to be . . ." She leaned into the room and saw the gruesome scene.

"Oh my goodness," she said in a whisper.

Rockin' pushed her way through the crowd behind Chanel. She tried not to show any emotion as Chanel screamed and cried.

"Oh no! Not this! What . . ." She looked around the crowd in search of answers.

Kyle and Tara heard her and ran into the sauna. Tara started to cry and ran out. Kyle stared at his father and Eryca. He looked at his mother, who was crying hysterically, but he didn't share her emotion. Instead, he felt like a weight had been lifted off of his shoulders and hers.

He took Chanel in his arms and called out, "Somebody, please call 911."

When the police and ambulance arrived, they secured the crime scene, retrieved the weapon for testing, and closed all entrances and exits. No one was permitted to come into or leave the hotel. The Gray Pearl was shut down.

"Rockin'," Chanel said as she collapsed in Kyle's arms. "You—"

"Shh, Ma. It's going to be all right," Kyle assured her.

Wow, Robin said. *You better come through like that for me when you kill my father.*

"Don't worry," Rockin' said, looking at Chanel but responding to Robin.

A police detective approached them.

"Miss? My name is Sergeant Fama. I'm going to be heading the investigation. Can I ask you a few questions?"

"Yes, and it's *Mrs.* Mrs. Chanel Kendricks. Todd," she pointed at him, "was my husband, and this is his ex-wife, Eryca."

"Kyle," Rockin' said, "take your mother up to her suite and get her comfortable. I'll bring these gentlemen up in a few minutes."

Kyle and Chanel got on the elevator and went upstairs.

Now, remember your name is Robin not Rockin', and speak correctly. I'll help you.

"Sergeant, my name is Robin Sessoms. I'm the general manager, but I've been on vacation for the last week or so. The hotel has never had anything like this happen. Ever! I'm shocked and very saddened that someone was killed here when people come here to relax and get some quiet time. If there is anything that you need, please don't hesitate to contact me. I'll be more than happy to assist you."

"Thank you. And you said your name was Robin?"

"Yes. Robin Sessoms." The detective wrote her name in a small notebook.

"Okay then, Ms. Sessoms, I'd like to go upstairs and speak with the widow of the deceased and does . . . " He flipped to another page. "Eryca have any family that needs to be contacted?"

"She and Mr. Kendricks have a son. His name is Reggie, but I have no idea how to contact him. Maybe Chanel can help you with that."

"Okay. Shall we go upstairs?"

"Sure. Follow me."

Good job, Rockin'!

Rockin' twisted her lips and looked to the side as if Robin were right next to her. She and Sergeant Fama went into Chanel's suite and he started his questioning.

Chapter Twenty-eight

It was 1:45 p.m. Lewis had Judge Haskins waiting in the wings in case Veronica decided to show her ass. He drove while Nelson sat and re-familiarized himself with his divorce decree. A squad car from the local police precinct was en route to meet them at Veronica's house.

During the twenty-minute ride, they made idle chit chat. Lewis knew that Nelson was nervous. It wasn't typical for him to talk about the weather and how green everybody's grass still was for this time of the year. Lewis entertained him because before they were business partners, they were friends.

Lewis was the only person Nelson considered to be a true friend. No one had ever gotten as close to him as Lewis, and no one else had ever known his personal business. From shopping to eating, to Nelson's taxes to the type of soap he used, Lewis was in control of getting and doing all of that stuff for him. And if he couldn't do it, then Lewis' mother would go shopping for Nelson's food and clothing, and bring him catalogs of Ferragamo shoes so that he could order them straight from the manufacturer. There was no in-between person in Nelson's life.

As they pulled in front of Veronica's house, she stood at the door with her arms folded over her chest, her hair disheveled, and a cigarette hanging out of her mouth. She wore a long, black sleeveless nightgown that revealed the needle tracks, like little ant bites on the insides of her forearms.

"Do you want me to go and get the kids?" Lewis asked.

"No, thank you. I'm going to get my kids just like I told them I would."

Nelson got out of the truck with his divorce decree in hand, looked at the squad car that kept its distance at the end of the block, and walked up to the door. Veronica began to scream at Nelson.

"You think you can bring your ass over here and just take my kids? You haven't been in their lives for months. Do you really think that I'm going to let you take them?"

Nelson held up the divorce decree. She snatched it from him and said, "So what? I got one of these. You and I both know that they mean nothing. Like I motherfuckin' said, you ain't taking them nowhere!" She blew smoke into Nelson's face.

Nelson looked at her arms, shook his head and turned around. He gave Lewis the nod, but he already had Judge Haskins on the phone. She gave Lewis the O.K. to have the police in the squad car aid Nelson in picking up his children.

As the police car approached, Veronica hurriedly closed the door. Meanwhile, Neeah and Naohme had come to their bedroom window. Unaware of what had just happened, they called out to their father.

"Hi, Daddy! We're coming."

Nelson looked up at the window then over at the officers.

"I don't want my kids to get upset. How can we do this so that they don't?"

"Officer," Lewis yelled. Both the officer and Nelson turned around. "Serve the warrant as a violation of a court order."

"There's your answer," Mr. Bray. "Please go back to your car and give us a few minutes.

The officer knocked on the door. "Ma'am, I have a warrant for your arrest for violation of a court order."

Veronica immediately opened the door. "I'm   a lawyer. Don't think that you're going to come in here and bully me around."

"Then you should know that you are in violation of a court ordered visitation of the children with their father. It is clearly stated in your divorce decree that he has the children every weekend. If you want to pursue this in family court, then you are free to do that, but right now, I'm here to enforce this court order. Now, get the children or you'll be placed under arrest."

Just as he said that, Neeah and Naohme hurried past their mother and out the door. Nelson got out of the car and went to meet them. Dannon was standing at the door next to his mother, with his overnight bag on his arm.

"Now, punk, look who's staying with me! You can take them, but Dannon wants to stay here. Isn't that right, Dannon?"

"Mom, we'll be back on Sunday," he said as he scooted past her and walked toward Nelson.

Nelson hugged his children and helped them into the car.

The officer thanked Veronica for her cooperation and left the residence. As Lewis and Nelson were pulling off with the children, Veronica came out of the house spitting venomous words. "I hate you, you fucking bastard. Those are my kids!"

Nelson put on the radio and Lewis drove them home. When they went into the house, Black and White were waiting at the door as usual. They hadn't seen the children in a while. Nelson had to carefully re-introduce the children to the dogs. After a few moments of sniffing them, the dogs fell back.

The girls shared a room, and Dannon had his own, right next to his father's. They took their bags up to their rooms and were delighted to see that not only were they redecorated, but each bed was covered with gift-wrapped boxes. These were the birthday presents Nelson had bought but was unable to give them when Veronica refused to let him see the children.

"Lewis, please order some food, sodas and juices, and dessert. We're eating in tonight. I'm not taking any chances by taking them out with that crazy woman out there. Call the liquor store and have them send over the usual, and well, that's it." Nelson went to make sure the kids were situated and comfortable.

Back at the hotel, Sergeant Fama, Chanel, Kyle and Rockin' were still talking.

"So, you said that Ms. Sessoms called you this morning to see what you were doing. Todd wasn't here when you woke up. You got up, sat in the kitchen and talked to your son. After that, you made plans for lunch. He went back to his room and you went to Ms. Sessoms' suite. Is that correct?"

"Yes. And my son's name is Kyle. I haven't really said more than a few words to Todd since I put him out the other day."

"And you, Ms. Sessoms. You called Mrs. Kendricks when you got up this morning. You two talked for a minute and then you took a bath. Mrs. Kendricks came to your suite around what time?"

"Well, I washed my a—"

Rockin', don't talk like that, Robin warned her.

"I took a bath for about an hour. Just chilled out and relaxed. Chanel must've come in at around 12 o'clock or so. It was around lunchtime because she was on her way to meet her son. He made plans in the meantime, but we were going to eat anyway. That's when we saw the crowd around the sauna and well . . . blah, blah, blah!"

Sergeant Fama looked at Robin, noting how unconcerned she appeared to be about Todd and Eryca's deaths.

"All right, I believe I have all I need at the moment, but I can contact you if I have any further questions, right? Oh, and I would like to get a copy of the security tape if that is at all possible."

"Security tape?" Chanel asked. "We don't have security cameras within the hotel. They're located at the entrances and exits only. I don't believe in invading the privacy of the people who patronize my establishment. We've never had to be concerned with this type of problem in the past, so I'm sorry, I don't have any tapes to give you."

"Thank you, Mrs. Kendricks. I'll be in touch." Sergeant Fama got up and let himself out.

Chanel, Kyle and Rockin' sat in silence. Kyle moved over to his mother's side. He could feel her trembling. She was breathing deep and rubbing her temples. Rockin' sat back in the chaise lounge, put her hands behind her head and closed her eyes.

You know you left Brenda doll in the car all this time.

"I'm telling you right now, I ain't carrying that shit. I'll get it and put it away, but forget about me hanging out with a fucking doll, okay!"

Leave me alone, Rockin'.

"What the fuck you mean, leave you alone?" She sat up and yelled into the air. "How you just gonna shut me out like that? You know what? That's peace. Be like that, and be careful what you wish for. Scary bitch!"

"Mom?" Kyle asked. He had never witnessed Rockin's outbursts before.

"Kyle, why don't you go and relax? I want to talk to her alone."

"Are you going to be okay?" he asked.

"Don't worry, little homie. It's all good," Rockin' reassured him.

Kyle reluctantly went to his room. Chanel fixed a drink for both of them and sat on the foot of the lounge chair. By that time, Rockin' had blocked Robin out and lay back in the chair again. She looked at Chanel through squinted eyes.

"Rockin', do you know anything about this?" Chanel asked in a whisper.

"What you think? I told you that I bet' not find out that Todd got Junie. Didn't I? So, don't cry over spilled milk. I did you a favor. I mean, look at you. You ain't mad. Hell, Kyle ain't even upset."

"I know. I understand what you're saying. I guess I'm shocked more than anything." She put her hands up to her face and rubbed her forehead. "I don't know if I would have been able to do it Thursday. In fact, seeing what I just saw, I know that I'm not capable of something like that."

"So then consider it a gift. You know that the sergeant's gonna want to question you some more. You know, wondering how and why you dealt with him as a junkie and a cheating-ass husband. Probably even say that you had opportunity and motive."

"Anybody who knows me knows that I could really give a shit. The problem I had was when he had Eryca around Kyle and when he got high in front of Kyle. He could do it to her all day long. Kyle was and is my only concern.

"And as far as opportunity, I was here all morning. I talked to you first thing this morning. Kyle and I hung out for a few, and then I called Nelson. They can check the phone records."

Rockin' stared at Chanel.

"Oh shit. I forgot to tell you that Veronica, Todd's supposed lawyer, called here twice this morning." She told Rockin' about the two phone calls, realizing that in all the commotion she had not checked to see if Veronica had ever called back. "Wait a minute while I get his cell phone."

When she checked, there wasn't a missed call or message. Veronica hadn't called back.

"Wait. You saying that Veronica is one of Todd's get-high cronies, not just his lawyer?"

"Yes. I think she is."

"Did you bring that up to Nelson?"

"Mm-hmm. We talked about it briefly, but he was on his way to get his kids. And he wants us to come by, so let's go. I need to get out of here for a while. I'll get Kyle."

Chanel walked into Kyle's room. He was stretched across his bed, throwing a football in the air.

"I prayed for this day. I hated him so much. I'm sorry, Ma."

"Oh, Kyle, don't. I understand how you feel. And I too prayed for the day when he would just leave us alone and destroy himself by himself. Guess our prayers were answered," she said as she sat on the bed beside him. "Come on, baby. We're going out for a while."

"Ma, can I ask you a question?"

"Sure. What is it?"

"What's wrong with Miss Robin?"

"Kyle, Robin is sick. She has a multiple personality disorder. You do know what that is, right?"

"Yeah. That's sad. Is she going to be okay? She scares me sometimes."

"She'll be okay. She's working on getting better. Robin is harmless. She has a good heart, and that's what's important."

"Her name is Robin. Why do I sometimes hear you call her Rockin'?"

"Well, her other personality prefers to be called that. To keep her happy, I call her Rockin'. It's weird, I know, but that's just how it is."

"When Miss Robin is Rockin', is she dangerous?"

Chanel had never lied to Kyle before, but there was a first time for everything. "No. She requires a lot of attention, that's all."

Rockin' walked into the room. "You okay, man?"

"Yes, Ms. Rockin' Robin."

Chapter Twenty-nine

"Jiles, what can I do for you today?" Nelson asked after Lewis buzzed him and said he had a call from a Mr. Sessoms.

"Young brother, have you thought about what I asked you the last time we spoke?"

"Yeah, man. I said I got you. Be cool. It'll all be taken care of in due time. But I will see you Thursday, right?"

"That's right."

"Good. I have to go because I'm spending time with my kids right now."

"All right now. Bye."

Chanel, Rockin' and Kyle rang the doorbell just as Nelson hung up the phone.

"What's up? Come on in."

"Nelson, this is my son, Kyle. Kyle, this is Mr. Bray."

"How are you, sir?" Kyle reached out and shook Nelson's hand."

"Boy, you better give me some dap." Nelson grabbed him and gave him a hug.

"You know me, nigga, so beat it. Where's the food? And did you like the flowers?"

"Yeah, I liked them. Thanks. The food will be here shortly. Neeah, Naohme, Dannon. Come down here. I want you to meet my friends."

When his children came in, Nelson did the introductions. Kyle and Dannon immediately hit it off and gave each other pounds. They retreated to Dannon's room while Neeah, Naohme and of course Black and White stayed with Nelson. He got the girls some juice and sent them to their room to watch a movie.

Nelson, Chanel and Rockin' sat at the dining room table while they waited for the food to be delivered.

"So, what are you girls up to today?"

"Nelson, there's a slight change in plans for Thursday. This morning, Todd and Eryca were found dead in the sauna. Eryca was shot in the face and Todd was shot in the head and in the chest," Chanel advised him.

"Get the hell out of here." Nelson moved to the seat closest to Chanel so he didn't have to talk so loud.

"Nope. I'm so serious."

"Who?" He looked at Rockin'. She chewed on her cheek and looked around the room as if she wasn't listening.

"Rockin'! What happened? You hit Todd and Eryca with the gun I gave you?"

"Fuckin' A, I did. I told Chanel that if Junie told me it was Todd who beat him, then his ass was grass. And when Junie described the dude, I knew it was Todd, so I smoked his ass like it was grass."

Nelson started laughing. He got up from the chair, put his drink down and went into the living room. He sat in the middle of the floor and laughed, rolling backwards and side to side while he covered his face. He laughed so hard that his stomach began to cramp up.

Neeah and Naohme heard him and came running from their room. They laughed at their father rolling on the floor. Moments later, Kyle and Dannon heard the laughter. They put down the joysticks to the PlayStation to see what all the noise was about.

Chanel got up from the table and went into the living room. Rockin' got up right behind her. Once

Chanel was in the mix, Rockin' stayed back and watched as Black and White pounced around them, not sure if they were attacking Nelson or playing. Either way, even their gruesome growl didn't take away from that magic moment.

"I ain't never had that kind of love and affection from my family . . . or should I say yours." Rockin' said, but she got no response. "Robin? Robin? Robin!" she said in a harsh whisper.

What is it that you want?

"I know you ain't still mad."

Leave me alone, Rockin'. You're dead to me.

"Oh, really? But I think you da one on the inside. I'm running shit out here, so you's the dead bitch. Peace!" She threw up the peace sign.

Chanel and Nelson understood what Rockin' was doing, and even Kyle knew what was happening as she stood there and talked to herself. Neeah, Naohme and Dannon weren't aware of her illness, but simply dismissed her odd behavior. They weren't strangers to dysfunction. But what they didn't know was that Rockin' wasn't feeling this moment at all.

The doorbell rang. Lewis came from the back, answered the door, and paid and tipped the deliveryman. The smell of fried chicken, buttermilk biscuits, baked beans and coleslaw filled the house. The boys once again retreated to Dannon's room, carrying their plates and sodas. The girls, Chanel and Rockin' sat at the dining room table while Nelson and Lewis sat in the living talking quietly.

Nelson told Lewis what had happened at the hotel, instructing him to get the necessary paperwork together should Chanel or Rockin' be called on Todd and Eryca's death. He would call a few lawyer friends

and cash in on a few favors by retaining them pro
bono, just in case.

"Oh, and did the destruction go okay?" Nelson
asked Lewis.

"Yes. The yard is clean."

After dinner, Dannon asked if Kyle could spend the
night. Chanel pulled Kyle to the side to talk to him.

"Sweetheart, are you sure you're up to spending
the night out? Sure you don't want to go and get some
movies and chill out on the couch with me?"

"Mom, no. I'm fine. And guess what? Dannon and I
have more than you think we have in common. His
mother is an addict just like my father was. And he
goes to my school too. Don't worry about clothes.
Dannon said that I could borrow some of his." He gave
his mother a kiss on the cheek and softly closed her
mouth, which had dropped open. He walked
backwards to Dannon's room as he blew her another
kiss and winked.

"Who loves you, baby?" he chanted.

By that time, Lewis had gone to take care of some
other business after reminding Nelson that *his* dinner
was in the refrigerator. Rockin' fixed another drink,
popped in DMX's new album and started doing her
thug dance. Nelson fixed himself a plate and sat at the
dining room table. Chanel came back to the table,
dumfounded, and sat next to Nelson.

"Do you know what my son just said to me?"

"No, what?" he asked as he sucked on a chicken
bone smothered with Red Hot extra hot sauce. He
leaned back and sucked in some air.

"Damn, this is hot!"

"Kyle just confirmed what I said earlier about
Veronica. She gets high. Dannon told him."

Nelson remained seated, stuffing coleslaw into his mouth while he felt the churning of his stomach from eating the greasy food. He didn't tell her that he had already come to that conclusion after he saw Veronica's arms. The fact that the kids knew, and now apparently other people did too, was enough for him to put his wheels into action.

How does a parent ask his children if their mother or father uses drugs? And did he really have to? Wasn't it obvious already? Would they even tell him if he did ask?

"Mm-hmm. I'm up on that. I saw the tracks on her arm when I picked the kids up. Not that it matters, but I wonder how long she's been leaving the kids at home and going out and getting high. Maybe that's the way I'll address it. Some time during their visit, I'll ask them what the deal is about her leaving them home alone. Well, with Cella."

"Do you want me to take Kyle home tonight?"

"No. Let him chill."

"Okay. We're leaving, then. I'll get Kyle in the morning." Chanel and Nelson locked eyes for an awkward moment. "Ahem," she cleared her throat. "Bye."

Nelson didn't answer. Instead he enjoyed some more chicken and baked beans. Five minutes later, he was in the bathroom, butt whistling.

When he was done, he checked in on the girls. They had fallen asleep while they watched *Shrek*. Kyle was stretched across Dannon's queen-sized bed, wearing a pair of his pajamas and playing a boxing game. Dannon was in a pair of silk shorts and a white wife-beater, chatting on line.

"You brothers all right?"

"Yeah, yes Dad."

"Yes, Mr. Bray."

"Who? Boy, Nelson. Just plain old Nelson. Don't stay up too late. I'm going in my study."

In his study, Nelson thought about how happy he was about the progress he was making with his plan. Black and White were sleeping at his feet. They were tired from all the excitement. He slowly bent down and rubbed each of their heads. He loved them and they loved him. He sat back in his chair and smiled.

No one knew what Nelson was really laughing about earlier. They probably thought he was so shocked at what Rockin' had done that all he could do was laugh. But that wasn't it. Maybe they thought he was delirious because his children were there with him for the first time in six months. But that wasn't it either.

Good ol' Rockin'. She pulled off a hit. Man, who would've thought? I can pick them, he said to himself.

He grabbed a key from under the desk and opened the left drawer where he kept some of his important papers. Thumbing through the files, he came upon one labeled *Gun Permit, Veronica.* He pulled it out and opened the folder. The gun that Rockin' had used to kill Eryca and Todd was registered to Veronica.

"Thank you, God, for making me take this gun from Neeah."

When Rockin' and Chanel pulled up to the hotel, news reporters and cameramen rushed the car. They hooked their arms together and pushed their way through the obnoxious crowd. Sergeant Fama greeted them as they came through the doors of the hotel.

"Mrs. Kendricks, may I have a word with you?" he asked.

"Here? In front of all these mother—people?" Rockin' asked.

"We can go up to your room if you would feel more comfortable there."

As they headed to the elevator, they glimpsed around the lobby. Aside from the yellow *Do Not Cross* tape in front of the sauna, everything appeared to be normal. Guests were still checking in, and it was business as usual, as if Todd and Eryca's life didn't matter at all . . . to anybody.

Before Chanel could open the door to her suite, Sergeant. Fama started with his questioning.

"The gun that was used in this homicide, and that is what it has been deemed as, belonged to one Veronica Bray, a.k.a. Veronica Jordan. Do you know who she is?" He held up a picture he had gotten from the station. It appeared to be an old mug shot.

"Ah," Chanel sighed. "Yes. She was Todd's lawyer. He had been arrested for possession of a controlled substance and endangering the welfare of a minor child recently, and he retained her for counsel."

"Were you aware that they had more than a lawyer/client relationship? After asking around the hotel, she apparently has been here on more than one occasion and at various times of the day and night, or rather early morning."

"No. To my knowledge, my husband was only screwing his ex-wife. I didn't know about Veronica."

"Well, we took the bodies down to the morgue for an autopsy, although it is evident how they died. One could speculate and say that they maybe had a fight or that they were so high that they didn't realize what they—he or she—were doing, but that wouldn't make sense. The shooter knew exactly what they were doing.

"By the way, did your husband have a cell phone or pager? I'd like to take it and go through it. Maybe someone he talked to frequently could shed some light on why anyone would want to harm either of them." He closed Veronica's file and got up to leave. "Once we're done with bodies, you're free to start making arrangements and take possession of them.

"Them? I don't even want his ass, let alone her," she said then went to get Todd's cell phone. "I'll call you in the morning and you can put me in touch with whoever handles your John Does. I don't want to draw any more attention to my hotel, my son or myself by having a big, extravagant funeral. I'd just as soon have him cremated and call it a day. He doesn't own a pager."

Chapter Thirty

Veronica sat nervously at the edge of her bed as she watched the news. Her mouth was dry and her arms itched as she listened. Todd and Eryca's death made the headlines.

"One of the owners of The Gray Pearl was found dead, along with his lover, in his hotel early this morning." After describing the murders, the reporter said, "Authorities found a gun at the scene. It was registered to Mr. Kendricks' lawyer. At this time, she is not a suspect, but is wanted for questioning. Authorities have no suspects at this time. Stay tuned for upcoming developments."

Until she met Todd, Veronica had never done drugs. She was always curious, but too scared to actually take that first hit, even though she ran with a crowd who used regularly. Her boyfriend, Germaine Dewey, was a hustler. He had almost every corner on West Bangs Avenue in Asbury Park. He was fine, smart and knew the streets well. She was his trophy and decorated his already well-studded arm.

Her purpose was to hold his money and nothing else. She never saw or handled any of the drugs. When he got too large, other drug dealers in the area had a snitch rat him out. Germaine was immediately put under surveillance and the police learned his routine down to the minute.

They knew that every day at 8 o'clock in the morning, he went running along a street parallel to the Avenue so that he could keep an eye on his employees. At 9:30, he went into the bagel shop and bought a bagel with vegetable cream cheese and an orange juice. He sat outside the shop on a bench and waited for his man to bring him his money from the night before. At 10:15, he was at Veronica's house putting his money away.

After a year of surveillance, the authorities finally busted him. Veronica was forced to cooperate and tell them everything she knew about him or be charged as an accomplice. She fully complied.

Sitting in his jail cell, Germaine was confident that his lawyer, Lewis Weinstock, would help him beat the case. Lewis, who had just opened a new practice with Nelson, asked his partner to try the case since he was too busy with another client's case. Nelson represented Germaine and helped him get a light sentence. Germaine served a year in jail then was put on probation for five years and had to perform 1000 hours of community service.

Once he completed every portion of his sentence, Germaine was back out on the streets doing what he did best, slinging dope. Nelson and Lewis continued to provide his legal counsel, a relationship that was mutually beneficial. They kept him out of jail, and he supplied them with information and favors whenever Nelson requested them. He was the dealer Sharon's husband went to when Nelson wanted to take care of that problem.

Veronica had been caught with such a large amount of Germaine's money that she was sentenced to seven years probation. During that time, she kept herself out of trouble and even completed her education. By the time she finished her probation, she had passed the New Jersey Bar exam and began working in Nelson's law firm. Her past continued to haunt her, though, and she was never able to become a partner in the firm.

Filled with regret about her past mistakes, Veronica's life seemed to take another downward turn. Her temper became uncontrollable and her marriage fell apart. By the time she met Todd and Eryca, circumstances had her feeling weak enough to take that first hit. Her addiction escalated quickly from there, and now she was watching a news report naming her as a wanted person.

Veronica panicked. How could she have been so stupid? When Nelson took the gun and hid it, she assumed he had just put it among the many boxes in her closet. Now she wished she had been smart enough to search for it.

As she shuffled through her closet, she was sure that the police were mistaken. They couldn't have her gun. It had to be somewhere in her closet. She threw shoeboxes on the floor and pulled blouses and slacks from their hangers. Veronica was becoming more and more anxious because the gun was nowhere in sight.

She pulled out her built-in drawers and chucked her camisoles, stockings and teddies onto the floor. Still, she found nothing. She fell to her knees and pulled out her suitcases, duffle bags and old briefcases, hoping that she hid it there. With no success, she fell back and lay on the floor. She was bugging out. Her eyelids fit her eyes like a too-small shirt that puckered at the button right at the breasts. Her lips quivered at the reality that she could be tied to Todd and Eryca's death. She was in the hotel on numerous occasions, and eventually the police would find someone who had seen her there and could connect her to the dead couple.

Chapter Thirty-one

Nelson's weekend was great. The time that he and his children spent together brought them closer. Kyle ended up staying the entire weekend, and he and Dannon made sure they exchanged emails and phone numbers so they could stay in touch. Now that they knew they were students at the same school, they looked forward to seeing each other again soon.

Once they had cleaned their rooms, the girls and Dannon, grabbed their bags and put them by the door. Lunch was on the table and when they were done, Nelson planned to take them home.

"So, when do I get to pick you up again?" Nelson asked with a bright smile on his face while he ate his grapefruit and maple and brown sugar oatmeal. Dannon sat silently. Neeah and Naohme looked at each other and shrugged their shoulders.

"What? What's the matter?

"Dad," Dannon started, "the twins and I talked, and we were wondering if we could stay with you for a little while."

Nelson put his spoon down and wiped his mouth. "Dannon, what's the matter? Why don't you want to go back to your mother's?"

"She's never there. For the last couple of weeks, we haven't seen her. She has Cella come over every night while she goes out. I don't know where she goes. I mean, she's dressed in her work clothes and all. All I know is that she gets home when I walk in from school, dressed in the same clothes as the day before. And sometimes it's two and three days before she comes home."

"Yeah ,Daddy, and she stink sometimes, too. I thought you said that little girls are supposed to be pretty and look nice because we're sugar and spice," Neeah said as she looked at Naohme and laughed. Nelson forced a little smile.

"Dannon, you know, I've always tried not to involve you or your sisters in your mother's and my problems, but now that you've said something, I want to know exactly what's been going on. Have strange people been coming to the house? What about the phone? Does it ring all times of the night?"

"Yup. I never see her sleep anymore. She's always up and moving fast around the house, picking at the smallest things, and she doesn't have any patience to help the twins with their homework. When I'm done with mine, I bring them in my room and work with them there. I make sure their clothes are clean—well, Cella and I—and I get them fed in the mornings."

"Thank you, Dannon," Naohme shouted.

He continued. "Dad, I'm thirteen years old and I feel like I'm twenty. I haven't been able to play football or basketball because I'm been too tired. My grades have slipped. I'm only on the honor roll, not high honor roll like I used to be. And yes, all types of men come in and out of the house."

"What do you eat if she's not there?" Nelson asked, grinding his teeth.

"Cella goes shopping when we're in school and makes sure that there's food in the house. But we just don't want to go back there. Please don't send us."

Kyle sat quietly while they talked. He knew all too well what Dannon and the twins were feeling, but his situation differed in one way. He didn't have another place to call home. He was stuck with his father because his parents weren't divorced. He admired

Dannon for his honesty because he never said anything for the sake of his mother's feelings. He kept it all in until that day. Kyle and Dannon talked about all of this the night before in Dannon's bedroom and were bonded for life.

"Mr. Bray, ah, Nelson . . . " Kyle said. Nelson looked over to him. "I don't know how well you know my mother, but my father was an addict. Living with him, for me, was horrible. I never knew when he was going to make me come with him to go pick up drugs or put me in the other room when another woman came over. But I had my mother there for me, and I think that Dannon, Neeah and Naohme are asking that you take them before it's too late," he finished, lowering his head as if he had spoken out of turn.

Nelson sat at the table with his hands tightly folded in front of him, looking at his beautiful children. All the time that he hadn't reached out to them for fear of dealing with their mother, he had exposed them to a child's worst nightmare. How could he not keep them there with him now? But it wasn't that simple. He had to show just cause to break the court ordered custody arrangement.

"Okay. I'll call your mother after lunch and see what I can work out. How does that sound?"

"Yay!" Naohme exclaimed.

Dannon gave his father a huge smile. He kicked Kyle's foot under the table. Kyle looked up and Dannon whispered, "Thank you, bro." Kyle nodded.

As it turned out, Nelson didn't have to call Veronica. Once she had pulled apart her entire house, she had to face the fact that her gun was not there. She was in a heap of trouble, and she knew she had brought all this on herself by giving in to her insecurities and weakness.

I just wanted to try it. I only shot up two or three times. I'm not hooked. I can kick this.

She thought of her children and felt guilty for all she had put them through. She wanted to talk to them, so she picked up the phone to call Nelson's house.

"Hello."

"Nelson, what time are you bringing the kids back?"

"Funny you should ask. I understand that there's been some changes in the time that you spend with the kids and, well, the streets. What's up with that?"

"What are you talking about?" she asked as she lit a cigarette, her hands shaking.

"You know what I'm talking about. I'm gonna tell you this one time and one time only. You get high. I know this from the tracks on your arm. I've never wanted or tried to keep the kids from you, but as God as my witness, I will take them from you so fast your heart will stop. I'm not bringing them home tonight. I suggest you take some time to get it together, and the kids will stay with me. In two weeks, we'll touch base again, but in the meantime, you can call and speak to them."

She remained silent, trying not to let Nelson hear her crying.

"One chance, Veronica. One chance only. You mess up, and that's it. I'll sue you for custody. By the way, you need to be worried about what you're going do about your gun. I'm sure you watched the news." He hung up on that note, satisfied that she wouldn't try to argue with this new custody arrangement.

Veronica stared at the phone, knowing Nelson meant what he said, and knowing that he was right. She had no choice but to go down to the police station, turn herself in and cooperate in any way she could, and that included telling them about what happened the day that Neeah got a hold of the gun. But would that really matter?

Chapter Thirty-two

While Kyle was at Nelson's house, Chanel went through all of the drawers in her suite. She found vials, needles and thin rubber strips hidden in different spots throughout the place. She was numb. She couldn't cry because she truly couldn't stand him, even in death. She couldn't laugh because it wasn't funny that she dealt with his shit for so long. It was as if she lost her identity while she was with him. There was no way she should have stayed with him and let her son bear witness to his infidelities, drug abuse and self-destruction. She felt that she failed Kyle somehow.

Granted, there weren't much of Todd's things left in the suite since she had already put him out, but she still felt the need to clear his memory out completely. She called housekeeping and told them to organize a crew to disinfect the entire suite. From the counters to the floors, from the carpet to the doorknobs, she wanted his scent gone.

While the crew worked, she decided to go downstairs and see how things were going. As she approached the front desk, she looked over at the sauna area and noticed that the yellow tape was gone. She peeked through the window in the door and saw that the room had been cleaned. When she opened the door, her nostrils were assaulted by the strong smell of bleach, smothering the stench of blood.

She went to the front desk. "Who cleaned out that area?" she asked Paula, who had basically taken over Robin's position at the hotel as general manager.

"Robin. She did it this morning. I don't know how she was able to handle the smell of all that blood and picking up the pieces. Eewwwww!"

"Okay. Thanks for the details. Where is she now?"

"I think she's in the swimming pool area."

"Thank you, Paula." Chanel made her way to the pool. There, she found Rockin' sitting in a bikini with a matching do-rag on, and a pair of Air Force Ones. She was drinking a Corona.

"Ah, excuse me, Miss Thang. What are you doing out here all by yourself? Everything okay?"

"Yeah. I'm just chillin'. You know I cleaned up all that shit and just felt, well, nasty. Figured since I can't dip my ass in bleach, the next thing would be to swim in it. I turned up the bleach dispenser so that I could get bleachy clean."

"You are so corny. Want some company? I'm having the suite cleaned out, and that's gonna take a few hours. I have nothing to do but waste time until Nelson brings Kyle home or I go get him."

"He ain't home yet? Baby boy got himself a new buddy, huh? That's all right."

"Yes. And you know what? He goes to the same school as Kyle. And you know what else? Dannon told Kyle that his mother was an addict. What a small world. I feel so bad for all of them. Funny how you can think that your situation is the worst ever and someone is going through the same thing."

"So Kyle got a new daddy too?" Rockin' asked with a smirk.

"Daddy? What kind of question is that?"

"Mm-hmm." Rockin' sat back in the lounge chair and closed her eyes. "What time you gotta pick up Kyle?"

"I'm not sure. I haven't heard from him this morning. Are you finished swimming for the day?"

Rockin' lifted her head up. "Hell, nah. You want to get in?"

Chanel jumped up and stripped down to her underwear.

"Oh, no you didn't, witcha stank self," Rockin' teased in the same manner that Chanel did when she came to the door butt naked.

"Be quiet, girl. Last one in eats shit!"

They both ran and jumped into the pool. They splashed, swam under water, did back flips and jumped off of the diving board into the 15-foot deep end of the pool. Rockin' dunked Chanel. Chanel returned the move, but then Rockin' managed to get on Chanel's back and dunk her. This time, she tried to hold her underwater.

Chanel's arms flew in all directions, and she managed to get free from Rockin'. When she was finally away from her, Chanel was very upset.

"Damn, what are you trying to do?" Chanel asked Rockin' as she pushed her hair out of her eyes.

"Oh, what happened? My bad."

"Rockin', I don't think that's funny." Chanel got out of the pool, got a towel and dried off.

"I said sorry. Damn."

Chanel grabbed her phone and left the pool area. Checking the phone, she saw that she had missed Nelson's call. There was a message waiting, so she pushed the button to retrieve it.

"Chanel, it's Nelson. There's been a change of plans, so I'm going to need you to come pick up Kyle this evening."

As Chanel was listening to her message outside the pook area, Rockin' jumped out of the pool.

Don't blow it Rockin', Robin said.

"Oh, so now you talking to me? She's trying to get with my man. I'm not having that."

Just try and keep it together a little while longer.

"All right." Rockin' grabbed a towel and ran after Chanel.

"Ay, Chanel, wait. I'm—we not working here no more."

"Well, I kind of figured that much. What are you going to do? Are you going to still pick up garbage?"

"I got some money saved up and no, I'm not doing that either. I ain't doing shit. The only piece of garbage I'm handling is Jiles."

Say sorry, Rockin'.

Rockin' rolled her eyes in protest but said, "I'm sorry, Chanel. I didn't mean to play so rough with you."

"Okay, Robin." Chanel accepted the apology, knowing it was best not to upset Rockin'. Her behavior was already aggressive enough. She changed the subject. "But about Jiles, I know that you had the gun and assume you were going to use that. What are you going to use now that the police have it?"

Rockin' shrugged.

"Hey have you heard from Sharon?" Chanel asked, changing the subject as she thought about the group of people she met the first day at Nelson's house.

"Nope, sure haven't. Why?"

"She kind of just dropped off the face of the earth. Wonder if Nelson has been in touch with her," Chanel said as she reached for her phone. "Speaking of Nelson, I have to go over there and pick up Kyle. Want to ride with me?"

"No. I'ma go upstairs, change and take a drive to get some fresh air. I'll catch up with you later."

Chanel looked at Rockin' and saw how lonely she really was. She hasn't seen her talk to Robin lately, and wondered if Robin even existed anymore. Chanel took a stab at her theory as she was gathering her things.

"Hey, so, are you still seeing Dr. Christopher?"

Rockin' looked up at Chanel. "Nah. Don't really see a need because she mad. She not talking, so fuck it."

"Rockin', you are more than welcome to stay at the hotel for as long as you like."

"Right . . . "

Chanel left to get Kyle and Rockin' went upstairs.

Chapter Thirty-three

"Oh hey, what up? Come in. You're just in time for dinner." Nelson opened the door and let Chanel in.

"Cool. What are we having and where are the kids?"

"They're in their rooms. Kyle is with Dannon. I haven't been able to separate them the entire weekend."

As they walked into the kitchen, Nelson offered Chanel a drink. He gave her the details about the weekend and then about his conversation with Veronica.

"She always thought she could control me and what I did, especially when it came to the kids. They practically begged me not to send them back. Dannon was so upset about the whole thing. He's a teenager. He shouldn't have to be responsible for two little girls. Education is so important, and his grades have suffered because of her negligence."

"Wow, Nelson. Maybe we can get them together sometimes, you know, and let them hang out. They would be good for each other. And I don't know, maybe the girls would like to come to the hotel and swim."

Nelson was beginning to see Chanel in a different light. It had a long time since he'd been even remotely enticed by a woman. His mind was barricaded because he missed his children. The time he'd spent with his children this weekend confirmed that he wanted out of his current lifestyle. Now that he had his children back in his life, he wanted to be on the up and up. After Jiles, he'd be done.

"Why you wet?"

"Excuse me?" Chanel questioned.

"Your hair. Did you go swimming or something?"

"Yeah. Rockin' and I took a dip. She was kind of rough with me. She apologized, but I don't know. It was almost like she was trying to drown me."

"Shit! She's out there, but she wouldn't drown you, Chanel."

"Maybe I'm reading too much into it." She shook her head. "Nelson, your party is supposed to be this week. But with the kids here now, you can't do anything with Jiles. And you know fire will be coming out of Rockin's ass when you tell her."

"You're not lying." Nelson's eyes were pleading with Chanel to help him out of this new dilemma.

"All right, I'll tell her. I guess you'll call and tell everybody else that it's cancelled?"

"For sure. I'll call Jiles," Nelson responded.

At dinner, they all sat around the dining room table, talking and laughing as if they'd known each other forever. The girls appeared to take to Chanel, and she looked like she was in her glory with them. It made Nelson think about how much he truly missed the surroundings of a family unit. And although he had one malfunctioning part, Veronica, getting up with the kids, getting them breakfast and getting them off to school was what he looked forward to every day when he lived with them. He was determined to get that back for the sake of his children.

After dinner, everyone helped clear off the table and put the dishes in the dishwasher that hadn't been used in a long time. Chanel and Kyle were getting ready to leave when Lewis walked in.

"Nelson, we need to talk."

"Okay. Give me a minute." He turned to Chanel. "You got plans tomorrow for dinner?"

"No," Kyle answered. Chanel shot him a look.

"As a matter of fact . . ." She paused. "No, I don't."

"I'll pick you and Kyle up after they get out of school, and we can go out to eat."

"That sounds great. We'll see you then. And I'll take care of that for you."

After they left, Nelson sent the kids upstairs and went into the living room with Lewis. Apparently, Veronica had called him wanting legal advice, and Lewis didn't know where Nelson stood with that. His loyalties were to Nelson and he wouldn't want to do anything to make him feel otherwise.

"She also wanted to know where you put the gun when you took it from Neeah."

"Don't give her any advice. She's counsel, and she knows what she has to do. I could give a damn about what happens to her with that gun business." He told Lewis about the conversation he and Veronica had and explained that the kids would be staying with him for at least two weeks, possibly forever.

After the girls took their baths, Nelson went upstairs to tuck them in. He kissed each of them softly on their cheeks. Smiles lit up their faces as they looked at their father.

"Daddy, you leaving tonight?" Neeah asked him.

"No, baby girl. I'll be right in the other room. You don't have to worry about me ever leaving you again."

"We love you, Daddy," Naohme chimed in with dreamy eyes and kissed him on the nose. Neeah and Naohme cuddled up together and closed their eyes. Nelson pulled the covers over them and left them to their sweet dreams. He went into Dannon's room.

"What's up, Mini Me?"

"Dad. What's up?" Dannon gave Nelson a hug and some dap. "I'm glad we're staying here for a while. Do you think we can come and live here for good? When can Kyle come back over? Are you and Mrs. Kendricks boyfriend and girlfriend?"

"No. It's not like that. We're just friends. Good friends."

"Whatever happened to Crystal?"

"Well, things just didn't work out. Get some sleep and I'll have breakfast ready for you in the morning."

With a huge smile on his face, Dannon pulled back his sheets and jumped into bed. He placed his hands behind his head and stared at his father.

"What?" Nelson asked.

"I don't remember feeling this safe and secure."

Nelson sat on the side of Dannon's bed. It was hard for him not to set his son on his lap and hold and hug him in an attempt to make up for the lack of affection he'd lived with lately. But Dannon was a little man now, and he was going to treat him as such.

"Dannon, I love you and your sisters with all my heart. I had no idea that you were going through this or I swear, I would've come to get you a long time ago. I wished you would've called, but then I understand why you didn't. She is your mother. But not to worry, little brotha. I got your back from now on. Had it then, but now you'll see."

"Okay, Dad."

"See you in the morning." Nelson bent over and gave Dannon a kiss on the cheek. Dannon rolled over with his oversized basketball pillow and closed his eyes. Nelson got up, put the stereo on because Dannon loved to fall asleep to music, and closed the door behind him as he left the room.

Chapter Thirty-four

As Chanel pulled up to the hotel, she wondered how she would let Rockin' know that the plans for Thursday were off. She sent Kyle upstairs, and she went to check on the front desk. After she saw that everything was under control, she went up to Rockin's room, eager to get this over with.

She knocked but there was no answer, so she went to her suite. By then, Kyle had taken his shower and was relaxing in his room. She said good night to him, took her shower, painted her nails then tried to call Rockin' on her cell phone.

"Hey, you. What are you doing? Where are you?" Chanel asked Rockin' when she answered the phone.

"Chillin'. Cruisin'. Doin' my thing. What's up?"

Chanel decided just to come out with it. "Rockin', we have to cancel our plans for Thursday."

Rockin' slammed on her brakes in the middle of the road.

"What the fuck you mean, we have to cancel Thursday?"

"Nelson will have his children there, and he doesn't feel like it would be a good idea if you hit Jiles while they're there."

"Is that right? So when, then?"

"Well, I think for right now it's off."

"You fucking kiddin' me?"

"Rockin', I know how you feel. Don't worry. We'll make it happen."

"Oh, I ain't worried, doll. And you right. I'm gonna make it happen." She hung up the phone and sat fuming in her car, which still in the middle of traffic. She was totally and completely pissed off. Fire was coming out of her ass, and her ears were wet. She felt brushed off by Nelson and Chanel.

Rockin' put her car in gear and drove until she was in front of Jiles' house. She reached in the backseat and pulled out a crow bar and the Brenda doll. She slid the crow bar into her sleeve, stuffed the Brenda doll in the front of her pants, got out of the car and walked up to the front door. She knocked.

"Who is it?"

She didn't answer

"Who is it, I said?"

"Open the fucking door. I want those got-damn ashes."

"Is that you, you ugly bitch? I got yo' ashes." He came to the door, opened it and threw her mother's ashes in her face. Rockin' stood in disbelief but welcomed the excuse to finally put his old, funky, mildew-smelling ass to rest. As she turned and pretended she was getting ready to walk away, she slowly let the crow bar slide down her arm.

"There, you crusty cunt. How you like them ashes?" he spat at her.

She turned and swung, landing a blow to the left side of his head. He fell against the door frame. She pushed him in and closed the door behind her. Rockin' threw the Brenda doll on the couch and commenced to beating him in the head and ribs. Kicking him in the mouth and smashing his fingers weren't enough, so she dragged him onto the back porch, into the backyard and to the homemade bonfire pit that he'd made to burn Toscha's belongings.

Rockin' doused him with gasoline and lit his sorry ass on fire. She ran to get the Brenda doll and together, they watched as he burned to an oversized, crunchy piece of shit.

"Brenda, how you like them ashes?"

Rockin' looked at the doll. She hated carrying it around. Robin wasn't really speaking to her, so why should she carry her doll around? She looked at the flames then back at the Brenda doll.

Don't!

"Don't what? Oh, now you want to talk. Well, guess what? Fuck you!" Rockin' chucked Brenda into the fire.

"I'm sorry, I ain't hear you," Rockin' taunted. Jiles' burning body began to snap, crackle and pop, and the smell of his flesh was rising in the air.

How could you?

"How could I what? I ain't heard from you in God knows how long because you got yo' ass on your shoulders, and now you want to call the shots. Fuhgettabout it! Brenda doll is a done deal."

You were meant to be his daughter, Robin told her. *You're a little Jiles. You should've fallen in the hole first. You probably knew what it was going to be like and couldn't handle it. You figured you would flow to the side and send me to endure his wrath. But look at you. You're a messed-up chick. And you're miserable. You're crazy now. I may be in here, but I'm okay. And you may have tricked me into being born before you, but I think the joke was on you.*

"What-everrrrrrrr. Forgot my wings on purpose. Bye, you simple girl. Go back to your corner."

Once the fire died down and Jiles was unrecognizable, Rockin' hurried back into the house. She saw the mess she made but wasn't worried about it. She went into the refrigerator to find only bologna, a loaf of bread and a case of Colt 45. She grabbed a beer, cracked it open and downed it like a glass of water. She grabbed another and went into the living room.

"Old Jiles had some funky-ass taste." She looked over at the coffee table and saw his money clip. It had to be about a thousand dollars in it. She picked it up and put it in her pocket then went to his room.

"P-fucking-U! Rotten-ass nigga," she said, shaking her head. She pulled open his drawers. They were a mess, just like they were when she was a little girl. As she fumbled through his sock drawer, she found a picture of Toscha, sitting in the kitchen, peeling potatoes. Robin was sitting next to her. Rockin' tossed it to the side and continued looking through his things.

As she went to his nightstand, she noticed a metal box under the bed. She bent down and opened it up to find a loaded .45 Magnum.

"Ooooooh, lucky me," she said as she held it up. She went over to the mirror and struck a few poses.

"Bam! Bam! Bam! I was so made to carry a gun." She tucked it into the back of her pants. "Okay. With that, I think I'm done here." As she left the house, she could hear the sirens in the distance. A few neighbors had come out onto the street. She waved to them in her rearview mirror.

When she got back to the hotel, she took a shower and fell into a deep, dreamless sleep.

Chapter Thirty-five

"I don't know when it was taken from my residence. I told you before that I had that gun for protection only. I only handled it once, and that was the day that I bought it. I've never had to use it, and as far as I knew, it was still in my house," Veronica explained, practically begging the detectives to believe her.

It was Monday morning, and she had gone down to the police station to turn herself in. She knew it would look better than waiting for them to come get her.

"Ms. Jordan, how do you explain the gun being at the crime scene? I mean, you had to have taken it there with the intentions of shooting Todd and Eryca, right?"

"No! I'm telling you, I didn't kill them. I was his lawyer, for Christ's sake. We were friends," she said, scratching her arms through her long-sleeved jean shirt.

"Friends?" Sergeant Fama asked in a snide manner. "Get-high buddies, too? Okay. Well, how do you explain this?" He pulled out the file containing all the reports filed and complaints signed against her when she was married to Nelson. On the top was the last report taken when she shot Nelson in the arm.

Veronica sat in silence. She gathered that Sergeant Fama had been around the block a few times and knew a user when he saw one, even if she had only been on the scene for a little while. With her background in law, she knew that this didn't look good for her. To try to deny that she used drugs or had a history of violence would just make her look like a liar, so she decided to tell him the truth.

"Yes. I recently started getting high, but it was just a phase. I was curious, so I tried it. Todd was able to get it, so whenever he had some, we hooked up. I'm not addicted, though. I can stop at any time. As far as those reports about my ex-husband, I . . . Well, you know, everybody argues."

"Ms. Jordan, I'm not concerned at the moment with your drug use. My concern right now is finding out why those two were killed. We found one of your prints on the gun along with Eryca's, but the magazine had only your prints on it. You had opportunity, and you had the means. What I need to know is why."

He leaned in close to her face and spoke quietly. "You can tell me. Did a deal go bad? Ms. Jordan, we have witnesses that can place you there early that morning, and to be quite honest, that may be all we need."

"I want to call a lawyer."

* * * *

As Nelson and Lewis sat at the dining room table going through some paperwork, the phone rang.

"Nelson, its Veronica." Nelson motioned Lewis to record the telephone call.

"Yes, Veronica, what is it?"

"I'm down here at the police station. My gun was involved in—Well, you know why I'm here. I need a lawyer. Are you going to help me out and send one of your boys down here? It's the least you could do considering you know you took that gun from Neeah and put it away. You were the last one with it, and I'm being blamed for murder, you fucking bastard!"

"For somebody who needs my help, you have a lot of nerve calling here with a nasty-ass attitude. You want me to send a lawyer, or excuse me, one of my boys down to get your ass out of this mess that you got yourself into? Maybe if you'd stayed home with the kids instead of running the streets all time, this wouldn't have happened. Maybe if you didn't have all kinds of people in and out of the house with my kids there, your ass wouldn't be in a sling."

He sounded almost overjoyed when he told her, "I'm not helping you do anything. Who knows, you probably took the gun out for whatever reason and left it out. Ask one a them dudes if they stole it. Don't ask me for nothing. Find your own counsel, counselor, and like I said, you have two weeks to get a handle on your business. If at that point you don't have it *completely* together, I will petition the court for sole custody of the children."

"Nelson!"

He hung up on her without reservation. As she dropped the receiver, Sergeant Fama was there to read Veronica her rights and place her under arrest for the murder of Todd Kendricks and his ex-wife, Eryca Kendricks.

After Nelson and Todd finished their paperwork Nelson ate the lunch that Lewis' mother sent over. His appetite had increased since he'd been with his children, and he suggested to Lewis that his mother should move in to be there on a full-time basis. Lewis was sure that she would oblige Nelson, as she treated him like he was her son. He assured Nelson that he would have her there as of the next morning.

At 2:30, Nelson headed over to the school to pick up Dannon. Kyle was with him.

"Li'l man, does your mother know that you're coming with me?"

"Yes."

"All right. Let's go get the girls."

"Dad, can we go play basketball at the park up the street from the house when we get home? A couple of the boys are meeting to play at 4 o'clock"

"That's cool. But we're going out to eat at six, so you boys need to be showered and ready to go by then."

Kyle and Dannon went to the mini basketball courts located at Neeah and Naohme's school to pass time while Nelson waited for the girls to come out. He cracked the windows to let the brisk air flow throughout the car. As he waited, he decided to call Jiles and let him know about the card party being cancelled.

The phone rang but there was no answer. Jiles didn't have an answering machine, so he couldn't leave a message. It was important that Jiles didn't show up at his house because he didn't want the kids to be exposed to someone like him in any way, for any reason.

He looked out the window and saw Kyle and Dannon carrying Neeah and Naohme on their backs to the car. They jumped in and gave Nelson a big kiss.

"Hey, Daddy," the girls greeted as all the kids climbed into their seats.

Neeah and Naohme played Miss Mary Mack in the back seat while Nelson and Dannon talked about a test he took that day. Kyle looked out the window and saw a vagrant sitting on a bench at the bus stop. Something about him looked familiar, but Kyle couldn't put his finger on it. The young man had on a dirty pair of jeans, a white Phat Farm T-shirt, a pair of sneakers with no laces and a baseball hat turned to the back. His head hung low. As people walked by, he held out a jar, begging for coins. Kyle felt bad for the young man, thinking he was probably not much older than he and Dannon were.

Nelson slowed at a stop sign, and Kyle continued to watch the young beggar. His eyes opened wide when the young man lifted his head and Kyle realized why he looked familiar.

"Reggie," Kyle said softly as his eyes locked with the young man's.

"What, bro? What's up?" Nelson asked Kyle.

Dannon turned and looked in the direction that Kyle was staring. "Oh, man. He looks young. You know him, Kyle?" Dannon asked.

"Yeah, that's my half-brother, Reggie."

"What!" Nelson responded.

"Please, just let's go." Kyle fell back in the seat and leaned his face against the window, watching Reggie fade out of sight as they drove away.

Neither Nelson nor Dannon knew what to say. They all rode in awkward silence. As they pulled into Nelson's driveway, Dannon went to help the girls out then called out to Kyle, who was making his way to the door.

"Ay, we're still playing, right?"

"Yeah," Kyle answered.

"Don't forget be back in time to be ready to leave by 6 o'clock," Nelson reminded them as he walked into the house.

The girls were at the dining room table doing their homework when the phone rang. It was Chanel.

"Hey, Nelson."

"Chanel, we should be there around ten past six to pick you up for dinner. Did you have a chance to contact Rockin'?"

"Yes, I did, and she wasn't happy. That was yesterday after I left your place. I haven't heard from her since."

"Well, I know she's gonna be mad, but you know, my kids come first. Damn, she'll have to understand."

"You're right. I'll be out front when you get here."

Chanel pressed the elevator button for the lobby, but it stopped on the fourth floor. Rockin' stepped on.

"Hey, Rockin'. Where've you been all day?" Chanel asked with caution.

"Where I been? Where you going all dressed up 'n shit?"

"Nelson and I are taking the kids out to dinner. What are your plans for tonight?"

"Dinner. Must be nice. What, you all playing house now?"

"Rockin', please. It's nothing like that. The kids get along really great, and with everything that's been going on, we figured we would get them out a little bit."

"I was going to see if you wanted to chill by the pool, but seeing as though you have plans, maybe next time, huh?"

"Well, yeah," Chanel answered, starting to feel uncomfortable. "Maybe we can hook up tomorrow and get a facial or something."

"Facial. Yeah, okay. I ain't Robin. I don't do that shit."

Chanel looked away and breathed heavily, placing her hand on her hip. "Rockin', I know you're not mad because we had a change of plans. His children will be there. You wouldn't want them to see anything and get all upset, would you?"

"Your situation was handled. You're good, right? No more husband." Rockin' paused. "You right. And yes, I understand the plans have changed."

The elevator doors opened and they stepped out into the lobby. Nelson was waiting outside for Chanel.

"See you later, Rockin'."

"Let me go say hey to my homie." Rockin' ignored Chanel's obvious brush-off.

Nelson got out of the car to open the door for Chanel.

"Rockin', how are you?" he said as Chanel climbed into the car and said hello to the kids. "Sorry about Thursday. You know I have my kids, and I don't want any static coming to them for anything or anybody. You understand, right?"

"I understand. And don't worry about Jiles. He understands now too."

"What?" Nelson questioned.

"See, you think I'm playing. I ain't playing. You said Thursday was cancelled, so I took care of things myself. You don't need to set up no card game or anything else because he won't be coming. No big deal. Plans change." She left him standing there and went into the parking garage. Nelson walked around to the driver's side and got in. He looked at Chanel and shook his head in disbelief.

"What's going on?"

"We'll talk later."

The wait at the restaurant wasn't too bad, maybe 45 minutes. "Bray, party of six," was announced and Nelson went to get the kids. Dave and Buster's was the best place to go with kids. There were plenty of things to take their minds off their hunger while they waited.

A waitress introduced herself and took their drink orders. Nelson encouraged Chanel to have a glass of wine, but declined to have any alcohol since he was driving. She ordered a white wine spritzer and Nelson ordered pitchers of Sprite, Pepsi and orange soda for the kids and himself.

As they ate, Chanel continuously wiped ketchup and mustard from Neeah and Naohme's hands while Dannon and Kyle gulped down bacon double cheeseburgers, onion rings, mozzarella sticks and mini tacos.

"Playing basketball made me really hungry, Dad," Dannon said as he took a sip of his drink then burped.

"Oh, dang," Kyle said.

"Dannon, that's nasty," Neeah and Naohme said as they giggled.

"I know you know better," Nelson said to Dannon.

"I'm sorry, Dad. I just needed to break the tension."

Nelson tried to give a stern look but was hardly upset with Dannon. Boys will be boys, and he was so overjoyed that he was actually spending some time with his children after such a painful separation.

Chanel smiled at Nelson as she stared in his eyes. Avoiding it long enough, Nelson took to her gaze, softly touching her hand and smiling at her.

Later as they drove home, the girls fell asleep and Kyle and Dannon popped in a DVD. Nelson and Chanel sat in the front seat, an awkward silence between them.

"So, what was that stare all about?" Nelson finally asked.

"As if you don't know," she responded, positioning herself to face him. "Did it bother you?"

Nelson licked his lips and shook his head.

"Good, 'cause there's more where that came from."

"Ma, do we have to go home?" Kyle asked, popping his head into the front seat. "Can we go to Nelson's house for a while? Me and Dannon got a game going on PS2 from last weekend, and we want to finish it up."

"Sweetheart, it's a school night, and I'm sure Nelson is tired. Besides, he has to get the girls ready for bed and clothes ironed, and—"

"What you scared of?" Nelson asked.

"Ooooooh, got her," Dannon and Kyle teased in the backseat.

"Yeah, right. Please."

Nelson took that as a yes and drove them to his house. He and Chanel each took one of the girls, while Kyle carried in the doggie bags. Dannon went to the curb and pulled up the recycling cans.

Inside, the girls sat on the couch still bundled in their coats until their bath water was finished running. Chanel got them undressed while Nelson laid out their pink and yellow pajamas. Once they were in the tub, they were wide awake. To settle them down after they got out, Chanel suggested that they drink warm milk, and Nelson gladly let her make it while he sat at the table and opened his mail.

"I hope you didn't mind Kyle coming over this afternoon. He called and asked me, and I told him that as long as it was okay with you, it was okay with me. Shoot, I was glad, because I was home taking a hot bath and listening to the tropical rain forest on the surround sound. I thought I was in somebody's paradise for a minute," she said with a laugh.

"It was cool. They went to play ball, and I had him do his homework first."

"Thank you, Nelson." She turned back around to the stove because she heard the milk rising and said, "Okay, get the girls. It's ready."

Nelson got them out of the tub, dried off and into their pajamas then brought them to the kitchen where Chanel had found some cookies for them to dunk in their milk. Nelson stayed back and let her do her thing with them. Neeah and Naohme seemed to be quite comfortable with her, and that made him feel good, especially with these unexpected feelings he was allowing himself to have for her.

When Rockin' first introduced them, he thought Chanel was conceited and too independent for him. Now he saw why she had that *I'm me and you don't matter* attitude. She had no choice but to be confident and in control of herself with that fool of a husband.

Once the girls were in bed and Dannon and Kyle were into their game, Chanel and Nelson went into the living room and sat on the couch. Black and White were asleep in the middle of the floor, Lewis was gone for the night, and Mrs. Weinstock was in her room. Other than the light from the curio, Nelson and Chanel sat in darkness, quiet for a few moments while each got their thoughts together.

"A penny for your thoughts. Or better yet, let me give you mine for free. I don't know what's going on here, you know, with these subtle hints of attraction and everything, but just for the record, I'm liking them," Chanel said as she crossed her legs and leaned back into the couch.

Nelson sat back and let himself fall into the couch too. He turned to look at Chanel, wondering if he could see himself with her five years from now. He was comfortable so far, but he'd been out of the relationship game for some time now and felt a little intimidated by the idea of starting over with someone new.

What could I do for her? he asked himself. *We're from two totally different sides of the spectrum, yet we seem to be making some kind of a connection.*

Finally, he spoke. "Me too. But I'll be totally honest with you and let you know up front that I'm scared to totally give myself to anyone else. Yes, you can blame it on being hurt over my divorce. Veronica was the only woman I ever truly loved. But on the other hand, I can't allow myself to shut out the possibility to ever love again."

He moved closer to Chanel. She uncrossed her legs and wiped her sweaty palms on her thighs. He stared deep into her eyes. As he licked his lips and leaned in to kiss her, Kyle and Dannon came into the room. Nelson tried to play it off.

He blew in Chanel's eye and asked, "Is it out? I think it was an eyelash."

"Yes," she answered, rubbing her eye and praying the boys couldn't see her blushing. She pushed her hair away from her face.

The boys were not fooled. Dannon turned up the lights and he and Kyle looked at each other as if to say, *Oh yeah, another five minutes and their clothes would have been off.*

"What are you doing?" Dannon asked his father with a devilish grin on his face.

"Nothing, bro. Chanel had something in her eye and I was trying to blow it out." He got up off the couch. "You guys want something to eat?"

They followed Nelson into the kitchen, and Dannon opened the freezer and took out mozzarella sticks with marinara, chicken and cheese sticks, and jalapeno poppers. He turned on the oven and set the timer.

Chanel sat at the table and watched as the boys gave Nelson every detail of their PlayStation competition. He was listening intently to them, but every time he had the opportunity, he snuck a peek at Chanel. She caught him each time, and on a napkin she wrote "ICUINME" in big letters and held it up. He tried not to smile but couldn't hold it in any longer. He gave her a playful smirk. Kyle noticed and looked over at his mother.

"What are you guys doing? Dannon, I think our parents are flirting with each other. Oh, man. Call us when the food is ready. Come on, Dannon. I told you they was about to get busy."

"Gimme some dap, Dad. She a cutie!" Dannon followed behind Kyle. "You kids be good while we're gone," he joked, shaking his finger at them.

Nelson sat at the table with Chanel.

"Rockin' took care of Jiles."

Chanel sat in silence as he continued.

"When I came to pick you up, she told me. I was speechless, you know. I mean, she couldn't wait? It was almost like she did it just to spite us for canceling Thursday's plan. Now I can't be sure if she did a clean job. She might have left behind evidence to get herself into trouble."

"I told you she was pissed off. And something inside of me knew that she was going to do something, but I just didn't know what. Did she say how she did it?"

"Nope. I didn't give her the opportunity. I was so shocked that I couldn't say anything. Besides, the kids were in the car and I can't let them see or hear any of this mess." He looked deeply into her eyes. "I want out. I don't want to do this anymore. I don't want to be responsible for setting up anything anymore. I'm out of this game. Done!"

"It's that easy?"

"That's right. This was my thing. Anybody who knows about it or had me take care of something or someone for them is in debt to me. I wasn't taking care of business for the guy next door, okay. I hold secrets that belong to many important people who had thorns in their sides and wanted them out. I'm not worried about anybody ousting me or pulling my cards."

"Well, I would say that if you're going to have your kids then you're right. You need to bow out gracefully and start raising your kids in a loving and caring environment." After a few moments of silence, Chanel asked, "Whatever happened to Sharon?"

"She and Cory moved to Michigan so she could be closer to her mother. Not that she was sick or anything, but I guess to get away from here. Know what I mean? I still help her out because she did a lot for me. She was there for me when I needed her, and I can trust her with anything."

"That's nice, Nelson, to be able to have a friendship like that. I thought I had that with Rockin'—ah, Robin, but now I don't know. You know, I think Rockin' is jealous of the time we're spending together. She got snippy with me when I told her that we were taking the kids out to eat. And the pool incident . . . I don't know, Nelson, I think her illness might be getting more serious. And she's not seeing Dr. Christopher anymore."

"I know. I speak to him every now and then, and he told me that she hasn't been there recently. I agree. She took Jiles out without even, you know, talking with me. What do you really think?"

"She's gone."

The oven timer went off. Nelson got out the food and called the boys.

"You're not going to get the girls?"

"They're out cold. They don't need this stuff anyway. This is growing boy grub."

"That's right," Dannon said, rubbing his hands together in anticipation. Kyle was right behind him.

"Kyle, after this we need to go. It's getting late."

"Okay, Mom."

"You guys can stop acting like you're not feeling each other. It's cool. We talked about it," Dannon announced.

Chanel blushed.

"You talked about it?" Nelson asked. "And what do you know about feeling something, chump change?"

"Oh, got 'im," Kyle said with a laugh.

"You throwing fifties," Dannon joked, "with your short sweats. Look, Kyle, he got on watermascants." Dannon got up. "Repeat after me," he said.

"Watermascants, ants, ants, you got on short pants." He did the dance too.

Chanel, Nelson and Kyle were laughing hysterically. For the next half hour, Nelson and Dannon engaged in cracking on each other, giving Chanel and Kyle a show. It was obvious that Nelson and Dannon were close even with the time they had spent apart.

"I love you, Mom," Kyle said, putting his arm across her shoulder.

"I love you too, baby." She kissed his cheek.

By the time Chanel and Kyle got settled in at home, it was 10:30. Kyle went into Chanel's bedroom, where she was reading *Antwone Fisher* in her bed.

"Mom, you're really digging Nelson, aren't you?"

Chanel closed the book and patted the mattress for Kyle to sit next to her. "I think so, but if you're not okay with it, I'll just leave it alone. You and Dannon could still be friends, though."

"I haven't seen you smile this much in a long time. Go for it. You deserve to be happy, finally." He planted a kiss on her forehead. She watched the love her life, her son, walk out of the room, then she turned out the light and rested peacefully.

Chapter Thirty-six

The week had gone by quickly. Chanel was busy with advising the appropriate people of Todd's death, removing his name from the bank accounts and speaking with banks in regards to their overdrawn accounts. There were loans taken out and promissory notes that weren't paid off. Although it was painful, she managed to get it under control. She would have to double up on a couple months' payments to catch up. Her personal account had enough to hold as collateral, and the hotel was going to be okay. It would just take time.

Nelson, after staying up with Naohme three nights during the week because she had a stomach virus, got the full effect of being a single parent. Nothing was helping—not ginger ale, crackers, or even tea. Whatever she ate, she vomited up. Dannon was helpful. After all, before they moved in with Nelson, he had been taking care of the girls when Veronica was nowhere to be found. Since being released, she only managed a day or two sober before she was right back on the block to get a hit, then another, and another.

On Friday morning, Nelson dropped the kids off at school then decided to pay Chanel a surprise visit. She was in the office when Paula came back to punch out after her midnight shift. In an attempt to regroup and get the hotel's finances together, Chanel had to cut costs, which entailed letting some people go. When she wasn't working the front desk, she would help in Breezes. She was tired but happy that it seemed she would be able to keep the hotel even after all of Todd's excessive spending.

The bell at the front desk rang.

"I'll get it, Paula. You go ahead home and get a good night's sleep."

"Thanks, boss. See you tonight."

Chanel put on her jacket, as she wasn't in uniform. She flipped through paperwork as she walked out of the office to the reservation desk.

"Nelson, what a surprise. What are you doing here? Have you had breakfast?"

"Yes. Thank you. The kids and I ate and I just dropped them off at school."

"How is Naohme feeling? Better, I hope," she said as she came from behind the reservation desk and directed Nelson to a couch in the middle of the lobby.

"So, what are your plans today?" she asked.

"I don't know. I thought I'd go down to the mall and do some shopping. Want to come?"

"Well, I'm kind of stuck here until my lunch, which is usually around 12:30 or so. But I don't want to keep you just waiting around for me. Why don't you go spend some time in the spa? That will kill at least three hours."

"Yeah, okay. Manicure and facial. What do I look like getting that mess?" he joked as he patted his face.

"Come on, you'll enjoy it, and you deserve it after a long week in the new life of single parenthood."

Chanel was finally able to coerce Nelson into getting a day of relaxation and rejuvenation. She watched him as he walked back to the body therapy area. He turned back to her and she shooed him away. "Go on. You'll be okay. They'll take good care of you."

She looked at her watch and headed back to the office. Her morning was full. She had to cater a corporate meeting in the main conference hall, meet with a bride-to-be about her wedding reception and meet with the construction crew who would be blowing out the walls in the sauna and replacing them with custom tile. By the time Nelson was finished being pampered, she should be finished with her to-do list.

Twelve-thirty came faster than Chanel had expected, and the construction people still weren't there. She decided that she would leave a note to have them reschedule, and she also left a note for Nelson to meet her upstairs. All that running around with the overzealous bride made her work up a sweat.

Once she exited the elevator and approached her suite, she could hear music playing inside. Kyle was in school and Nelson was downstairs. She wondered who was in her room. As she reached for the doorknob, she noticed the door was already cracked. She pushed it open and found Rockin' sitting on her couch, drinking.

"What are you doing here and who let you in?"

"Kickin' back, and I let myself in. Since you ain't never around, I figured I be here whenever you got in. Whatchu doin' for lunch? Want to eat?"

"Actually, I have plans to meet with Nelson and go shopping at the mall. I just came up here to freshen up. And I don't think I really appreciate you just breaking into my place and waiting for me. I'm a big girl, and last time I checked, I didn't have to answer to anyone."

"Oh, really." Rockin' slammed her glass on the coffee table. Her drink splashed all over. "I guess I'm out. I see how you do."

"Rockin', what is that supposed to mean? You act like I just up and dissed you. I have a hotel to run, and since I no longer have *Robin,* and since I had to let almost half of my staff go, I have to manage and maintain this hotel—which, by the way, is also my home. Is that okay with you? And so if I don't have time to hang out and shoot the shit with you as much as I used to, then excuse the fuck out of me. Besides, you are not Robin!" Chanel shouted, finally getting to the heart of her issue with Rockin'.

Rockin' grinded her teeth and headed for the door.

"I'm sorry. I didn't mean that. It just slipped out. I miss my friend," Chanel exclaimed. She followed Rockin' only to walk into a door that was closed in her face.

On the other side of the door, Rockin' stood, pointing the .45 Magnum directly at the peephole. A jingle of keys made her pull back and put the gun away. She quickly retreated, got on the elevator and headed downstairs.

As she was coming off the elevator, Nelson was getting Chanel's message from the front desk. He turned around to go upstairs. Rockin' slowly walked by with a very angry look on her face. She flipped him the middle finger.

"What?" he asked, putting his hands up in the air. Rockin' ignored him and kept walking out of the hotel. She got into her car, which was parked on the street, and drove off.

Nelson immediately rushed upstairs. He lightly tapped on the door and Chanel quickly opened it. She tried but could not hide her aggravation.

"Chanel, what's the matter?" Nelson asked as he came in and closed the door.

"When I came upstairs, I found Rockin' sitting on my couch, kicking back, as she so eloquently put it. She fucking broke into my place. She said that since I've been so unavailable this past week she thought she would wait for me here."

"How long had she been here and how did she get in?"

"I have no idea how long she was in here. She had to come after seven this morning because I left out around then. And . . . " Chanel walked over to the door and found that the lock was busted. "Here's your answer." She pointed at the door.

"Okay. Let's relax. You want a white mine bitcher?"

"What?" Chanel laughed.

"You know what I mean, girl. Stop playing," he said jokingly.

"You can't be serious," she said as she turned down his "white mine bitcher" and requested a martini.

"My titi. You want a my titi," he said as he headed for the cart that held the liquor.

"You are sick, Nelson," Chanel said as she started to take off her shirt and walk into her bedroom. Nelson couldn't help but stare at her defined back under the sexy camisole she wore. It wasn't until he heard the liquor spilling onto the cart that his daze was broken. He cleaned up his mess and stood outside her bedroom door, holding her drink and periodically trying to catch a glimpse.

"I can't drink it if you keep it in there. Can you bring it to me please?"

By that time, Nelson's penis miraculously came back to life. He walked into the bedroom where mauve, soft purple and pale yellow created a cozy room. A bouquet of fresh cut roses sat on the dresser next to a crystal jewelry box. He heard the water from the shower and was even more enticed by the sound of Chanel humming.

As she washed, she noticed that he extended his arm into the bathroom to hand her the drink. "What are you doing? Come in. Who's scared now?" she teased.

Nelson pushed the bathroom door open. Chanel wiped the fog off the shower door and looked at Nelson. With a sexy smile, she wiped the entire door so he could get a full view. Nelson brought his legs closer together in an attempt to hide his hard dick. It was to no avail.

"I think I better set this down and I'll see you when you get out." He placed the drink on the counter and backed out, but remained in the bedroom until he heard the shower stop.

"Okay. I'm going out into the living room so that you can get dressed."

Chanel stopped him before he got out the door. "There's more where that came from," she called out.

He stopped in his tracks, did an about-face and went back into the bedroom. Chanel was bent over, drying her legs and feet. She stood up quickly and turned around when she saw his feet. There she stood, butt naked in front of Nelson. For the last fourteen years, Todd was the only man who'd seen her in the buff. Before she had Kyle, she wore a size four, but he was a big baby, and she never got rid of the stretch mark after his birth. Now, her stomach was the only part of her body she was self-conscious about. But she wasn't going to let her anxiety blow this one. No, no. Not only did she talk shit, she was hot and horny, and it was time to cool the kitty.

"So, someone is happy to see me," she said, looking down at his penis. Nelson looked like he was frozen in his spot, so she walked over to him and took his hands. Slowly, she guided them to her face, down her neck, onto her breasts, where she hesitated and let him softly caress her nipples, down to her stomach, where she allowed him to squeeze her abdomen, and finally to her vagina. She guided his fingers inside of her, swirled them in her wetness then slowly took them to his mouth. He sucked on his fingers, tasting her juices and moving closer to her. Their lips softly touched then their tongues engaged in a wrestling match that landed them on the floor in the middle of her room.

"Are we sure?" he whispered.

Chanel hesitated for a moment then said, "I   don't know."

He stopped kissing her. Gently, he pushed her hair back and wiped the perspiration from her forehead. He got up then helped her up. As he went to sit on the bed, Chanel asked, "Can you dress me, please? My underwear are in that drawer."

He walked over to the dresser, removed a bra and panty set and went to her. Seductively, he bent down, helped her step into her panties and gently pulled them up. He turned her around so that her back was facing him, put the bra around her, fastened the hooks and slid the straps onto her shoulders. Then he sat as if waiting for his next orders, but there weren't any.

Chanel went into her walk-in closet. She put on a burgundy-and-cream sweat suit and a pair of Reeboks. When she returned to her bedroom, Nelson wasn't there. She grabbed her purse and went out into the living room where he sat waiting for her.

"What's wrong?"

"I don't know that anything is wrong. If anything, I think it's right. I just want to be sure."

"Me too," she said with a smile. She leaned her head toward the door and said, "Let's go."

After she advised the front desk that she would be coming back a little late and ordered that they send a locksmith up and repair her lock, she and Nelson headed down to the mall.

"How you like me? Do I smell good? My feet feel really good," he said with a smile.

"See, I told you you'd like it. And yes, you look good, Nelson. Oh look, there's Junie." They walked over to his stand, where he was shining a customer.

"Hey, Junie, how are you doing? I see you're back to work."

"Yep, back in my old spot. I guess I should've stayed here to begin with. Business hasn't been better, and I need all the business I can get to pay off those hospital bills."

"Not to worry. Send them to me and I'll take care of them. Junie, this is a friend of mine, Nelson." Nelson extended his hand shook Junie's.

"What they feed you, boy, when you was coming up?" Junie asked, marveling at Nelson's height. "You know, I haven't heard from Robin since she took me home from the hospital. Then this afternoon, she walked past me and didn't say a word. Is everything okay with her?"

Chanel tried to dismiss his comment about Rockin', only answering, "I really don't know, Junie." After a bit more small talk, Nelson and Chanel went on their way because they had to pick up the kids in less than an hour.

"She's here, and it's like I can feel her presence now that he mentioned her name. Do you think we have anything to worry about?" Chanel asked Nelson.

He was looking around in case Rockin' was nearby, but tried to soothe Chanel. "Nah, we don't have anything to worry about, baby."

They stopped at the food court, and while they ate, Chanel's cell phone rang.

"Mom, can I go over to Dannon's for the weekend?"

"Oh hey, Kyle. Nelson, its Kyle, and he wants to know if he can stay over your house for the weekend."

"Tell him we'll talk about it over dinner tonight at my place. And tell them to be out in front half an hour."

"I heard him, Ma. See you guys later." As soon as she hung up the phone, it ran again.

"Peek-a-boo, I see you." The voice on the other end sent chills up Chanel's spine. She closed the phone quickly, and before she could even get the words out to tell Nelson who it was, his phone rang. From the look on his face, Chanel knew he had just received the same call she had. They looked around the food court nervously.

"Over here!"

They scanned the immediate area until they saw Rockin' waving to them from a Verizon booth. Nelson excused himself and went to talk to her. Chanel sat nervously and watched their encounter.

"What's your problem? You been acting stupid lately, and to be perfectly honest, my patience is running real low. Now, if there's something on your mind, say it. Otherwise, I suggest you take a vacation and get it right because you're becoming a pain in my ass," he said, pointing in her face. "You need to be out!"

He walked back to the table where Chanel was sitting. Rockin' followed him.

"Well, well, well. Isn't this nice and cozy? Hmm, let me think why seeing you here rings a bell. Oh yeah!" She snapped her fingers. "This is where I saw you and your girl, Sharon. Just friends. Yeah, right."

Chanel looked at Nelson for some kind of explanation. He told her, "Don't even worry about it. I'm not sweating anything she has to say right now."

"Rockin', what do you want? Can't you see we're having lunch? And we have to hurry because we have to pick up—"

"The boys, right. Can I be of some assistance and pick them up for you? I can get the girls too so that you two love birds can have some private time together," she said sarcastically and in a failed attempt at Robin's voice.

Chanel, too through, tossed her napkin on her salad and got up. "I'm not sitting here and listening to her. I'll see you in the car." She left.

"You go anywhere near my kids or Kyle, and I will kill you. You can count on that, Rockin' Robin."

"Pussy motherfucka, you were supposed to do that anyhow. Remember, Jiles asked you to take care of me. So, what's up?" She stood there with her arms to her side, ready for him to strike. Nelson turned and walked away.

"She's buggin', I know. I'm going to handle Rockin'. You got my word on that," he said when he got in the car with Chanel.

Chanel didn't respond because she was trying to keep herself calm so Kyle wouldn't notice anything when she picked him up. She looked at Nelson then out the window. They drove down Main Street.

"Oh yeah, look at that young brother right there. The other day when I picked up the kids, Kyle said something about that being his half-brother. Man, he has on the same clothes."

Chanel looked at Reggie and insisted that Nelson pull over. Cautiously, she approached him. He reeked of urine and alcohol.

"Reggie?"

He shook his can, keeping his head down. She put her hand on his chin and lifted up his smudged face. She never had a relationship with Reggie. Todd had always used him as an excuse to be around Eryca, and as the reason why he never had any money. She tried to be in his life to some degree, but Todd always put up the roadblocks to hide the truth. At that moment, she had to put all of those issues behind. It was apparent that he was homeless. He was Kyle's half brother and in theory, her stepson. She couldn't very well just let him stay out in the cold.

She carefully collected him and his change jar and put him in the truck. Nelson pulled some blankets out from the back and put them around him. As they drove, Chanel and Nelson were silent. She looked back about ten minutes later and saw that Reggie had fallen fast asleep.

Dannon and Kyle were waiting in front of the school. Nelson and Chanel figured they should give them a heads up on what was going on. They stepped out of the car to talk to the boys.

"Hey, guys. Um, Reggie is in the back seat. I don't know what I'm doing, but when I saw him on the bench, shaking his jar for money, I couldn't just let him stay there. It's going to be dark soon, you know," Chanel explained carefully.

Nelson gently rubbed her back. Kyle walked up to the truck and looked at Reggie. Dannon came up and stood next to him.

"It's all right, bro. Everything will work out."

After they picked up the girls, they all went to Nelson's house. It was difficult to answer the questions that Neeah and Naohme were asking, as Nelson and Chanel didn't really have any answers to give them. Reggie was still asleep in the truck, and they decided to let him rest while the girls got settled down and did their homework. Kyle wanted badly to be there when Reggie awoke, so he went back outside and waited by the truck. When he couldn't wait anymore, he quietly opened the door and climbed in.

He shook Reggie, but he didn't wake up. After he shook him a few more times, he went back into the house and told his mother.

"Well, honey, he's probably exhausted. I mean, who knows where he's been sleeping? Where did they live anyway?"

"I don't know. We never talked like that. Any time he was around he was quiet, and when he came to our place, all he did was eat. He used my stuff, but I think that was to appease his mother. I don't really think he wanted to make me mad or anything, but he did what his mother and father told him to do."

"That's a shame," Nelson said. "Dannon, go in the attic and get some clean clothes down for him."

"I'll order some food then go and wake him up," Chanel said.

"No. Let me." Kyle went out, opened the door and got back in the truck. He wasn't quite sure what he would say to Reggie. For so long, they were strangers.

He shook him again, and this time he woke up immediately.

"Hi."

"Hi," Reggie responded, still groggy.

"You hungry?"

"Yes."

"Come on inside. You can take a shower and change into some clean clothes. My mom ordered some food and it will be here soon."

Nelson was sitting in the living room when Reggie came in, and Chanel was on the phone, checking on the hotel. Black and White stood like soldiers, growling at the stranger. Nelson asked Reggie to come and pet them so they could learn his scent. Bashfully, he patted the dogs on their heads. At first, they weren't receptive, but with Nelson there to rub their backs, they slowly calmed down and at least stopped growling.

Dannon ran the shower, laid out the clothes, a towel and washcloth, then came out into the living room. Everybody just stood there and said nothing. Reggie, who was so embarrassed, sensed that the quiet was because of him. Tears welled in his eyes and he held his head low. When his body started to jerk from his crying, Nelson put an arm around his shoulder and led him to the bathroom.

"Take a shower, get cleaned up and we'll have dinner. Everything will be okay." He closed the door and went back into the living room.

"Dannon, you and Kyle go to your room. I need to talk to Chanel."

Dannon went to his room, but Kyle paused and looked at his mother, wanting to know what she was going to do about Reggie. He knew in his heart that she would do what was right for him. He didn't really even have to ask. He turned and left the room.

"What are we going to do with Reggie? Do you know of any other relatives he can stay with?" Nelson asked Chanel.

"No. I know absolutely nothing about his side of the family. Todd always kept a wedge between us. He never allowed us to get close."

During dinner, they had basic conversation. Dannon, in between bites, attempted to have a one-on-one conversation with Reggie, but got no response. Kyle took a shot, and he too got nowhere. The girls stared, and that made Reggie feel uncomfortable, but he still didn't say anything.

After dinner, Nelson sent the girls, Kyle and Dannon to their rooms because he and Chanel needed to talk to Reggie. Chanel started.

"Reggie, first I want to say that I'm truly sorry for your loss and unfortunate circumstances. For you, I wish things were different. Where have you been staying? Do you have any family that could take you in?"

"No. I've been staying in parks, bushes, any place that would keep me from either getting wet or being cold."

"How do you eat?"

"I get a few dollars a day in my jar then I go to either 7-Eleven and get coffee and a roll or go to McDonalds and get something from their dollar menu."

"How do you wash?"

"In gas station bathrooms."

"If you leave here tonight, where will you go?" Nelson asked.

"Back to the park. It doesn't look like rain tonight."

"I tell you what. You can stay here for the night. Tomorrow, I'll make some calls and see what we can do."

"Thank you, sir."

"Would you like to go and hang out with Dannon and Kyle?"

"I don't think Kyle wants to hang out with me."

"Don't worry, they won't mind," Chanel assured him.

Reggie got up and followed the sound of the games. Kyle and Dannon accepted him with open hearts.

"Oh my goodness, Nelson. What am I going to do?"

"Tonight you can't do anything. Let's not think about it right now. Like I said, tomorrow I'll talk to Lewis and see what his rights are and what you can do as his stepmother. How old is he?"

"Well, Kyle is thirteen, so I'm guessing he must be around fifteen or sixteen. That is so terrible that I don't know how old he is."

"He's definitely not old enough to be on his own. We'll deal with it tomorrow. I'm going in my bedroom to watch a movie on cable. Are you joining me?"

"Sure. But wait. Can we handle the sleeping arrangements before we get comfortable?"

They went into Dannon's room. He, Kyle and Reggie were sitting on the floor, talking. When they noticed Chanel and Nelson, they became quiet.

"Reggie, there's an empty guest room downstairs, and you can sleep there tonight.

"Thank you," he said, making eye contact with Chanel and Nelson for the first time.

"We're going into my room to watch a movie if you need us."

Dannon looked at Kyle and they both said, "Yeah, right." Reggie cracked a tiny smile.

Chanel plopped on Nelson's king-sized bed, feeling emotionally drained. "I have to believe that there's a reason why all of this is happening. I just have to." She heard a click. Nelson closed and locked the door.

"What are we watching?"

"Nothing," he said.

She turned over and sat cross-legged. He climbed onto the bed and sat in front of her. Seductively, he blew her a kiss. Without another word, she took off her shirt. He was immediately drawn to her nipples. Softly, he nibbled on them, twirling them with his wet lips. She moaned as the wetness between her legs soaked her panties. He pushed her back and they engaged in a passionate kiss.

She moved from under him and took off the rest of her clothes. He put on the stereo to mute any noises they might make. Chanel climbed back onto the bed and propped pillows against the headboard, leaned back and started to masturbate. Nelson turned up the music even louder as he removed his clothing and stood at the end of the bed. He stroked his staff as he watched her tease herself. She had her legs wide open, rubbing her lips and grinding her hips.

He crawled up onto the bed and buried his face between her legs. Lightly he pulled and sucked on her clit while he fingered her. He was driving her crazy.

"Oh damn, Nelson. Mmmm, right there. That's it."

As she climaxed, he climbed onto her. He entered her and started to slowly slide in and out, feeling the pulsating of what now was driving him crazy. He licked her breasts as he made love to her. Then he turned her over and took her from behind. He softly pulled her hair with one hand and lifted her up with the other until she came again.

"Let me taste it," she moaned.

He turned her around and allowed her to swallow him whole. As her wet tongue glided up and down, his nuts tightened. She softly tickled his thighs with her fingertips. That drove him wild. Up, down, in and out, with a little swirl here and there, made him grab onto her head tighter and help her take all of him. She stopped, looked up at him and said, "I want it there," She pointed to her butt.

Nelson, with no hesitation, carefully and diligently inserted his cock into her.

"Take it." She moaned.

That was Nelson's cue. He took her. He pumped her ass and filled her with every bit of his nine inches. She reached under and lightly caressed his balls. He leaned forward so that he could feel her body on his, and as he continued to go deep inside of her, she turned and slipped him her wet tongue. Over the edge he went as he pulled out and came all over her.

"There you go. Some brotha butter for those fat buns," he said as he pumped the rest of his cum onto her ass. Chanel turned around and lay back on the bed, watching as he stood there with his head tilted back. His dark chocolate, muscle-bound body was tight, and he exhaled after coming for the first time in a long time.

Chanel sat and watched him come down from where she knew she had taken him. She chuckled softly.

"What's so funny?"

"Nothing. That was good, baby."

"There's more where that came from," he promised.

"I'm sure it is."

"I'll go check on the boys." He threw on a pair of sweats and a T-shirt and went to check on the boys. When he stuck his head in the door, Dannon was on the phone and Kyle and Reggie were still sitting on the floor talking. He went to see what the girls were doing. They were sitting in the room at their desks, painting. The television was on, their radio was on, the ceiling fan was on and they were in their glory.

"Daddy, we're waiting for the Power Puff Girls to come on. Wanna watch? Look at my picture."

"It's beautiful, Naohme. No, baby girl, I don't want to watch. I was just checking on you. You'll need to take a bath tonight to wash off all that paint."

"Okay," they said.

Nelson went into the kitchen. He pulled out a block of pepper cheese, crackers, pepperoni and some fruit. He filled a pitcher with apple juice and grabbed a two-liter bottle of soda. Black and White were scratching to go outside, so he let them out the back. He set the food and drinks in the middle of the table then yelled, "Anybody want a snack?"

Kyle, the girls and Dannon, with the phone glued to his ear, came running into the kitchen. After Chanel got up and went into the bathroom to wash up, she came out of the bedroom. When she passed by Dannon's room, she noticed that Reggie was still sitting on the floor. His head was lowered.

"Reggie, you okay? Don't you want a snack?" He didn't answer. Chanel went in and knelt down in front of him.

"You don't have to be ashamed. You had nothing to do with what happened to you parents. You had no control over what they did to you or themselves." She lifted his chin. He looked into her eyes and began to cry. She held him close, softly rubbing his hair and rocking slowly.

"We're going to get you through this, I promise. Okay?"

He nodded.

"Come on, let's go in the kitchen and sit with everybody else."

Eventually, Reggie became more comfortable with Chanel, Nelson, Kyle, Dannon and the twins. He felt badly because although he didn't have any control over what his parents did, he knew exactly what they were up to and could have warned Chanel. The relationship that he so badly wanted with Chanel was voided by his mother's ill words about her and compounded by his father co-signing them. So even if he wanted to go against them and start to develop a relationship with Chanel, he would have risked losing his parents altogether.

He was very envious of how Kyle and Chanel interacted. His mother didn't give a damn about what he ate, where he slept or if he even went to school. That's why although he was all of 135 pounds, he had gas all the time, his heart felt like it skipped beats, and his teeth hurt. One might look at him and say how unfortunate he must be to have lost both parents and be homeless, but then again, one might say how lucky he must be to be taken in by the one person who was presented to him as the enemy. Had his parents been alive, he wouldn't be in a warm house surrounded by loving people who made him feel like he mattered.

Everyone had gone to bed. Nelson had just finished cleaning up the kitchen when he heard an engine running in front of the house. He opened the front door and found Rockin' sitting in her car outside. She waved then pointed to the back seat. Black and White were in the car with her.

Nelson started to come out of the house and walk toward the car, but Rockin' put it in drive and fishtailed away.

"Rockin'!" he yelled. "Fuck!" He turned around, rushed into the house and closed the door behind him.

Think, think, Nelson told himself. It was late. Everybody was settled. He didn't want to get anybody upset and worried, so he'd have to wait to get Black and White back from Rockin'.

Chapter Thirty-seven

After Nelson talked to Lewis, who in turn spoke to other colleagues, it was determined that Reggie would become a ward of the state if no other family members stepped up to the plate and took responsibility for raising him. Since Chanel didn't want that to happen, she found out what she had to do to become his legal guardian. He was Kyle's brother, and he had been through enough. Her heart couldn't stand sending him away, separating him from Kyle, who could be faced with the possibility of never seeing him again. Money wasn't an issue, and besides, Nelson had her back.

Lewis was able to get an emergency court date and they were in court the very next day. The presiding judge was known for his soft side for children in distress, so this was in their favor. As they sat in the courtroom and waited for the judge, Chanel had done some thinking and came to some conclusions. It was no big secret that Reggie was damaged goods, but when she thought about it, so were she, Kyle, Nelson and his kids. Taking Reggie in could totally work out or totally blow up in her face, but it was a chance she had to take.

They stood as the judge entered the courtroom and took his bench. Lewis remained standing while Chanel and Reggie sat at his side.

"You may sit, counselor. In all my years of practicing law and even as a judge, I have never seen such cruel and unfortunate circumstances brought onto a child by his or her parents. I understand, Mrs. Kendricks, that you were married to the late Todd Kendricks, who was the biological father of Reggie Kendricks." He took off his glasses. "You must know the responsibility of raising children, as I see your son," he flipped through the paperwork submitted in Chanel's petition for guardianship, "Kyle is in the court in support of your effort to aid in making this boy, his stepbrother, into a young man. The court will find in favor of your petition with the following stipulations . . ."

He picked up a piece of paper read the court's decision. "It is understood that as of today, Reginald Kendricks will be in the custody of Chanel Kendricks," the judge said. "He will reside with you at The Gray Pearl, where you have a two-bedroom suite. I assume that you will make provisions to accommodate a third person living there. Since it is not known when Mr. Kendricks last attended school, you will enroll him in the appropriate school, have him academically tested for proper placement and start him in therapy."

Chanel nodded to show her understanding.

"Do you have a family therapist that you would like to use?"

"Yes, Your Honor," Lewis answered. "Dr. Shaun Christopher, located in Long Branch, New Jersey."

"Very well. It is duly noted in the file that Dr. Shaun Christopher will be seeing Reginald Kendricks. And Mrs. Kendricks, may I suggest that you and your son Kyle, after some time, attend therapy with Mr. Kendricks. If you are going to be a family, I think that a therapist can help you mesh together. In addition, he is to have a full physical and be examined by a dentist. The Court will expect a full written update every three months for the next year, and every six months thereafter, on Mr. Kendricks' progress until he becomes of age."

"Yes, sir," Chanel responded.

"There are benefits that will be paid out to you, and I trust that you will distribute them appropriately. Mrs. Kendricks," he said as he closed the file, "let me take this opportunity to commend you for your interest in taking an active and responsible role in Reggie's life. I can't imagine the loss he must feel, regardless of the relationship or lack thereof that he had with his parents or with you and your son. It takes a certain type of person to do this, and I'm sure when Reggie grows into a respectful and successful young man, he too will be appreciative.

"If there is nothing else, this court is adjourned."

The loud bang of his gavel shook everyone's emotions. Chanel started to cry and Kyle came over to hug her. Nelson sat back and watched as Reggie went to Chanel and quietly thanked her. As Chanel embraced both boys, Nelson went out of the courtroom to pull the truck up to the front. After he got the truck and parked it by the curb, he got out and saw Rockin' sitting on the hood of her car.

"Y'all just gon' dis me, right? Been blowing me off, and now she done went and so-called adopted this cat. I thought it was me and you. We had a good thing, and you letting a piece of ass come between us. I brought her to you. I took care of some shit for her, and now both of y'all giving me yo' ass to kiss. That's what's up?"

Nelson's relationship with Chanel, in Rockin's eyes, voided her relationship with him. Prior to Nelson, Rockin' hadn't been close with anyone except Robin, and when Nelson came into her life, she felt she had a real purpose for existing. He drove her and pushed her to limits that even Jiles couldn't. But now he had Chanel, Kyle and his children with him.

She had taken Black and White thinking it would drive him crazy to lose his two loyal companions. She figured taking them would be enough to get his attention and bring him back into her life. But now that he had his children, it looked he didn't even need Black and White anymore. He hadn't even come looking for them since she had taken them.

"All bets were off, Rockin', when you started doing things without getting with me first. You could've fucked up, and I wouldn't have known anything about it. You put me out there, as far as I'm concerned. So, breathe easy. I'm not trying to hear you right now. I'm going to pick up my kids and then we're going out to eat. Take a few to get it together and I'll call you, a'ight?" He started to walk away, then turned and said, "And I expect Black and White to be home today. Don't play yourself, Rockin'."

"You not gonna invite me to eat, homey . . . boo?"

"Bye, Rockin'." Nelson walked away.

"Ay!" Rockin' shouted. She went to her car and opened the door. Black and White jumped out.

"Black. White," Nelson shouted. Once they heard him call, they ran over to him. As they were running, Rockin' pulled out the .45 she had taken from her father's house and shot both of them. People outside the courthouse began to scream and run in all directions.

Satisfied, Rockin' got into her car and drove slowly, stopping only a few yards away. By this time, Nelson was kneeling next to Black and White. They were dead. He looked up at her with teary eyes and mouthed, "You're a dead bitch."

Rockin' got out of her car, pointed her gun past Nelson, aiming for Chanel as she and the boys walked out of the courtroom.

"Get down!" Nelson yelled. He turned to face Rockin' as Chanel, Reggie and Kyle fell to the ground. Rockin' got back in her car and sped off.

After Nelson got Black and White into the back of the truck, Chanel and the boys followed suit. As they were about to drive off, Rockin' came peeling back around the corner. Nelson threw the car in park and got out.

"You not gonna speak?" Rockin' said in an antagonistic manner to Chanel. "Hey, baby girl. It's me, Robin."

Police sirens became louder in the distance.

Chanel rolled down the window and yelled, "You're sick." Nelson opened his coat and showed Rockin' the gun that was tucked in his waist halter. He had pulled it out of the glove compartment as soon as they got in the car.

"Go home, Rockin'. It's been a long day. The police will be here any minute, and you need to enjoy the rest of your time, what little you have, because I'm going to kill you." He walked to the driver's side, got in his truck and drove off.

"Why did Ms. Robin kill the dogs, Mom?" Kyle asked tearfully.

"Not now, honey." She turned to Nelson. "I can't believe she killed the dogs," Chanel whispered.

"Why are you whispering? They know what happened and who did it." Nelson was pissed. He turned away as he let tears fall down his face. Chanel saw that he was crying. Reggie was sitting directly behind Nelson. He reached up and put his hand on Nelson's shoulder. Chanel tried to change the subject.

"Yeah, looks like everything went well. I'm not sure what—"

"Shh! Don't second-guess now. We don't second-guess around here. What you did was a very noble thing, and the right thing."

As they sat and waited outside of the twins' school, they watched as Kyle and Reggie bounced the basketball around.

"He seems so depressed," Chanel said.

"Weren't you? Maybe in a different way, but depression is depression no matter how you look at it. He's a child. He'll loosen up, trust me. Just give him time." Nelson rubbed his face.

"Yeah," she said as she let out a big sigh. "I need a drink. Let's go out to eat."

"No. After we pick up Dannon, I have to bury Black and White."

Chanel and the kids were in the house. Nelson sat on the back deck with Lewis standing beside him. Black and White were on a tarp in front of him. His insides hurt as he looked at their lifeless, bloodied bodies. Robin's aim was right on point. She shot both of them in the head.

"She's dead," he whispered.

"You want me to handle it?" Lewis asked.

"No." Nelson knelt down beside Black and White, his partners, his protectors, his soul mates on a level that no one could ever know. He kissed their faces then stood up. He loved them so much. They had his back, and now they were gone. Nelson was too angry to cry.

"Lewis, cover them up. Get in touch with a funeral home and plan for them to be put to rest peacefully. I want them buried back here."

Lewis looked at Nelson with concern. His eyes were blank. His face was emotionless. He was numb and on a mission. He was going to make Rockin' his last hit.

"I'm going to take my family out to dinner, Lewis. Call Ray's and let them know I'm coming. We'll be back in a while."

This dinner would be both a sad and special occasion. Nelson tried to appear like everything was okay or at least going to be, but inside, he burned.

"Nelson, it's been a long time, no see," the waiter greeted him at the restaurant where he was a regular. "And who are these fine people?"

"Jarvis, my man." He stood up and shook his hand. "I'd like you to meet my girls, Neeah and Naohme, and you remember Dannon. This is Chanel and her two sons, Kyle and Reggie."

"Nice to meet you all," he said with a pleasant smile. "Will you have the usual?"

"Yes, that would be fine." He invited everyone else at the table to place their drink orders. Thank you."

"Of course. I'll be right back."

"Nelson, this is really nice. And you are quite the spectacle," Chanel said, noticing several of his old clients nodding to greet Nelson.

"Thank you, Chanel."

Jarvis brought menus and everyone ordered their food. Thirty minutes later, they were eating and talking in between interruptions from the many greetings Nelson received. As they were preparing to leave, Jarvis advised Nelson that his tab was on the house and gave him a handful of after dinner mints. They left thankful for that day of their lives, even it if came through troubled times.

The valet went to get Nelson's truck as they stood outside the restaurant. Dannon, Kyle and Reggie talked in a huddle while Neeah and Naohme stood at Chanel's side. Once the truck arrived, Chanel put the girls in and got in the front. Kyle and Dannon started to get in the back. Nelson took out his wallet so that he could tip the gentleman, but dropped it. Reggie bent down to get it, and all of a sudden Rockin' called out.

"Nelson, you punk motherfucka!" A shot rang out, and Reggie was hit in the left shoulder. Nelson quickly pulled his gun and shot Rockin' in the chest. She stood firm.

"Oh my God!" Chanel screamed. The girls started to cry once they heard Chanel scream, and Kyle and Dannon ducked in the back seat.

Nelson fell to the ground to cover Reggie. Chanel was shaking as she tried to call 911. Kyle attempted to get out of the truck, but Nelson pushed the door closed with his foot. The onlookers scattered as Nelson got to his feet. His gun was pointed at Rockin's head.

"Chanel, come and get Reggie."

"Come on, Chanel. Come on out and get your son," Rockin' taunted. Chanel hesitated but was reassured by Nelson.

"Come on, baby. Rockin' don't want to catch another hot one."

Chanel got out of the truck and struggled to help Reggie onto his feet. She managed to get him in the truck and closed the door. Police sirens screamed in the background.

"Mr. Bray, you really thought that I was soft."

"No, I never thought that, Rockin'."

"Well, what did you think? That you could just come into our lives, show us love and then drop us like we hot?" Rockin' dropped then came up quickly like she was in a dance video. "I know, I'm crazy".

"Rockin', Rockin', Rockin'." Nelson shook his head. "You thought you had control. You made decisions that you weren't qualified to make and did things that you had no business doing, like what you did to Sharon."

"Fuck her! Playa, playa. You can tell me. Y'all was doing it, wasn't you?"

Nelson gripped his gun tighter. Rockin' had hers pointed directly at him.

"Okay, Rockin', you want to play with the big dog? Let's see who gets one off first."

Rockin' laughed as she pulled the trigger, hitting Nelson in the knee. At the same time, he pulled his trigger and hit Rockin' in the stomach. She went down as the burning sensation melted into her flesh. She rose up slowly after a moment.

"Nelson, shoot that crazy bitch!" Chanel screamed.

The space between Rockin' and Nelson was about 100 yards. He slowly limped toward her with his weapon still drawn. Rockin' held her stomach and took his challenge. She walked toward him.

They both let off shots. Rockin' was hit again in the stomach, and the bullet meant for Nelson's head missed and hit a light pole.

"You off, Rockin'," he said as he walked closer.

Rockin' fell to her knees. Blood flowed from her open wounds.

Stop now and you may live, Rockin', Robin said to her. The smile on Rockin's face faded. Her eyes were glassy and her mouth began to water. Nelson knew he had no choice but to put her down because if he didn't, this day would come again.

Just as he was going to end it all, a police officer spoke. "Put your weapons down!"

Nelson ignored his instructions and continued to limp toward Rockin'. She was still on her knees, and her arms were by her side. She was seriously hurt.

"I'm sorry, Rockin'," Nelson said as he raised his gun to her head.

"Me too, Nelson," she said as she lifted her arm and shot him in the groin area. He fell to his knees and was now face to face with Rockin' Robin. "It ain't over just yet, motherfucka."

Nelson fell back, and surrounding police officers hit Rockin' with rounds of bullets to her body. She fell to the side and onto the ground.

Epilogue

The healing process began. Reggie underwent physical therapy from his gunshot wounds. After his recovery, he started sessions with Dr. Christopher. In the beginning, getting him to say one word was difficult, but as time went on, he began to talk about his parents and how he hated having to listen to them when they said bad things about Kyle and Chanel. He hadn't seen his father for days before his death, and the last day he did see him, he left him in the park—the same park Reggie called home shortly thereafter.

It was also difficult for him to abide by Chanel's rules at first because he didn't want to live in the same place that his father did. This expedited the move to a totally different suite.

Nelson underwent extensive surgery to remove the bullet that landed in his upper left thigh, and after a few months of therapy, he was one hundred percent again.

After months of adjustments, Chanel, Kyle and Reggie had yet another situation to get used to. Nelson had proposed to Chanel. She accepted, and they decided to have a private ceremony. Nelson had two best men, Dannon and Reggie. Kyle gave his mother away, while Neeah and Naohme threw multi-colored rose petals at her feet.

For the time being, they lived between the hotel and Nelson's house until Chanel decided that she didn't want to run the hotel, wanting instead to be a full-time mother. Nelson bought the hotel from Chanel and changed the name to Bray's Black Pearl. He hired an abundance of staff to ensure that the quality of the hotel would remain the same, if not better.

One of the additions to the hotel was a dog kennel. Guests with pets no longer had to send them to kennels off-site. During the school year, Reggie, Kyle and Dannon worked there after their homework was done, and full-time during the summer. After taking courses in dog grooming and nutritional education for animals, they were the operators of The Brothers Kennel, a name all three of them came up with. To add to their entourage, Chanel bought a family dog, a gray Akita they named Gem. She understood clearly that it didn't replace Black and White, but she wanted Nelson to have that camaraderie feeling again. It completed him.

Lewis sat on the Board of Trustees for the hotel, and suggested they bring Junie back to the hotel to run the shoeshine stand. But Junie had bigger plans. One day, after he'd spit-shined a customer's shoes, the customer realized he left his wallet at home, so Junie accepted a lottery ticket as payment instead. Junie hit the lottery on that ticket, and got his pay of $375,974.31 from shining a shoe. Needless to say, he declined Lewis' offer, and instead rented a suite year-round at the hotel and pampered himself every day with room service, back rubs and an occasional shoe-shine. Occasionally, he helped the boys in the kennel when the boys took lunch, had a lot of homework or just needed some time off. He became a part of the Kendricks-Bray family, and was now known as Uncle Junie.

Veronica hadn't gotten herself together. In fact, she began using more. After Nelson learned of this, he petitioned the court for sole custody of the kids and won. He did, however, stipulate that she could see the kids every other Saturday for four hours under supervision. As far as being charged with Todd and

Eryca's murder, the police didn't have enough evidence, even with the gun, to make the charges stick. None of the people who said they had seen her come into the hotel could point her out in a line-up. The authorities had no choice but to let her go. She lost her house and eventually lost her license to practice law because of her drug use.

Because the hotel was the best in town and business was going very well, Nelson and Chanel were able to purchase ten-bedroom home on four acres of land in Colts Neck, New Jersey. They had a full basketball court, an Olympic-sized pool, a track, two swing sets and quads for the boys.

A year later . . .

Robin sat in a chair next to the window. The shots to her stomach severed her small intestine and she had a very difficult time eating. When she was able to eat after weeks of being fed intravenously, her portions were tiny. After a few more weeks, she was slowly fed normal food until her stomach grew accustomed to it again. Three of the bullets fired by the policemen hit Robin—one in the arm, one in her thigh and one in her wrist. Surgeons were able to remove all three and she was regaining use of all her limbs.

Her daily routine in the psychiatric ward of Jersey Shore Medical Center was to get up, get cleaned, go to physical therapy and watch television until she had her group meeting at 1 o' clock and her one-on-one with Dr. Christopher.

"Robin?"

"Yes," she answered Dr. Christopher.

"How are you today?"

"Good."

"How do you feel about getting out in a few weeks?"

"I feel okay about it."

"And how is Rockin' doing?"

"I don't know."

Dr. Christopher was silent for a moment.

"Do you have any remorse for your actions?" he asked after a while.

"Yes."

Robin's responses were short. She was depressed and had begun to pick at her hair. She started to cry.

"You're doing good, Robin," Dr. Christopher tried to reassure her.

"I don't feel good."

"You've been through a lot."

"How many people did I hurt?"

"You've been sentenced to five years in the psychiatric ward and mandated to see me every day for two hours a day. You were charged with aggravated assault, possession of a deadly weapon, terroristic threats and a slew of other offenses."

"My mother's dead." Robin covered her face.

With that, Dr. Christopher came to the conclusion that all the progress he'd made prior to Rockin's emergence had been erased by the recent events. Robin's therapy would start from that day, and she had a long way to recovery.